THE LIVING TREES

Clyde Sutton

THE LIVING TREES

Clyde Sutton

LIVING TREES PRESS

Living Trees Press
43 Waimaunga Road
RD 2
Raglan 3296
New Zealand

First published 2019
© Copyright 2019 Clyde Sutton

ISBN 978-0-473-48854-3

This is a work of fiction. The characters are both actual and fictitious. With the exception of verified historical events and persons, all incidents, descriptions, dialogue and opinions expressed are the products of the author's imagination and are not to be construed as real.

Design and layout of text: PressGang www.pressgang.co.nz
Cover design: Dunken Francis
Printed in Auckland by Benefitz www.benefitz.co.nz

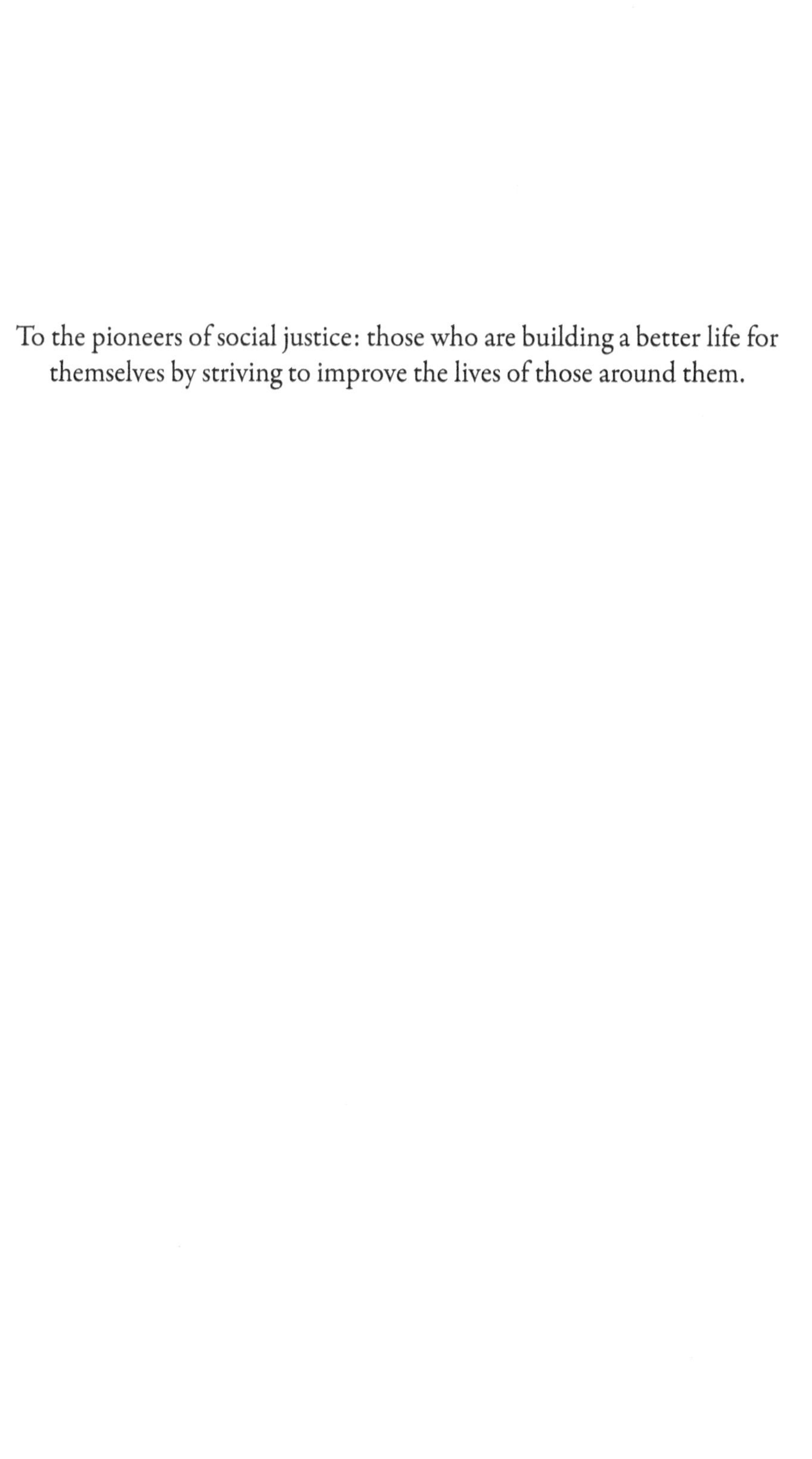

To the pioneers of social justice: those who are building a better life for themselves by striving to improve the lives of those around them.

1

Don't Mention the War

The attack was as short as its outcome was predictable. The tank had fired its cannon and destroyed a significant part of the small village with one shot. The few inhabitants left to show token resistance melted into the forest around their homes rather than be shot by the tank's machine gun. The stories were well known by now of how the machine gun had devastated the population of the first village attacked when its inhabitants had fought back. The tank contemptuously finished its assault by simply rolling over the rest of the houses and smashing them under its tracks.

Lestze and three men from the village had been pursuing the small tank since then. They were tired and hungry, with the lengthening shadows in their dim forest world telling them the day would soon be over. The tank was clearly headed for the next village, but that was close to a day's walk away and progress for the tank was painfully slow through the dense forest covering most of the vast, swampy terrain. It was simply not designed to cope with what its occupants were putting it through.

Lestze had been sent with the others, not because he was considered suitable as a fighter — he was seen as far too valuable to The People for that — but because he was sensitive to thoughts and feelings. His role was to monitor the tank and suggest ways it could be neutralized if possible, being as it was the most dangerous and destructive weapon they faced at the moment. He felt the frustration level inside the tank boil over when it bogged down for the fourth time that day and the hatch in the turret popped open. Two men got out, dressed in combat uniforms, while Lestze sensed a third still inside. The taller of the two outside carried an automatic weapon, while the other argued, "Aw come on, I've had to do it every time." His comrade laughed. "That's because having a famous father and wearing that uniform doesn't make you a soldier. You're worthless with a gun so I get to stand guard. Get on with it." He sat on the turret as the second man slid over the tracks to the ground.

The other man would have stomped to show his displeasure if he could have in the swamp. Instead he squelched around to the back of the tank to deploy the winch, floundering as he dragged the wire rope back through the mire to anchor it to the bole of a giant tree, of which there was no shortage, as far back as the rope could reach. He signalled the other man, who was still perched on top of the tank. The lookout shouted into the tank and the winch started turning, slowly dragging the tank back on to firmer ground. As the tank rolled back, its tracks turned slowly to help the winch pull it out.

Lestze was gratefully enjoying the respite from their pursuit when he recognized this situation might present an unexpected chance. Without telling the elders who had sent him, he had come prepared in a number of ways. Knowing his companions would disapprove of him risking himself, he moved back along the trail of destruction they had followed in the tank's wake then edged around behind other trees until he was near where he thought the tank would stop. He took some supplies from his bag and bided his time. He poured a powder carefully distilled from bamboo shoots into a wooden phial. Waiting for the winch man to start climbing into the tank, he quickly mixed in a concentrated acid distilled from vinegar and, being careful not to breathe as the mixture started bubbling, he pressed a slightly larger, tapered phial over the other, squeezing till they jammed tight.

Waiting till the man's head was disappearing into the hatch, he sprinted to the side of the tank and lobbed his concoction into the hatch. No one noticed the sound of a small wooden container dropping in over the other echoing noises within.

The hatch did not close as he dashed back behind cover. Instead he could barely make out the sound of arguing emanating from within and could sense the simmering resentment that had been coming from the third person inside the tank, along with the boredom and frustration from the two he had already seen, turning to anger. To Lestze's surprise, a young woman's head appeared out of the hatch. He should have realized she was a woman from the slightly different flavour to her emotions, but he excused himself on the grounds of his unfamiliarity with these people.

She took a few deep breaths from the cool afternoon air and looked around. Seeing no danger, she said loudly, "I don't give a shit what your orders say, I am going to take a piss outside this stinking tin can somewhere away from you fucking deviants." She climbed out with a little difficulty as she was carrying a pistol in one hand.

The guard stuck his head out and spat "Don't blame me."

She turned to confront him from the ground beside the tank. "Of course I fucking blame you. If you had brought a proper relief map that showed contour I could have followed higher ground instead of your stupid orders to go in a straight line from village to village," she stormed.

"But we don't have any relief maps for this world yet," he apologised.

This only made her angrier. "We are on a parallel world in a parallel universe. Use your fucking brains. The topography should be identical to the same area at home. Any relief map from home would do, and I could have told you that if your stupid fucking superiors had bothered to ask my civilian opinion before we started." She waved the pistol in his direction. "If I see your snoopy eyes show up while I am out here, I'll see if I can put a bullet between them," she finished pointedly. His head disappeared back into the tank.

While this tête-a-tête was continuing, the increasing gas pressure popped the two halves of the jammed container apart and a smell of bitter almonds spread rapidly through the cramped interior of the tank. Even if the two men had been able to notice it over the other odours that permeated the air, they would still have had less than two minutes to get out. They didn't.

Lestze was now in another quandary. He had expected to simply stop the tank by killing its controllers. If the hatch was locked down from the inside, there was no way he and his friends could break in before a search party came looking. But the hatch was up, which opened up many possibilities he and his friends might exploit. He had to stop the woman from getting back into the tank. He was of course completely at home in this forest environment, and could move silently and almost invisibly in the forest gloom if he was careful and slow enough.

He was on the move as soon as she turned her back on the tank, extrapolating on her possible destination from the direction she had chosen and aiming for that point. He miscalculated. She didn't go quite as far as he expected from his knowledge of the mores of her people, wisely choosing to stay within an easy distance of the tank and security. He was thinking that he had better freeze before she noticed him when psychology won the battle for him. She turned to face the tank to make sure there were no prying eyes before squatting, turning her back to him. He was torn between his need to stop her and his greater need to stay silent. If she turned with the gun, it was all over. He could tell from her state of mind she would not hesitate to shoot.

He was close but not quite near enough as she started to stand. He had been searching the forest floor around him as he moved to be sure he would not step on something that would crack and give him away. He had seen part of a rotten limb that had fallen from a tree above, a metre or two off to his right, and knew from long experience he could throw it easily. Abandoning stealth when she moved, he leapt to it, snatching it with both hands and throwing it in a single fluid twist then dropping flat on his face. The limb was over a metre long, well aimed, heavy, and turning horizontally end for end. Some part of it was bound to try to pass through the space she currently occupied.

She spun at the sound of his sudden movement, raising her gun as she did. Catching Lestze's shape and movement out of the corner of her eye rather than the branch in the dim light, she snapped off a shot in his direction before an end of the branch hit her across the chest. It continued its spinning flight, catching her diagonally upwards across the chin and left side of her head. Stunned, the gun fell from her hand as she tumbled backwards, only saved from broken bones and more serious injury as the rotten limb shattered with the impact.

Lestze had fallen on his hands and was up in an instant, reaching her in a few steps. She had already rolled on to her knees and was trying to crawl to her gun. His first instinct was to stop her rather than take the gun, which he despised as a symbol of violence and weakness. He put his hand on her shoulder and pushed her back. She rolled and grabbed his wrist with both her hands, pulling his hand to her mouth to try to bite it. He saved his fingers by making a fist, which she still bit. As he recoiled, jerking his hand up, she came up with it, swinging a vicious kick at his knee. He shifted his weight (and most of hers) on to his other leg, allowing him to take the weight off and bend the leg she was kicking at, protecting the joint as the leg could now move with the impact. He was astonished, appalled and confused by the ferocity of her attack.

He was off balance as she dangled from one of his arms with most of his weight on one leg and started to fall. Rather than fight to regain his balance, he did the only thing he could think of — he threw her down in front of him using the arm she was still gripping wildly and fell on top of her, his heavy bulk knocking out her breath and pinning her to the ground.

His companions were warily coming to his aid. Fear conflicted strongly with their desire to help their friend. They had now seen with their own eyes what they had once just heard of, what the alien weapons did to houses, let alone people in their way, and they remembered the elders' orders to stay safe and out of sight. Lestze called out a few words that indicated that the tank was safe and while not understanding why, they accepted his word without reservation, rushing up to help. When they got there, they were not sure what to do. When Lestze tried to get off the woman, she attacked him again. How can you reason with something that seems totally unreasonable? A strongly ingrained unwillingness to demean her dignity, to force her to do something against her will, slowed their response. After discussing the issue, one of them produced a rope he was carrying and together the men tied her hands as this seemed the solution least likely to harm her. Lestze was now able to stand up but, unwilling to leave her helpless, he helped her stand too.

The four men spoke rapidly to each other in their language; time was vital. Lestze was sure the tank would be equipped with a radio transponder and some sort of radio communication. A search party would be sent out come morning, if not earlier, when they did not hear from it. While the tank was a great prize, he did not delude himself they could keep it. If they tried to move it, the marks and damage it would make when moving through the forest would be child's play for anyone to follow, and they would eventually be confronted by a superior military force that they had no hope of defeating. There was no way they could strip it in time and shift it in smaller pieces, although that was how it had been brought through the gate between worlds.

The young woman interrupted their anxious deliberations. Looking down and pointing to herself as best she could with bound hands, she said slowly and deliberately in English, carefully enunciating each syllable, "Me Atawhai." The men looked at her quizzically, interested to see what would happen next. Lestze turned his head and lowered his eyebrows, irritated that her people had been coming here for nearly forty years and they still treated his people as if they were stupid, insensate brutes. 'Ah,' she thought, 'they must be able to understand.' She repeated the performance. "Me John—" he replied sarcastically, pointing to himself, "John Doe," and returned to his conversation with the other men.

She thought his reply over. His speech was oddly pitched, more musical than she had expected and oddly accented. He hadn't managed the 'o' sound in John and particularly Doe correctly, but eventually she figured out what he had said. "Hey," she interrupted again, "that can't be your name, and you can speak English, can't you?"

He said politely as best he could, "The name we are given or choose to use is simply a convenient symbol for us. The name I gave you is what you use for a nameless victim of a crime. In this situation, it describes the relationship between you and your culture and me and my culture perfectly, so it seemed an appropriate symbol to use."

It took a while for her to digest this and understand what he had said. By the time she had sorted out the words and what he meant enough to be suitably outraged by what she saw as his distortion of the truth, the conversation between the men was over. One by one they ran off in different directions, moving freely and easily in what she saw as dangerous and difficult terrain.

Lestze had his back to her, turning to bid them farewell, so she took the opportunity to dash back towards the tank. He tackled her from behind before she was more than halfway there. With her hands tied, she hit the ground hard. He turned her round and sat her up to face him. Now that there was little more he could do than wait, he looked at her properly for the first time. An accusing trickle of blood had run from the left side of her mouth to drip off her chin after her encounter with the branch and was drying there. As a telepath with very strong empathetic ability, he always did his best to avoid causing pain, not only because he felt it himself but also because he felt and understood the other's point of view.

"The chances are high you will die if you go back in there," he told her, gesturing towards the tank to let her know stopping her was in her own best interests and a kindness on his part.

"And the men inside?" she asked quietly.

"Dead," he replied succinctly, having no need to go and physically check.

He was one of a very rare few among his people, selectively bred over many millennia for his ability — to be able to sense pain or emotion in general, not just in people but as disorder in communities or disturbance to the delicate balance of the forest's ecology around him. He was compelled by his nature to nurture and protect as he tended to share the distress of anything around him, but if that meant he had to destroy invading organisms introduced by his people's travels or kill something in untreatable distress, he did so as efficiently and painlessly as he could. He felt little or no remorse for the dead men, knowing they would never have been able to fit into the civilization he was part of, delicately balanced between the requirements of its citizens and the environment in which it existed. They could bring only destruction. However, he felt her sudden anguish at his statement and it hurt him deeply. It might have been kinder to kill her too, he reflected, but he was already unable to do so. His instinct to protect now included her as well, unfortunately strongly as she was a fully sentient being, and on her own she could not be considered a threat.

"What are you going to do with me?" she asked plaintively. The question took him by surprise and confused him. It should be obvious to her he hadn't planned to be in this situation. He didn't know himself what was the right thing to do.

He dredged through his memory to try to grasp how her species handled situations like this. "You are my prisoner," he finally said, then adding after a little more thought, "a prisoner of war" — as this was supposed to guarantee decent treatment and should reassure her she was safe (her people pretended to have rules for war, he remembered reading).

Instead his words wound her up again. "It's not a war," she shouted angrily.

"Of course it's a war," he answered reasonably. "You are invaders from another world using advanced weapons to try to subdue or wipe out the intelligent, relatively peaceful species who live here."

"No," she insisted angrily, "we are refugees with no choice but to escape to this world. We are just trying to find a place. It is not a war!" she insisted again.

"Okay." He agreed with her just to keep the peace. To consider this a war, she would have to think of him and his people as equals, and that she couldn't do with her current set of values.

2

What Price a Man's Honour?

Lestze helped the woman up and led her away from the tank. He noticed her body starting to shake and realised shock was setting in. He would need to get her warm and comfortable if she was to survive the night. He looked around quickly for the highest point that he could clearly see in the fading light. It should be the driest point in this part of the swamp-forest from where he might still be able to keep watch on the tank.

He led her over to the spot and sat her down beside a fallen tree trunk then wandered in the forest to see what was available, while still keeping an eye on her. He collected some dry twigs and larger branches and came back to start a small fire. He would have liked to make a small ring of rocks to contain it, but there were none in the swamp, so he had to be content with clearing any debris from the ground around the fire. Besides, it was damp, and the fire spreading was not likely. Atawhai huddled beside the fire shivering slightly. He tried offering her the dried food he was carrying, but she was not interested.

He was only wearing a light sleeveless cloak, which he offered her, but she pushed it away brusquely. He left her to search for something dry, stripping off the dead leaves from the native palms and old fern fronds he found that were held above the wet forest floor. He took them back to the fire, laying them out on top of each other beside the log and persuading her to lie on them. He put the last few over her and when she rapidly fell asleep took off his cloak for the second time and laid it over the top.

He sat quietly to spread his mind, finding the group of elders who had sent him here once it was apparent their world was under attack. Some among them possessed a telepathic ability like his or better. They would pass his message on to their brethren who did not have this ability and to other groups of elders around the planet. Lestze had been the nearest telepath when the invasion began, even though it had taken him half a week of travel to reach the area of the jump station. His ability to report over large distances made him an irreplaceable asset, so he had been ordered to stay well clear of any fighting and well away from the station.

Once it was clear that the tank was destroying the villages around the station, Lestze had been sent to the hamlet ahead of the tank's arrival to keep track of it and report to the elders. He could sense their surprise or, rather, consternation when he told them he had stopped the tank. He had disobeyed their expectation he keep himself safe. As he explained further, though, he could sense they were elated he had stopped it but were equally concerned about retaliation. They were very interested to hear about the girl and asked him to stay with her to get any information he could from her. They already knew her people were escaping something, but they were not sure from what or why.

As he waited, members of his people started arriving from the swamps and, as the word spread, from the village where the tank was headed next. Lestze was accepted without question as commander of the operation to salvage what they could from the tank. He first set up a roster of people to keep watch over Atawhai then cautiously went to the tank and put his head in to sniff the air. He did not notice the particular odour he was looking for, but this was not reliable as there were too many competing smells, so he put his head inside, took a few deep breaths then hopped down to the ground to wait for any signs of nausea or dizziness.

While waiting, Lestze had asked two of the locals who knew the terrain to find a deep swamp that dropped off sharply from harder ground. It was important it was reasonably in line with the tank's next target. One of them thought he knew a place nearby and went with a friend to check. By the time they returned, the bodies of the two soldiers had been removed and had been stripped of anything of possible value, most importantly their weapons. The tank was quickly searched for any other weapons and yielded another assault rifle with extra ammunition. As soon as it seemed they had it all, Lestze sent the guns away, the load spread between a number of people to lessen the chance of leaving a trail of footprints, while several others went with them to lay some false tracks and obscure the real ones.

After the jump station had been built, The People (as Lestze's race thought of themselves, not knowing any other society) had established a number of hidden observation points in the forest around it and set up safe and defensible (as best they understood it) hiding places to act as marshalling points further away from the station. They were effectively arsenals set up as part of planet-wide plans to contain any attacks from the station's race, although the weapons were primitive by comparison to what The People were facing. Lestze had sent the guns to the nearest arsenal.

Lestze had decided the best they could do with the tank was strip it and destroy the evidence if possible. The two men returned to report positively of a deep area of swamp covered by scrubby bushes not far away. He intended to drive the tank there, but when he tried it was beyond him. His education had included a considerable section on the theory of the aliens' machines and technology. It had unfortunately been largely theoretical as his teachers had no concrete examples to work with. His people possessed almost perfect memory, so he had in his mind explanations or ideas of how the tank worked but dealing with the real thing proved much more difficult than he expected.

Quickly accepting defeat, he left the tank and ran to where Atawhai lay next to the fire. He sat down beside her and composed his mind while her current watchers faded into the forest night, knowing it would be impolite to intrude. Telepathic contact, even for those with the talent for it, requires a great deal of training and a clear mind. You need to learn to recognize and separate the first few wisps of thought you detect from another's mind from your own tangled thoughts, emotions and dreams. Equally, you need to be able to maintain an unalterable awareness of who or what you are and what are truly your own thoughts. Until you can, telepathy is often meaningless and a curse rather than a gift.

He sat for some time getting the feel of the stream of thoughts and emotions coming from her. Once he had a proper feeling for someone, he could find or contact them over huge distances but, until then, he was effectively blind to them. The process usually happened quickly with other telepaths, but for people without the talent (most people) it could take days or weeks of familiarity to achieve. She was asleep, dreaming, which paradoxically made his task much easier. The simplicity and one-dimensional nature of the dreams made her mind much easier to sense in a way he could understand. He had considered asking her for the help he needed but knew she would adamantly refuse to give him any information if she could. She may not be willing to admit this was war, but her actions and the emotions she emanated made it clear she regarded him as an implacable foe.

Once he had a sense of her mind, he passively watched the dream images flash by, usually without understanding their significance or what they meant but chilled nonetheless by the barbarity they suggested. When he was reasonably confident he would see what she dreamed, he sent an image of being inside the tank and an urge to move it. Her subconscious mind took over, mixing in some of the trauma of her capture earlier as her dream jumped to her running from a dark, foreboding forest to find refuge in the tank. She started it and drove it away, feeling she was fleeing from some unbearable fate she had only just managed to escape, consumed by irrational terror.

At one level Lestze experienced the dream as if he was driving the tank himself, but most of his mind was simply observing. When he had the information that he needed he made the effort to harden the walls around his mind or maybe re-establish the normal filtering we all possess that prevents our mind from being engulfed by all the stimuli, information and influences, thoughts and emotions that flood around us all the time. The connection to her thoughts disappeared.

Violence was so unusual between The People that most never came across an instance of it in their lifetimes, and even in those rare occasions it was the result of mental illness. To use force on another was repugnant, as a mature and responsible person would inevitably choose for the common good, even as it was acknowledged that following your own calling or doing what you were best at usually did contribute to the common good. A civilized person could not help but consider the impacts of their actions on the community and environment around them.

Two weeks previously, Lestze would have considered invading another's mind to experience their thoughts without their permission an unthinkable act of aggression. To his way of thinking, no society whose citizens did not treat each other with complete respect and consideration could be considered even mildly civilized. He had been told by his teachers that in times of 'dire need', if it was necessary for the well-being of the community, the basic rules of civilized conduct could be overridden, but to his knowledge that need had not arisen in generations. It had never occurred to him he would have to be the one to overturn cultural expectations established by many thousands of years of careful consideration and development.

He stood up feeling angry and somehow unclean. It seemed there was now a new category for people in his mind — enemies for whom the rules of decent conduct didn't apply. Expediency can excuse anything, he reflected bitterly as he hurried back to the tank, and war brings out the worst in us as well as in them.

3
Even the Unexpected Can Be Unexpected

It was still not easy for Lestze to operate the tank as he had to rely on his memory of someone else's actions. He knew what to do now intellectually, but he didn't possess the instinctive or reflexive actions that are only learnt through practice and experience. The tank moved off in a laughably slow, stop–start manner, as Lestze had to think about every action as he tried to follow the two locals around the obstacles in the forest. Watching them wait placidly for him to keep up only added to his frustration as Atawhai had seemed to do it so easily. He reached the edge of the swamp and stopped as the guides frantically waved their arms in front of him.

The place looked perfect. Lestze could not see any obvious transition from solid ground to treacherous swamp. The only thing that gave it away to his experienced eye was the sudden change in plants that grew on the ground.

The rest of the helpers who had answered his call were waiting as he climbed out, having followed the tank easily through the forest. He set them to strip anything that could be reasonably carried away, including ammunition for the machine gun and shells for the cannon. They were hampered by not having enough adequate tools for removing even things as simple as bolts and screws for some of the larger parts and had to rely on the repair tools the tank carried. Lestze also had to be sure the drive mechanisms were not damaged, so he tested them from time to time as parts were disconnected to see if it paralysed the tank. He intended to destroy the evidence of his people's part in the tank's disappearance.

It was still two hours before dawn when he called a halt to their labours. The scavenged parts had mostly been taken away as they had been removed, but several groups of people left with the last few pieces as Lestze climbed into the tank. He checked out how to lock down the hatch from the outside in the dim torchlight before descending into the brighter interior. Looking at the interior light, he was torn by the desire to take the irreplaceable batteries, but he did not know if the engine would run without them and was unwilling to take the risk. He set the machine going as slowly as he could, jamming the controls in the forward position, and climbed out the hatch.

Lestze was sealing the hatch as the nose of the tank lurched downward when the front of the tracks broke through the thick crust of debris to sink rapidly into the swamp. He would have lost his footing and fallen on to the tracks if he had not been holding on to the hatch levers. Shuffling as far back as he could on the tank, he sprang back towards what he hoped in the flickering shadows was solid ground. He sank almost up to his hips as he landed heavily in the soft muck at the edge of the swamp churned up by the passage of the tank. His initial exasperation turned to a smile as he heard the good-natured chuckling from the few remaining onlookers at his expense, even as they rushed to help him out.

He reached solid ground and turned wistfully to see the last of the tank disappear into the swamp, the swirling eddies of sludge showing the tracks were still turning. He hoped it would stop before it dug itself in too deep as he couldn't put a value on how much the tonnes of metal would be worth to his people. When circumstances allowed they would come back for it. Most importantly, the invaders would not be able to take it back and, with luck, it should look to them like an accident.

The People used bows for hunting and had learnt how to make crossbows since the invaders had come. By this stage they had soldiers too — people being trained, not just in fighting and weapons but strategy as well. In open country the range of the invaders' guns made resistance suicide, but in the close quarters of the denser parts of the forest, and with the ease with which The People could move through it, they were more than an even match for the invaders. As the invaders were uncomfortable in the forest and afraid of the cover it provided for Lestze's people, the area around the jump station had been rapidly cleared of trees since the invasion started and the clearing was continuing.

The tank was being used to destroy the nearer villages beyond the reach of the forest clearance to force The People to retreat from the station. It was being handled in a remorseless fashion, but it was clear to Lestze that the invaders were still trying to avoid bloodshed while they had the upper hand. So long as The People retreated without any sign of resistance, the tank's weapons were not used on them. It was not a bloodbath yet. Lestze did not want to change this policy by leaving evidence of The People's hand in the tank's fate. Without doubt there would be a rescue party sent to find what had happened to the tank once the sun came up, but they would not dare during the night.

Lestze wearily turned his back on the swamp and walked back along the tank's path, those with him erasing some of the tracks as they went. Lestze wasn't worried about a few footprints as the enemy was too intelligent not to assume there would be observers watching the tank's movements and following it, but he didn't want the scale of their night-time activities obvious.

He said a few words to his companions as they reached the place where he had stopped the tank. They used their torches to search the ground for Atawhai's boot-prints leaving the tank's path and erased them as they followed him over to her.

Atawhai was awake and had obviously been so for some time. He quietly asked her guards if she had said anything. They told him she had tried to communicate with the previous guards, but neither of them were as fluent in English as Lestze was and she had quickly given up. She had taken some water from them but was still refusing to eat anything. He was pleased to see that at some time during the night someone had brought a homespun, hand-woven blanket for her. She was sitting with her back to the tree trunk, the blanket wrapped tightly around her, staring into the embers of the fire.

He walked over to her and said quietly, "Atawhai, we have to leave now." She looked up at him and he wryly considered how he must look to her, covered in sweat and grime from his labours with the tank, topped off with a liberal coating of foul-smelling mud. It had to be anything but reassuring. She shifted her gaze to look out into the darkness then back to the men and women in the half-light, waiting with a few torches at a polite distance while he talked to her, and said, "What will you do if I refuse to come?"

"We will carry you if we have to," he replied matter-of-factly.

She scowled but struggled up to stand. He saw her hands were still tied as he hadn't remembered to untie her, but as he looked closer her saw the coarse rope had been changed to a softer material strip. Obviously, one of her guards had had the good sense to check her bonds during the night and make them more comfortable for her. He also realized she would not have been able to wrap the blanket around her as it had been with her hands tied. He made a mental note to thank her guards for the care they had shown her when the occasion arose.

Lestze asked her to hold her hands up and she meekly complied. As he untied the strip, he apologized to her for forgetting to untie her. He signalled to the others and the group ambled over, one of the locals taking the lead, and they disappeared into the forest heading north, at right angles to the line from the jump station to the tank that a search party would follow.

Lestze was still worried and wanted to put as much space between them and possible pursuit as he could. He had put Atawhai in the middle of the column, if such it was as The People were spread out to minimize damage from their feet leaving trail signs, while he followed near the rear, consumed by his own thoughts. He was feeling frustrated again. His knowledge of their technology was so small he realized he was trying to anticipate possibilities he didn't understand or could imagine. At some stage he was thinking about radio communication between the tank and the base, and it suddenly occurred to him Atawhai might be able to contact the base directly.

He sighed, feeling he was about to provoke another confrontation with her, as his signal to halt was passed quickly up the line. Accepting the inevitable, he walked up to where Atawhai was standing and asked directly, "Are you able to contact your friends?"

"No, I can't," she answered emphatically, but he was familiar enough with the feel of her emotions now to know she was lying.

He was confident enough in his own ability to accept this conclusion without question, so after thinking about it for a moment he asked, "Are you carrying a device that can contact them?"

Again, she answered firmly, "No," and again he could sense the lie.

Knowing what he had to do, he replied, "I apologize in advance, but I am going to have to search you." He sensed a surge of emotions from her, the anger, fear and resentment he had anticipated, but just as strong were shame and humiliation; he couldn't think why and with his cultural innocence, asked why she felt that way.

She said, "You are a man. I don't want you touching me without my permission." He thought about this, remembering being taught that these people have lots of taboos around bodies and sex but not really understanding what that really meant.

"There are several women in the group and I will ask them to search you." As an afterthought, he remembered how she had fought him last night and added, "If you resist them or injure them, I will have to do it myself."

He called over two of the women who were with the party and tried to explain to them they must search Atawhai carefully and remove anything they found. This introduced a whole new order of complication. While they were not sure Atawhai was in her right mind or whether, given her barbaric behaviour, she could really be considered a person, it was still a violation of her dignity to do such a thing without her permission when she didn't offer any danger to them or herself.

Atawhai looked on in confusion as the women continued to ignore her and started discussing the ethics of his suggestion, not only with Lestze himself but also the other members of the group. Lestze almost ground his teeth in frustration. The tank represented something completely new to their experience and was so obviously dangerous they had no cultural or habitual patterns of behaviour concerning how to treat it, so they had followed his orders immediately and completely concerning it. Atawhai, on the other hand, as a living and thinking being, ought to be treated with the same consideration they would extend to any other member of their people.

Lestze raised his voice a little, something impolite enough to catch everybody's full attention, and pointed out Atawhai's people were invading their world and had killed their brothers and sisters, even brutally beating the elder who had gone to reason with them when the invasion started. What was imperative right now was to find out if she had any devices that could call her friends to her because if so, they would come and kill everybody here as well. There were no precedents they could rely on to tell them how to act honourably in this situation.

Grudgingly and hesitantly at first, the two women started searching her clothing, but as various devices and small weapons started appearing from the pockets of Atawhai's combat uniform their attitude changed to one of grim determination. When they had finished her clothes, they even decided to pat down her body, something that hadn't occurred to Lestze, and discovered several more unrecognizable objects.

Lestze had watched the process with increasing bemusement and embarrassment at his own naiveté and had made a very strong mental note to make sure the elders got a full update on the incident. In particular, they needed to give directives that any future captives must be searched very carefully.

He walked back to Atawhai and asked, "Do you still have anything you could use to contact your people?

"No," she answered, and this time her state of mind, along with emotional overtones of resentment and anger, convinced him she was telling the truth.

Unfortunately, he could still sense an undercurrent of what seemed to be smug superiority or even triumph, without any sense of compliance or surrender. She seemed to feel she still might have won. This worried him so much he gave his companions a harsh "Guard her carefully" and walked away from the group to be able to sit down and think clearly for a while. After reviewing the events methodically, he was sure she was not telepathic enough to let her people find her so that only left her tiny machines. They must still be traceable.

He walked back to the group who were waiting patiently and confronted Atawhai. "We have to destroy those machines to be safe, don't we?" he stated tersely.

Her face paled, seeing the destruction of her only possible lifeline to her people in this alien world. "Please don't," she almost begged. "I will tell you anything you ask." Despite her concern, she still tried to misdirect him several times before his accuracy in detecting her lies forced her to identify for him a device, calling it a 'mobile', and admitting under questioning it could be found so long as it was turned on.

He made her show him and two other men how to turn it on and off, then asked the men to take everything they had found on her to the elders at the village two to three days' run to the north. They borrowed a backpack and the others handed over any food they were still carrying to the two of them. Lastly, they collected everything found on Atawhai and putting it in the pack too, ran off.

As she saw her links to her own people evaporating with the disappearing runners, Atawhai turned on Lestze. "You knew every time I lied to you, didn't you?" she accused. He tried to say no, but she continued on relentlessly: "You can read my mind or something, can't you?"

He started to say, "I don't know what you mean" with a straight face, but she cut short any further comment, exclaiming, "You are the worst liar I have ever seen" and turned on her heel, anger and indignation searing from her.

He stared at her retreating back, desperately wanting to fix the damage he had inadvertently done but, seeing no possible way of to take back what she had deduced, gave up in disgust. He called over the most senior of those left in the group and ordered: "Keep her hidden under the trees, but get her to the armoury as soon as you can. I have to get there as fast as possible — can I have a guide please?"

When a guide was chosen, or rather volunteered, he sprinted off with Lestze at what was breakneck speed for the terrain, driven by Lestze's desire to get to the armoury to check what small devices had been taken there from the dead men the previous night. He had not thought to look properly at what had been taken from the bodies at the time; he had been busy enough as it was. That oversight could still be disastrous if there were other devices there that could guide the enemy to the armoury. Lestze's concentration was focused to a knife edge by the need to watch every step of the treacherous footing in the forest's dim, early-morning light, yet even that was not able to stem the stream of recriminations that flowed through his head. He had messed up over the mobile and even worse, much worse, he had somehow managed to give away one of their most precious secrets to the enemy — that The People numbered telepaths among them.

As he ran, his mind boiled with new precautions his people would have to adopt. First, we will have to search any captives very carefully in future but more importantly, how can we find common ground with people who can lie so easily? We will have to teach everyone not to believe anything they hear from the invaders. Then anyone dealing with the enemy will have to learn how not to give away secrets, which seems to mean how to lie convincingly. Mostly he wrestled to understand why anyone would need secrets in a society that consciously worked for the common good (and wouldn't any rational society function that way?) knowing that system gives the best chance for all members to get what they want.

4
Pride and Privacy

Lestze wanted to search the sky, so despite his haste he asked his guide to detour out on to patches of true swamp where the big trees could not grow. The second time they did so he saw what he feared, a flying machine, knowing it was called a helicopter from his reading, flying from the jump station towards the tank. It would be a reconnaissance mission. Depending on what they found or decided, a ground force or rescue attempt might follow. He and the others were well off the line of flight now, but he reflexively headed back in to the deeper forest. Bitter experience had showed his people the helicopter could find enemies in the dark or under light forest cover.

Hours later he made it to the armoury. Dug into a rocky knoll near where the two rivers joined north of the jump station and hidden in tall forest, it was almost impossible to find. He walked in and looked at some of the most advanced weapons his people had produced, but it seemed somehow futile to him now. The crossbows had been easy to make once they had the concept, but developing reasonably good quality spring steel for the bow had taken time. Since the arrival of the invaders, The People had developed gunpowder and made a few flintlocks on other continents, but there were none here yet. They had developed from a peaceful, cooperative civilization to adeptly wielding medieval weapons in less than forty years. Lestze knew it was an impressive effort, although it still looked paltry when compared to tanks, aircraft and artillery.

One of the two caretakers (the concept of guards hadn't occurred to The People) on duty had watched Lestze approach and had followed him in. He noticed Lestze's introspective mood and waited politely for Lestze to speak him. Normally, Lestze would have been aware of another person's presence some distance off, but today he was too agitated. He turned and almost jumped in surprise at seeing his friend Apakta standing unexpectedly behind him. Wordlessly, Lestze hugged him warmly. Because of his telepathic ability, Lestze had been chosen as an infant for accelerated training that, as he got older, had often meant leaving his family and village. The arrival of the world jumpers caused the elders around the world to establish new schools and institutions, including a military with the beginnings of an army. Lestze had met Apakta during the year he attended one of the new military schools. He had worked hard, being expected to learn the whole curriculum in that year, including weapons use and strategy, though the latter kept evolving and being rewritten as The People rapidly developed their own military science. He and Apakta had become fast friends.

Without another word, he asked to see everything that had been brought in the night before, starting with the smaller items, and was chilled to see two more mobiles. He struggled to turn them off, not knowing he could have removed their batteries or that he might inadvertently call the station if he pushed the wrong buttons. After looking over the rest of the things, he resigned himself to waiting for Atawhai as he could not guess their functions. He spent the time talking to Apakta as they looked through the armoury and the surrounding area.

It took most of the day for Atawhai and her companions to arrive. The People were relaxed and fresh, having spent the day ambling along, from their point of view, while Atawhai was tired and angry. For her, it had been like a forced march. Having reached their objective, they sat down happily to prepare a meal in a clearing nearby where some sunshine reached the ground, while a few people ambled over to see what could be spared from the arsenal's stores to add to their meagre fare. The People automatically included Atawhai in the social event as it didn't occur to them not to. One or two of them knew a reasonable amount of English and although their pronunciation was terrible, Atawhai relaxed a little in the obviously friendly milieu.

Lestze sensed the arrival of the group from out in the forest and returned to the armoury. On the way, he sat down to compose himself and clear his mind as he wanted to be aware of every nuance of Atawhai's emotions when she looked at the different machines. When he was ready, he walked over to her and asked her to come to the armoury with him. She was in a better mood by this time and followed him without rancour, asking if he could tell her where they were.

"Near the second village you attacked," he replied a little caustically. "Its name would translate as Two Rivers," he finished as they entered what appeared to be a cave mouth in a hillside.

Lestze could sense her surprise — actually, shock — as she saw the weapons lined up in racks along the walls in the dim light. Questions streamed from her in a non-stop torrent. "What are they for? Aren't your people peaceful? Where did you learn to make weapons like this?"

Lestze waited patiently, and when he was able to get a word in, said, "I will answer your questions honestly and completely later if you will first answer the questions I am about to ask you with the same candour."

She laughed at his earnest delivery, saying, "If you want to make a deal with me, you should sell it much better than that, make it sound like you are doing me a huge favour or something. The way you put it sounded like you really want my help and I will be doing you a favour if I tell you the truth."

"But I do want your help," he answered with painful honesty. "However, you know I can almost certainly find out what I need to know even if you try to deceive me, but I was hoping we could treat each other in a dignified or respectful manner, maybe as friends."

"But we are enemies," she replied thoughtfully.

"Why are we enemies," he asked. "Do you want to hurt me, kill me?"

"No, but if I had to kill you to get back to my people, I would."

"I can understand that," he stated, "and I will do what I have to in order to safeguard my people too, but not at any cost. We don't want to hurt each other, so in that sense we can't be enemies. Let's leave it at that for the moment."

He took her to the pile of objects removed from the two dead men, squatted on the rough-paved floor beside her and asked what each was for, whether it needed to be turned off and if it could be found. She answered each question fully and honestly (he was almost certain) until he showed her the third object. He sensed her emotions change as he showed it to her. She called it a land-based GPS reader, saying it was turned on and could be traced. She also said she would turn it off if he gave it to her. He could sense the hidden layers of thoughts behind the words and knew she was lying and put it behind him. The last two were the men's mobiles and she confirmed they were turned off with an accompanying feeling of sincerity behind her words.

They talked a little more and as they talked he laboured to connect his mind to her thinking. Partly, this meant relaxing the boundaries around his mind while focusing on hers, and partly quietening his own mind, removing himself from his mind, his thoughts, opinions and memories, so there was a place for him to experience hers. Even with his natural talent, it had been an absurdly difficult discipline to master.

When he could sense the flickering images that passed across her mind, he reached back for the mystery object and held it in his hands in front of her. As she looked, he knew now it had belonged to the soldier and that each soldier carried one when in unknown territory — it told them where they were in relation to a chosen coordinate.

He asked her again, "Is it turned on?" and her reply "Yes" was indeed the truth and that she could turn it off was also true.

What she had hidden earlier and was now clear to him was that it could be triggered to send an emergency distress call. It could even be turned off to conserve power without disabling the distress signal, which would continue for many days until the battery ran out if that mode was chosen. He could see now how to turn it off without setting off the beacon and he did it himself before putting it with the other objects.

He was almost swamped by the emotions that flooded though his mind as she realized that his action implied he had seen the truth in her mind. Fear at what she saw as a magical or supernatural ability, fear for herself, despair as she saw her last hope dashed, self-pity for herself and a rabid rage that boiled with resentment towards him at the same time for what she saw as his mistreatment of her.

Lestze shot to his feet, certain she was about to attack him, and kicked the pile of equipment behind him in a single fluid movement to make sure she didn't try to grab the GPS beacon. Atawhai recoiled from him, falling on her back before coming to her feet in a combat stance, breathing hard as she faced him. The sudden movement and focus on his own body had brought his mind back under his control, but he sensed mostly confusion from her now. She had no idea why he had behaved the way he had.

As he paused, not sure how to break the deadlock without winding her up again, she took the initiative. "What the fuck was that about?"

"I didn't mean to alarm you," he explained placatingly. "You were suddenly so angry I thought you were going to attack me." Wrong answer, he realized belatedly. The anger was back again.

She took a step menacingly towards him. "How dare you ferret around through my mind, my thoughts and feelings," she fumed, her fists clenching. After a few moments of uncomfortable silence, while her impotent rage still boiled about his mind, she finished vehemently: "You have no right to invade my privacy."

He was angry himself now. In the small communities that existed on these islands, where everybody knew intimately everybody else's business, privacy was a meaningless concept. Community — working together to ensure everybody's survival — and equally important, well-being, was paramount.

He probably should have shouted back, but it still did not occur to him to be so rude as he stated, "A few moments ago you said you were willing to kill me to get back to your friends. You seem to feel that is fine, but you find the thought of me checking up on your lies unbearable. You would butcher us all with less concern than you feel for some imaginary slight to your pride. I have done you no harm whatever. If what you hold in your head is so shameful that you can't bear the thought of another seeing it, you should have removed it. It is your choice to think as you do. It is the only thing you are completely responsible for."

He turned towards the entrance, gestured towards it with a curt "It's time to go" and followed her out.

5

Life is Worth the Effort

The local people had packed up from their meal and were anxious to return to their homes before it got too dark. Out of deference, they had waited for Lestze to come out of the armoury to make sure there was nothing more he needed before they left.

One of them wandered over as he emerged to say they were leaving, catching him by surprise again. He had no idea what to do with his 'prisoner of war' and wanted to be rid of her disturbing presence. He had assumed the local people would look after her until the elders had arranged to come and get her, but when he and the spokesman went to discuss it with the rest of the group they were horrified by the idea. Their village, situated where the rivers met, had been the second to be destroyed since the invasion, shortly after the small settlement that had been set up on the riverbank near the jump station to act as a buffer between the outsiders and the rest of The People. Their village had been the biggest in the area around the jump station. The two rivers were the main form of transport for this part of the island, so where they joined had been a natural place for the key village to develop for commercial and social reasons. The armoury had been hidden near the village for transport reasons also.

The old people and a few of the others had already been relocated to settlements further away, but most were living in temporary shelters, hidden in the forest, rather than withdrawing from the region as the invaders were trying to force them to do. While not being a violent people, their self-possession gave a strength of character that was resilient and unbowed. Aside from survival, they were being trained as auxiliaries by the few soldiers currently in the islands, with the intention of forming the nucleus of a resistance force. However, they had little enough for themselves to survive and nothing to offer a level of hospitality to Atawhai that, as a guest, would not shame them if they had to look after her.

At the same time, the memory of the tank's destruction of their town, killing some of their friends, and the knowledge now that Atawhai had been driving it, created a raw wound that stretched even their charity to the limit, despite their respect for Lestze. No family was willing to act as her host at first, but they grudgingly agreed to look after her for a day or two so long as he came along too.

Before leaving, Lestze spoke to Apakta and the second caretaker who had arrived back with supplies while Lestze had been in the armoury with Atawhai. He asked them to make sure all the machines were sent to the elders and scientists as soon as possible but asked them to keep the three pistols, two assault rifles and any ammunition for the guns until he had contacted the elders. He realized that having the sophisticated weapons without their enemies knowing potentially gave his people a huge tactical advantage, so even though he wasn't responsible for military defence or attack, he wanted to hang on to the weapons in the meantime.

They left as a group as the sun was setting, spreading out but talking and passing opinions around using a language interspersed with what sounded to Atawhai to be more like bird calls, whistles and screeches that carried better in the still evening air in the forest than normal human speech. Lestze had placed her near the head of the group and deliberately gone to the rear to avoid her, but she had worked her way back to be near him almost unconsciously. He seemed to be the only constant or security in the darkening forest and her present captivity. The prospect of another fear-filled night in the gloomy, sinister loneliness of the forest filled her with dread.

A little later the current spokesman (this was a very fluid position in any group of The People, changing imperceptibly by usually unspoken agreement within a group as they assessed who was most suitable to be in charge for a particular situation) or leader for the group dropped back to speak to Lestze as they walked. He said the group would break up soon, as there were several encampments in the forest and those still here wanted to go back to their families.

"If it is acceptable to you Lestze," the older man suggested uneasily, "there is a home that is far enough from the village to have been untouched during the attacks. We feel it would be best if you took the girl there rather than one of the camps in the forest; it would be a much nicer place for her. I'm afraid it is over an hour's walk from here." He paused then finished hopefully, "Of course I will come with you as a guide."

Lestze sighed inwardly, knowing Atawhai was on the edge of collapsing from exhaustion, along with suffering from shock and almost certain concussion. She needed rest and protection from the chill fog that was settling in as night fell. Unfortunately, he could also sense the man's continued discomfort at the thought of having to look after her at any of the camps, so he quietly but reluctantly agreed.

The old man moved forward and Lestze could sense a wave of relief radiate through the group as news of his decision spread. The group began to fragment immediately as people regrouped to go to their respective families. Atawhai asked him what the man had come to say and Lestze paraphrased, saying, "There is a home some distance north of here where you will be able to stay the night." She sighed with relief but was too tired to ask more.

Within minutes there was only the three of them moving slowly north, following the big river. The old man led with Atawhai in the middle and Lestze bringing up the rear, keeping a close eye on her. Hours later she stumbled, and he sprang to catch her, jerking her upright from behind by catching the collar of her uniform. He took her arm to steady her and noticed she was sweating, though her skin was cold and clammy. He stayed beside her, holding her upright, and cajoled her into moving again, while telling the old man to find paths that would allow the two of them to walk side by side.

This proved a difficult task and their progress slowed even more. Another hour had passed before Atawhai finally slumped against Lestze, semi-conscious, unable to walk further. Lestze could sense no one near and knew intuitively there was still a long way to go. He also felt Atawhai's condition would become critical if nothing was done soon. It would be dangerous for her to keep going but more so to stay in the cold of the night, even if he made a temporary shelter. He took off his cloak and picked her up, putting one of her arms high around his neck so her head rested on his shoulder, then asked the old man to put his cloak over her so she was protected from the cold while his body heat would warm her as he walked. He got a clear direction from the old man, which he knew he could follow even though the fog obscured the moon and stars, then sent the old man to get help from the home urgently.

He managed to carry her for almost half an hour before being finally forced to admit defeat. Carrying someone through the almost pathless forest while the gathering darkness made it nearly impossible to see his footing, or to avoid entangling them both in the cold, wet vegetation, was a fool's errand and he knew it. Even so, Lestze continued till his path neared one of the giant swamp trees with large buttressed roots running from the trunk. He made his way to the north-east side of this Old Man of the Forest, away from the prevailing wind wafting the damp fog. Finding some relatively dry ground there, he backed towards the trunk and sat down, squeezing between the buttresses that seemed to make a room with no roof, holding Atawhai still cradled in his arms.

He knew he should make the effort to gather leaves and branches to cover them both and conserve their body heat but was too exhausted from his two days of struggle to care. Another distant voice suggested that not caring was a bad sign, but he was not interested in listening to that voice either.

Time past unnoticed as he slumped with his back to the tree and his mind, vacant from fatigue, seemed to float free of his control. He sensed the swirling, semi-conscious half-dreams in Atawhai's mind and recoiled from their confusion, the disjointed maelstrom of fears, hate and longings tangled with genuine love, lusts for power and possessions and status strangling the impulses and kindness of a warm heart.

He was drawn by the consciousness of the giant tree behind him, if consciousness it could be called. The wisdom of its fifteen hundred years of existence could be summed up in one all-consuming imperative — grow. It had waited for over a century as a forest floor seedling before a long-forgotten forest giant crashed to the earth, from age and from its own immense size and weight, in a hail of destruction. The unexpected light had beamed down to spur the growth of the carpet of seedlings in the new clearing and all had grown together, but the Old Man had won the race. As a seedling, his growing tips had been eaten back many times by the giant grazing birds, and even now he was still food and shelter for a vast army of tiny living things that infested his canopy, but he knew nothing of resentment or despair or failure, just the will to grow.

The innocence and strength of that hunger for life was the tonic Lestze needed. He slowly forced his errant thoughts back into order and checked his own body. His body core was still warm from carrying Atawhai and the heat he was radiating in the still air of their little cranny was showing signs of warming her too, though her hands were still terribly cold when he touched them. He was weighing up whether to leave her to try to start a fire when he sensed people were coming but still some time away. He settled for shifting his position a little to try to get more comfortable and ease some of the pressure of roots poking into his back and legs. He still cradled Atawhai as much as possible to keep her off the damp, cold ground.

The helpers arrived sooner than he expected as they knew the territory well and could travel it easily in the night with their glowing torches. Lestze whistled from time to time and when they were close enough to hear, they whistled back. Not long after, a middle-aged man with his two sons jogged up. The boys gently lifted Atawhai from Lestze's lap and wrapped blankets they had brought around her while the older man gave a hand to Lestze to help him up, introducing himself deferentially as Dginze in the process. Atawhai roused, trying to stand without being held but quieted again as Lestze reassured her that all was well and she was with friends.

The young men volunteered to take turns carrying Atawhai, saying it was not so far to get home and they had not thought to bring a stretcher — the task was not as difficult as it might seem as The People are more muscular than humans on average. Lestze agreed, wanting to get to shelter as soon as possible.

With the help of the torch and their knowledge of paths through the forest, they made rapid progress, shifting Atawhai from person to person before the one carrying her tired and slowed the others down.

The forest finally receded, giving way to surreal glimpses of orchard trees, shadows dimly seen and vaguely menacing in the swirling fog and hazy moonlight, weirdly unsettling and ephemeral after the solid darkness of the forest. Moments later a building loomed out of the mist, surprising Lestze by the suddenness of its appearance. No light sneaked out to give warning to travellers as shutters had been closed over the windows before sunset to keep out the insidious autumn chill. This changed as Dginze swung open the door. Light from the fire at the side of the large central room streamed out, promising welcome and security to the weary travellers.

Atawhai was taken to a bed in a small room, more a nook built into the wall of the communal living and dining room, under the watchful eye of Dginze's wife Thsermi, while Lestze was led to a seat by the fire next to the old man who had been acting as his guide earlier. The old man shamefacedly whispered he had intended to come back with the others to look for Lestze but Thsermi would not allow it. Shortly after, Lestze was given a bowl of steaming thick soup with a generous slice of a coarse dark bread made mostly from flour from a kind of tuber.

Once Atawhai was settled, Thsermi returned and told Lestze that Atawhai was doing as well as could be expected and she would keep an eye on her from time to time during the night. She then sat and joined the conversation between the five men as the family from the settlement were keen to hear news of the latest developments. However, she quickly noticed Lestze's exhaustion and called a halt to the discussion, sending one of her sons to tidy his room so Lestze could sleep in it. Lestze was embarrassed at the thought of putting the family out and said he would be happy to sleep on the floor in front of the fire, but she bridled at the suggestion, clearly feeling such an arrangement would be an insult to any guest. He was asleep as soon as his head touched the rudimentary pillow.

6

The Ignominy of Babysitting

Lestze woke early the next morning feeling tired and troubled. While he had been looking for specific information in Atawhai's mind, his subconscious had picked up and stored all the peripheral, disjointed images and emotions that constantly pass through the mind of any conscious being, hers being no exception. His sleep had been troubled by a maelstrom of confused dreams filled with experiences and attitudes he did not have the contextual information to be able to understand.

He tried to sneak out into the forest to be alone to collect his thoughts, away from people and the confusion they inevitably caused him, but Thsermi caught him tiptoeing out the door, insisting he eat a hearty breakfast before she would consider letting him leave. While he ate under her watchful gaze, she told him Atawhai was sleeping deeply but was running a fever and wouldn't be fit to leave for days. As he tried to escape for the second time, she informed him when lunch would be ready and that she would be angry if he wasn't back in time. He left hurriedly with the feeling or knowledge she thought him too skinny and with her motherly instincts sure he needed looking after as he did not seem to be doing the job properly himself. There also seemed a faint suggestion in her thoughts that while she did not have a daughter of the right age, she had a niece that should fit the bill nicely.

As he reached the edge of the forest proper, he looked back at the homestead through the morning mist. The home was on higher ground, set a long way back from the river to avoid winter flooding and surrounded by a patchwork of gardens and orchard trees. It consisted of a large central living and dining room with small rooms off each side that would be warmed by the main room's fire. The walls were thick to keep it warm, with a wide, thick thatched roof to keep out the weather. Other small buildings were tucked between trees, and he could tell more people lived here than just the immediate family.

He wandered deep into the forest with no direction in mind until he felt relatively free of the influences of others' thoughts and sat down, taking time to find a relatively dry spot as these were few and far between in the swampy landscape, even at this time of year, the end of summer. It took him more than an hour to clear his mind to his satisfaction of all the alien thoughts that were plaguing it. Eventually, he felt focused enough to make the effort to contact the elder, Senden, he had talked to two nights before.

As he felt the comforting sense of Senden's calm presence enter his thoughts, Lestze lost some of his equanimity. Rather than giving a concise and coherent account of the last day's events as he had intended, he blurted/said/thought: 'Being around Atawhai — an image of the girl mixed with unintentional conceptual tags that included alien, violent, deceitful untrustworthy, dangerous and confusing — is extremely uncomfortable for me. She isn't in any condition to move from the house over the next few days, so can I leave her with the family here to wait for some of you (meaning elders or their representatives) to come and get her. I could go back to my observational duties for you,' he added hopefully.

The strong wave of gentle humour his outburst elicited convinced Lestze that Senden was probably laughing out loud as well as mentally. Lestze flushed with embarrassment, then, knowing Senden would experience the emotional or mental overtones of that embarrassment directly because of their mental link, flushed even more.

An image appeared in his head of Senden laughing uproariously accompanied by the thought: 'My, my, Lestze, she really has managed to disturb your much-vaunted composure. As to returning to your duty, you have very successfully put an end to the threat of any more tank attacks, despite orders not to put yourself at risk I might add. Your observational duties there are at an end for the meantime. The knowledge the girl has about what her people are running from is vitally important to our people's survival, so she must be your first priority.'

A feeling of reproach replaced the humour as Senden continued, 'She and her people are fighters, killers by the selfishness of their cultural heritage. You are one of very few among us who has had the military training to be able to deal with those like her. Your experience and awareness of how she thinks, along with your superior strength and psychic talents, mean you can easily face her and win if you have to or choose to, and, for the good of us all, you must make that choice. That family would have no chance against her as they have no way to conceive what she is capable of. How can you even think of leaving them at her mercy (or lack of it) just to help yourself feel comfortable?'

Where Lestze had felt embarrassed before, now he felt absolutely wretched. These were the harshest words of censure any elder had ever spoken to him. Senden paused for a moment, leaving Lestze to consider the likely consequences of leaving Atawhai unguarded.

He cut back in to Lestze's thoughts. 'Enough self-pity. Only children try to avoid the consequences of their actions. As an adult in our culture, you must accept responsibility for the consequences of your actions, even unforeseen ones like these, and do your best to anticipate what the long-term effects might be, compensating for them if possible. At the same time, there is no one else where you are located equipped to cope with Atawhai, so by default, she has become your responsibility. You are her minder, warder or jailer if you think that's a more appropriate description, until we can come up with a better solution. Yes,' he emphasized and started laughing again at the thought as it crossed his mind, 'you can consider your official position as babysitter for the foreseeable future.'

'As nobody is all-knowing, you must be prepared to rely on others to point out what you have overlooked. There is no shame in that, so stop feeling so crestfallen. And by the way, good morning Lestze and, yes, I am not busy right now and have the time to deal with this. So good of you to ask.'

Lestze was stung for a moment by what he saw as another rebuke but sensed Senden's laughter behind the comment as he added: 'Her defensiveness is certainly rubbing off on you. Now wait a moment as I want to contact some of the elders groups in other areas. Since I passed on your previous messages, many of them want to question you directly.'

Lestze watched inwardly, fascinated as Senden concentrated, contacting an individual on another continent who in turn started contacting others, then he moved mentally on to another contact. It was a laborious process as many were asleep in other time zones and others busy for one reason or another, but soon enough there was a spider web-like tracery of connected minds around the globe. 'This is a Great Council,' he thought to himself with something akin to awe. He knew they occurred regularly, being effectively the planet's government, but had never expected to be part of one.

'Yes, impromptu as it is, this is still effectively the Great Council,' Senden's thought answered unexpectedly. 'Don't be too surprised. We are convening almost daily since the war started. Now, rather than telling us what you have seen, please start from before you stopped the tank and recall exactly what happened, everything you experienced and thought.' As Lestze shuffled through his memories of the day in order to find an appropriate point to begin, an image of the tank destroying the village passed before his eye and a cacophony of voices and thoughts stopped him. Very few of the assembled elders in other parts of the world had ever seen large examples of the invaders' technology or machines, let alone weapons, and consequently were very keen to see the tank through Lestze's eyes. He ran through the memories exactly as he had experienced them, his perfectly trained memory recalling every detail, while those watching lived them as if the events were occurring to them. He could feel many emotions from the assembled minds, surprise from some that intelligent people could be so callous, anger, consternation, fear, impotence but also an impersonal sense of calculation as information was added and compared and conclusions considered. It caught his attention, and once something caught his attention he could seldom be diverted.

Lestze jumped in his memory from the attack to the fourth time the tank became bogged down late in the day. He was linked to the gathering through Senden's mind, but as time progressed he began to sense directly individuals further away in the web and his conscious mind drifted. He became absorbed in the huge amount of data available to the council. Memories of events, wars and calamities from millennia ago passed down from mind to mind for untold generations. People even now were sorting his own memories as he passed them on, considering what was important enough to be passed down or be added to the collective memory, and what should be left to disappear with the rest of his individual memories. He could see how they reached decisions through careful consideration of huge amounts of information. The council was determined not to repeat the mistakes of the past, even the far distant past, because some of its members still remembered them!

What suddenly caught his mind and was particularly interesting were memories of the arrival of Atawhai's people. The skeleton of the jump station had been put together by tiny machines and was well under way before any of The People noticed. When they did, the elders decided not to interfere as they had no idea what was happening. Once the jump gate was operational, bigger machines and finally people came through and together they built the remainder of the station.

The station had been under observation for some time by this stage by the local people and telepaths who had been sent as soon as word of the strange events reached the elders. When the aliens arrived, representatives of The People tentatively went to meet them. The consensus reached by the elders, after a month or two of contact with the aliens, was that war between their cultures was inevitable. This decision was not as simple as it sounds. Lestze could see all the events that had occurred, along with observations from experienced telepaths who had gleaned a great deal of information about the aliens' culture and degree of civilization from their minds and so much more. Once it was clear an equal meeting of cultures was impossible, the village near the station was scaled down and people with sensitive knowledge moved from the region (actually from the islands altogether). The aliens couldn't be trusted not to kidnap someone to take his knowledge if they thought they had something to gain. Making sure that the thought they might have something to gain did not occur to them was vital.

There was a sudden change and Lestze became aware of himself as an individual mind again that retreated or was being forced back to his own memories and to awareness of his own body, back to an anchor point in physical reality. He could sense the link to Senden's mind and the other minds beyond, but as he tried to reach out towards them again, it was simply not possible, though he couldn't tell why. It felt like trying to push through a wall that you couldn't see or even feel and yet was utterly implacable. So, Senden had brought him back to where he should be. As this realization percolated into his consciousness, Senden's thoughts cut through his disorientation: 'Bring your thoughts back to your memories; many people are waiting.' Habit and self-discipline kicked in immediately. He quickly found the point where his mental narrative had trailed off into incomprehensibility and picked up the thread again. He was questioned, or rather grilled, a number of times by different people. Each time the interrogator was not interested in the events so much as why he had made the decisions he had — to poison those in the tank (and why he had the poison with him anyway), why he decided to stop the girl getting back into the tank, why he chose to sink the tank into the swamp, and so on.

The elders examined his memories until Lestze had passed on all the events at the armoury, at which point a sense of urgency ignited in a mind somewhere and spread almost instantly through the assemblage. Without the need for individual consultation, the decision was made to end the interview with Lestze, and awareness of the council vanished from his mind.

He was left locked in what felt like an empty head with an intangible sense of loss and isolation that was on the edge of tipping over the precipice into self-pity. Worse, he had embarrassed himself again, this time in front of the council.

'Yes, addictive, wasn't it?' Senden's thoughts suddenly echoed though the emptiness. 'So much knowledge, experience and wisdom. All at your disposal. How sad to lose it. Still, self-pity is another form of mental addiction. Pity is for the weak. You are not weak and to offer you pity would be an insult to you. Don't expect it from me. If you can clear your mind by tomorrow, contact me then.'

7

On the Nature of Mastery

Lestze opened his eyes and looked around. The early morning fog had not burnt off as the sun rose but had thickened into a cold, grey, dreary day that he could feel would turn to cold rain by the end of the afternoon or evening. His inbuilt time sense told him it was nearing lunchtime and he needed to hurry so he stood up with little stiffness from his hours of immobility and began to jog back towards the homestead, fearful of incurring Thsermi's wrath by being late.

Oddly, Lestze was happy. Senden's seeming curt dismissal was a gesture of faith. He believed in Lestze's ability to sort himself out and was leaving him to do it. Lestze loped through the forest, relaxing his body, and paying attention to every detail he could as he passed, feeling the flow of life that he loved. He had experienced far too much over the last few days for his conscious mind to make sense of and rather than remain caught in the maelstrom, he chose to remove himself from it and simply bask in the sensations of the moment.

The softness of his footfall in the forest litter beat a rhythm that only accentuated the beauty of the calls of the birds as they sang to mark their territories or to chorus a warning of his passing far below. He sometimes touched their simple but agile minds as he passed, respecting their right to exist as much as his own and revelling in the intensity of their joy of life, or felt the serene flow of life from the giant trees, greeting them with the respect due a brother.

When he reached the house, there was a basin of warm water waiting for him to wash himself while a communal meal was being put on the table. It was clear the meal had been ready, but Thsermi had waited for him to arrive to present it. Dginze was there with the two boys from the night before, along with an older sister and her husband and Thsermi's parents. He was introduced to those he had not met earlier and assumed they lived in the smaller outbuildings he had seen nestled in the trees away from the house.

The meal was a lively and happy affair that took some time, partly because meals among The People were seen as a social event where discussion was as important as the food, but also because Lestze was new and interesting and was wrung dry of every bit of information he was happy to give.

Eventually, he held his hands up, saying good-humouredly, "It must be time to get back to work. Besides, it looks like I will be here for a few days, so we can talk more later."

As Dginze nodded to him and stood up, he added, "I have nothing better to do, so is there anything I can do to help?" Thsermi frowned, making it clear to anyone paying attention she felt it was demeaning his position as an honoured guest to expect him to work, and Lestze was aware Dginze picked up her feeling too.

Lestze looked at him and raised his eyebrows with a smile. Dginze shrugged back with a clear suggestion of 'I will have to deal with this later' but said cheerfully, "Come with me," and led the way out the door.

Lestze silently followed him through a patch of garden and out into the forest. They soon entered a small clearing, more a patch of light that centred on the devastation created recently when a large limb had broken off one of the giant trees that formed the canopy high above and crashed through the understorey below.

Dginze gestured towards the pile of logs cut from the broken branches and said, "The boys have been working on this for a couple of days. I would appreciate your help carrying it back to the house." With that, he lifted the log from the top of the pile and carefully balanced it on his shoulders, turning it till there were no lumps digging into him, then started to walk back. As Lestze struggled to get the next piece on his shoulders, he noticed Dginze had paused and half turned to see how he was doing. When Dginze saw the log balanced on Lestze's shoulders, he turned and continued on his path, showing neither approval nor dissatisfaction.

As the afternoon continued, Lestze was soon acutely grateful that lunch had run late and there was not a huge amount of the day left. What had seemed to be a random pile of sticks had been cut with a particular goal in mind. Thicker limbs had been cut shorter, thinner branches were longer and the pieces had been cut so each would weigh about what a man could 'comfortably' carry with a precision that surprised him. At least you would be comfortable if you had been carrying logs all your life, he reflected glumly.

As they got back to the homestead, the logs were stacked in piles in layers at right angles to each other and with a little gap between them to allow air movement to help them dry out. As the piles reached shoulder height, the sides were sloped inwards to allow a steep-pitched, thatched layer or 'roof' to be laid over them to keep the ever-present rain out.

Lestze realized they were carrying firewood, though not for this season as winter was already upon them and the wood would take some time to dry. Better lengths of timber, thicker, straighter and undamaged by the fall, had been left to be cut later when the debris and less valuable waste wood had been cleared away. It was more efficient to carry the firewood in as big a piece as possible to cut later than to cut it up where it had fallen, then have to carry lots of small pieces back to the homestead.

However, he became more interested and a little bemused as the afternoon wore on. For all intents and purposes, this was just an old man carrying wood and yet Dginze moved serenely through the forest, at one with and as much part of the forest as any of the forest's other denizens. He turned and sidestepped without effort to ensure the branches he carried never tangled with all the obstacles, the ferns, saplings and fallen debris, of the forest floor. He was careful where he put his feet and changed paths regularly to minimize the damage their passing made.

He moved gracefully with a natural economy of effort and energy despite the heavy weights he carried. Lestze could only marvel at the old man's completely unconscious display of virtuosity. He had often seen great dancers perform and heard many great singers sing. He had been suitably impressed by their great artistic ability and charisma, though not necessarily by their character. He finally realized he was watching a degree of mastery that was every bit as real as that possessed by those great artists and equally only achieved by a lifetime of effort and mindfulness to what he was doing. Mastery of the sort Dginze displayed without self-consciousness or affectation had always gone unnoticed, at least by him, because it seemed so ordinary and commonplace, and yet — was it any less important or admirable?

8

A Change of Heart

Dginze called a halt to their labour early, at least well before sunset. "If you're too tired to talk this evening, I'll be in more trouble," he commented dryly. However, instead of walking back to the house, he angled his way down to the river and threaded his way between the trees that lined the bank.

"In a way," he observed conversationally, "the river has become our Achilles heel. We have always been able to use it for transport so have no roads in this area, apart from the tracks we use from time to time. As you are aware, the invaders' flying machines easily see whatever is moving on the river and have, in the last week, warned off our boats on the river too. You probably haven't heard yet that they have found a new use for the small boats they had near the jump station for exploring when they first came. The boats are patrolling the river from time to time, crewed by soldiers, and they are much faster than anything we have. While they have not attacked anyone yet, we have stopped using the river for the meantime.

"The reason I bring this up is there are no proper tracks north from here through the hills and it would not be easy for an experienced group of The People to make the journey. Your guest is certainly not up to it. You will have to decide whether taking her further is worth the risk of being discovered if you go by the river. You are welcome to stay here with her, though I understand keeping her near their bastion is also a substantial risk."

Lestze was aware the invaders had other ways of seeing besides helicopters or planes and may have had the capacity to launch small satellites among other things. Seeing people moving on the river would be easy for them. The two men rambled silently along the river while Lestze collected his thoughts. He sighed inwardly to himself and accepted the inevitable. "I had intended to get Atawhai to the elders (the thought 'and off my hands' passed accusingly through his mind too, but was filtered out as he spoke) as soon as possible but I agree it seems best to stay here for the meantime, at least until she is stronger," he replied after a little thought. "I hadn't considered the difficulty of moving her on land either, but your observations are obviously correct. Not only would it be too difficult, it would waste too much time in the present crisis."

They continued walking companionably for some time. Dginze strolled downriver till they reached a decaying jetty, timbers of different ages clearly indicating regular repair, running out into the river. It went out into deep water and could only have been built during a very dry summer. The size of the timber poles buried in the river bed suggested a significant number of people had worked on the project. Dginze commented, "This was once an important staging post for development upstream, but its importance dwindled as the village at Two Rivers grew. Commerce along the river has been steadily scaled down since the jump station was built with new development being focused where the Greedy Ones would be less likely to interfere."

They walked back into the forest and continued parallel to the riverbank until they reached a small river that flowed into the large one. Dginze showed Lestze the boats his family looked after for The People to use when needed. They had been recently paddled up the tributary and pulled out on to the bank under thick forest, hidden from prying eyes. He said, "The boats could do with being cleaned down and repainted to preserve the wood while they are not being used if you are looking for things to do."

Lestze groaned to himself as they walked through the forest. Spreading the thick, tar-like oil on the boat hulls would be much easier in the heat of summer and it would soak more quickly into the wood too. He could see, though, that as the boats were not likely to be used in the near future, it was a convenient time to get the task out of the way. Dginze was all too aware it would be an unpleasant job and had been polite enough not to ask him directly to do the task, leaving it to his own inclination to do the work or not.

Having said what he wanted to say, Dginze headed straight back towards the house, if straight described a route that mostly followed the contour, unless that created too big a deviation, while detouring around trees and swamp, a route that seemingly unconsciously made the most efficient compromise between effort and time.

When the house came into sight, they washed well in the cold water at a sandy bank of the river, then cleaned their feet again at the door before going in.

Thsermi walked over and touched her husband gently by way of greeting before saying to Lestze, "Atawhai is awake and asked for you some time ago. Would you come to see her?"

He followed Thsermi the few steps to the alcove where she stood aside to allow him to push aside the curtain and walk in. Atawhai started a little at the sounds he made, jerking her head to look up, then softened a little, letting her head sink back to the bed. He asked quietly how she was feeling and instead of replying to his question she asked, "Can you take me outside please."

He looked down at her, saying ruefully, "No, that wouldn't be right. You are still too unwell for me consider that."

She pulled herself up to a sitting position and said with a quiet sincerity that affected him more than any amount of histrionics would have, "I really want to do this. Help me please." He thought silently for a few moments before nodding his head and calling for Thsermi.

Thsermi was there almost immediately, walking in quickly in case there was something wrong. When Lestze told her Atawhai wanted to go outside she tensed to protest but glanced at Atawhai before saying anything. Their eyes held for a long moment and Lestze could sense some unspoken agreement passed between them. Without missing a beat Thsermi said to Lestze, "I will get a robe. It will be easier for her to get into and should keep out the evening cold." She bustled out, shooing Lestze in front of her, and was back in a moment, thick winter robe in hand. Thsermi helped Atawhai put it on before calling Lestze back in.

Between the two of them they helped Atawhai to the front door where they stopped as Lestze asked her what she wanted to do. She looked around before pointing to some higher ground away from the river that was still highlighted by the setting sun. The late afternoon was looking brighter than earlier in the day as the fog had finally lifted and the rain was still holding off, though not far away.

As Lestze picked her up easily and carried her down the steps towards her chosen position, Thsermi turned back into the house then followed after them with a blanket in her hand. She hurried to reach the knoll at the same time Lestze did and folded the blanket in two before putting it on the ground for Atawhai to sit on. Without a word, Thsermi turned and walked back towards the house as Lestze lowered Atawhai on to it.

Not knowing what was expected of him, Lestze sat beside Atawhai and watched Thsermi walking away, aware there was already an understanding between the two women that surprised him. He turned towards Atawhai, noticing her body trying to sweat and shiver at the same time. After a moment he realized she was staring intently northwards.

He followed her gaze towards the Mountain that reared up there, its summit hidden by the thick grey clouds ominously poised to pour rain on their parade, trying to see what was absorbing her interest.

"I know where we are," Atawhai commented wistfully.

"What?" he exclaimed, confused by another rapid change in subject.

"I know where we are," she repeated in a more conversational tone this time. "That mountain, I know it, some of my family are buried there. We call it Taupiri." She frowned for a moment as if the name was a bad taste in her mouth. It reminded her where she really was as she trailed off, "At least I would if I was on my world."

He could sense the undercurrents in her head. Where she had been disoriented by all the travel through the forest now she had a reference point and therefore knew approximately where or in which direction the jump station was. Escape was a possibility once more.

Her words, innocent enough on her part, reawakened the spectre of responsibility and fear in Lestze's mind. They had reached the home on the riverbank after a long day's walk, crisscrossing between swamp and drier ridges covered with dense forest. He had taken for granted Atawhai would be lost, but knowing where she was would also tell her the jump station was not so far away as it might seem. She could get there easily in two days — much less if she put her mind to it, just by roughly following the river upstream. He would have to be on his guard again for any signs of her trying to escape.

Atawhai put her hand gently on his arm to catch his attention and spoke his name.

He grunted noncommittally, still absorbed by images of the consequences of her returning to the station with the knowledge that some of The People were telepaths. It would be a catastrophe from a tactical point of view.

Atawhai tried to wait patiently for Lestze to remember she was there and pay attention, but knowing a lady could never rely on a man noticing her when it was in his own best interests to do so, impetuousness won the battle. Remembering wrestling with her elder brother, she lifted her hand slightly and pinched the inside of his upper arm, twisting a little as she did. As expected, she had his full attention instantly, along with a satisfying flinch and a very reproachful glare.

Feeling exhaustion creeping rapidly up on her and the need to say what was on her mind before it won, Atawhai exclaimed, "I was wrong about you. You — no, your people — are not the savage brutes our government has always said you are. You have treated me as kindly as you could under the circumstances but your people, even those who know what I have done to their friends and family, have treated me better than I deserve. I feel shamed by their graciousness." She paused, both for breath and to emphasize her next words. "I give you my word I will not try to harm you or your people." After another pause, she looked up into his eyes and with an eerie kind of prescience added, "I will not try to run away either; I promise.

You can look into my mind and check if you don't believe me."

Lestze did not have to. He could feel the sincerity in every word she spoke. He shook his head as Atawhai slumped back, drained by the effort. She sighed, "I had hoped I would feel better if I was out in the sun, but I need to go back."

Wordlessly, Lestze picked her up, putting his hands under the blanket and doing his best to wrap her in it then carried her back to the house, through the dining room to place her gently on her bed. She was already asleep, so he called Thsermi to make Atawhai as comfortable as possible.

Lestze would have liked to be alone with his own thoughts but members of the family were already assembling in the dining room in preparation for dinner and it would have been rude for him to walk out. He was soon enmeshed in a turmoil of laughter, conversation and seeming random participation in the tasks of setting up the meal. There were more places being set at the table than there was for lunch and provision being made for others who could fit there. He sighed as he realized this was shaping into a major social event.

The evening turned out as he expected. People turned up from some distance away. The family there had obviously sent one of their number around to invite their neighbours. Lestze was of course the centre of attention. What stood out for him was the interest in Atawhai shown by the group. Thsermi and those of her daughters who had spent time with Atawhai looking after her when she had been awake had thoroughly discussed their thoughts during the night. Atawhai did not make sense to them. She had killed people and her society was insane. How could she seem so ordinary and decent?

9

Calm before the Storm

Lestze woke early the next morning feeling, surprisingly, happy. Thinking about it, he realized it was because all he could do was wait — there was nothing he had to try to organize or be responsible for. He was in the eye of the storm. Nobody was expecting him to be the solution to their problems or know the right thing to do in any situation, just because of who he was. In a way, just for a moment, he felt free.

Lestze waited, relaxed in his tiny alcove, when normally he would be diving into his day as soon as he woke. He listened peacefully to the noise of activity in the living room building in a crescendo as the family prepared for breakfast and went out to join them.

After an extended breakfast, Lestze stepped out the door into a fog so heavy he could see little more than an arm's length, while the temperature had fallen overnight and was close to freezing. He deliberated only a few moments before stepping back inside and closing the door.

The family chatter paused as he returned to the table. Dginze winked at him when he sat down. They had already written off the morning and were interested to see he had come to his senses.

An hour later, he borrowed a blanket and a woven mat and stepped out again, much to the family's amusement.

Lestze walked tentatively into the grey to get away from the immediate presence of other minds. He followed his memory of the day before into the forest to a dense understorey tree. The thatch of leaves channelled the airborne moisture outwards into a curtain of rain around the drip-line, but it was dry enough near the trunk. Lestze sat on the mat, wrapped the blanket around him and set his mind to contact Senden.

Lestze felt a subtle change that told him Senden was aware of him and waited patiently. Almost half an hour later, Senden's thought greeted him, 'You are more settled than yesterday Lestze.'

'Yes. Atawhai is still sick and should not be moved for a few more days. Aside from that, the family here think it would be unsafe to move her even if she were well. The river is being monitored and traffic disrupted sometimes. She might be noticed.'

Senden thought privately for a few moments before communicating, 'I was hoping to see her as soon as possible. Is there anything else you observed that might be useful?'

'No, she hasn't given any further information and the situation has not changed.' Then as an afterthought, 'Atawhai appears to be friendlier than I expected.'

'Explain?' with a strong undertone of interest.

'She promised me yesterday she would not try to escape.'

Senden insisted on seeing the event as Lestze had experienced it, paying particular attention to Lestze's empathetic awareness and assessment of her state of mind.

'She is not inimical to us, even if she is not on our side. That is better than I had hopped. I will sail down to you immediately.'

Dismissal was inherent in the last statement, but Lestze had not finished.

'I was amazed yesterday by the complexity of the Great Council. It is far more than a telepathic meeting of elders from around the world. Why wasn't I told? It should have been a major part of my education.'

There was a pause again as Senden decided whether to deal with this now.

'The council has maintained a stable society for many millennia. The original incursion showed us how vulnerable our stability has made us to a technologically advanced race. Relying so much on what has worked in the past has made us overly cautious and set in our ways. Part of your training has been to ensure you are not reliant on wisdom and values learnt from the past.'

'Is that why the council members interrogated me so ruthlessly yesterday? I was being tested?'

'Yes. The council is trying unusual innovations to make our culture more flexible and able to adapt. You are only one of many. As an experiment you have been successful beyond our expectations. Your behaviour is spontaneous and completely unpredictable — even by your mentors who know your mind well. You represent the best we can produce, of what we are, without being constrained or defined by the weight of experience. However, you can't blame the council for being careful. From some points of view, you are more dangerous to our culture than the invasion is.'

The link ended without so much as a goodbye as Senden was already considering the logistics of his trip.

Lestze returned to the house to warm up and wait for lunch. He was surprised when Thsermi brought Atawhai out to eat with them. After lunch, Lestze broke the news that Senden was on his way. This caused a flurry of activity as Thsermi organized the family to prepare. Lestze spent the afternoon with one of Thsermi's sons catching and cleaning fish and eels from the river for dinner. Any excess would be preserved by smoking or drying.

Atawhai was still up when they returned with their catch. Lestze was shepherded over to sit by her near the fire. She asked him what he had been doing so he described his last two days' work for the family, finishing with "What do you usually do?"

"I was trained as an exo-biologist. I study the biology of other planets or, rather, other timelines of the Earth. More recently, I have been looking at the feasibility of large-scale settlement of other timelines for the company I work for."

"Is that why you are here? So this really is an invasion of our world. I had assumed you were a soldier. You were the one driving the tank, after all."

Atawhai blushed. "Please don't judge me by that. It was not my choice."

"Why not?"

"The place where the jump station opens in my world is Hamilton, by our standards an insignificant city in a small country. The station has not been used much for many years so was effectively unguarded. I work at a much larger station in one of the world's most powerful countries. I was home with my family when a group of rich men decided to illegally escape to your world to establish their own colony. I was the only specialist on alternate worlds in my country at the time, so they effectively kidnaped me — forcing me to come and help them survive to build a viable society here. It is a relatively small group and not intended as an invasion."

"In that case, why did you attack the villages with the tank? When the jump station was built your people got along with ours reasonably well. They weren't hostile without reason or warning."

"The rebel leaders were taken by surprise when we arrived, and we found established villages both up and down the river and in the forest around the station. It was a panic reaction really, as the surveys done when the station was built showed no population centres nearby. Those in charge of security, military contractors, or mercenaries to be honest, had assumed none of your people would know we were here. When they found those unexpected villages right on the doorstep, they decided to scare the population away. I know the first surveyors wouldn't have missed something like that. Those villages have recently been established around the station for a reason. Why were they?"

Lestze refused to comment, feeling he had given away enough secrets already. The silence between them was starting to become awkward when Thsermi asked them to help set out the meal.

Next morning, Lestze was set to restocking the firewood at the house with enough to last the next week or so. It took him all morning, but as lunchtime approached he slipped into the forest to contact Senden and check on his progress. Over lunch, he told the family Senden was on a ship coming south down the east coast and should be able to cross to the west coast where the two harbours almost met before nightfall. By sailing early next morning and catching the ingoing tide up the river, he should make it to the house by nightfall.

Atawhai was uncomfortable talking to Lestze when the family was gathered. The younger ones could speak English after a fashion and tried to do so around her out of politeness. Normally, they seldom used the language and they often lapsed into their own when the topics were more difficult or interesting. Atawhai didn't like missing out on large parts of every conversation so she apprehended Lestze before he could disappear after the meal.

"Who is Senden?"

"He is a representative of the planetary government."

"Why is he coming here?"

"Well, we do have a war here you know."

Atawhai ignored the comment and thought for a while. "No, why is he coming here *now*. The family had no idea he was coming until you told them yesterday. Then you told them today when he is going to arrive. . . . You must be in contact with him. There is no other way you could know. You can talk to him with your mind in the same way you know what I am thinking."

He sighed, feeling inept again. Damn, she is quick. He is supposed to be in charge of the resistance here and despite his best efforts it was clear he was unable to keep anything secret.

Atawhai laughed at the downcast look on his face. "And now I know how you can have a planetary culture and government without any apparent form of global communication. All our surveys concluded this planet held isolated splinters of a dominant culture on the different continents. It didn't make sense that there was no fragmentation and cultural differentiation. We were wrong. You do have a global government and it was your government that set up those villages around the jump station, wasn't it?"

Lestze decided there was no further point in trying to conceal the truth. "Yes, the families in those villages are volunteers."

"But why? You can't have been waiting for an invasion for nearly forty years!"

"Not exactly. The villages have only been established recently, even though forty years is a very short time from the point of view of the council. When the station was being built the Great Council studied your people and came to the conclusion that war between us was inevitable.

They estimated it would be close to a hundred years before overpopulation, pollution and resource depletion would force your governments to attack another populated timeline. They are preparing for that now and are obviously thinking a long way ahead. Our government is so stable it didn't occur to them a rebel group might attack so much sooner."

"Back to my original question. Why is Senden coming now?"

Lestze gave in. "He wants to speak to you."

"That's what I thought. Why not just tell me?"

He frowned, "It honestly had not occurred to me as an option. I have no idea if we are still enemies or not."

"You can be amazingly dense sometimes." Atawhai laughed happily. "What is his position in the government here?"

"He *is* the government for these islands."

"That doesn't make sense. There must be more government representatives here. What about you?"

"I was appointed by the council, so I guess that makes me a representative too."

"What do you mean you guess? You can't run a country with only two people."

"Why does anyone need to run the country. A properly organized society is largely self-governing. However, its citizens need to be trained from an early age to consider the effects and consequences of their actions on the wider society and to take responsibility for them. Your whole culture is based around the assumption that people are stupid, that they need someone to tell them what to do and organize their lives. That is wrong. Intelligence is a product of education and learning, not the other way around. If you teach people that they are dependent on governments, investments, jobs provided by others, you end up with a whole world of learned helplessness. If you teach people to be self-reliant and to be able to make whatever they need to live a happy life, they are inherently much harder to manipulate or control. They don't need a government's interference to survive. They cooperate with a government out of intelligent self-interest and only if they believe the government operates out of concern for the greater good of the society. In that sense, the everyday people you see *are* the government and can be trusted to be the government because they are willing to govern themselves first."

He stood up to forestall any further conversation and, after thanking Thsermi for the meal, walked out to find Dginze, hoping to be given something useful to do for the afternoon that didn't require thinking or subterfuge.

Lestze worked late, if it could be called work, foraging through the forest far from the homestead. He was searching out the last flush of forest mushrooms before winter, picking fresh edible fern fronds and looking for higher populations of birds where he could set traps. Mostly, he was avoiding returning to prying questions.

10

An Unexpected Request

Lestze was surprised to see a young stranger chatting animatedly with the few family members present when he returned to the house. Thsermi greeted Lestze happily, with the news that Yensen was here to see him, but that any business would need to wait till after dinner.

Lestze was intrigued, if not alarmed, assuming there had been some change in the status of the conflict important enough to send a messenger. However, he felt a little guilty as they had waited politely for him so they could start their meal, and he had the good sense not to argue with Thsermi. He could feel her disapproval of his tardiness.

Regardless of that, once the usual chatter that went with any meal was in full swing, Yensen caught Lestze's attention and said, "The leaders from the villages are unable to reach a decision about what to do next, and the uncertainty is quickly brewing into argument and dissension. They are asking you to come and intervene as soon as you can." He then passed over a small piece of thin leather folded so that a scratched glyph covered most of the front.

Lestze unfolded it to look at the few symbols on the other side, then sighed as he carefully refolded it to put it in his tunic pocket. "I will come with you in the morning, if that is acceptable, Yensen."

The boy just nodded. The family conversations that had died down while they watched the exchange sprang up once more.

Atawhai moved to squeeze in by Lestze afterwards.

"What was that all about, Lestze?"

"The people from the villages have asked me to come and help them decide what to do."

"Do you really have to go? I don't want to be left behind here."

"I had really wanted to be here when Senden arrived, but this is an unusually formal request. The leaders are worried. I can't turn them down without good reason."

"Can I see the message please?"

He handed it to her and she turned it over carefully several times without opening it. "What does this symbol mean?"

"It's a representation of an old pictograph really. From a language that isn't spoken any more, but everyone recognizes the more common symbols. The simplest or literal translation would be 'The Living Trees.'"

"Okay, but that still doesn't tell me what it means or why it is here."

"When I graduated my training, I chose it as a symbol to represent me in my governmental position or me in my official role. To differentiate that from me as a person. While it says 'the living trees', 'the forest ecology' would be a better way of explaining it, but still doesn't really describe it. A forest is a huge living system where all the seeming parts, trees for instance, are dependent on other parts of the system to maintain the environment they all survive in. It is a symbol of the total interdependence of living things. That any living thing is reliant on other living things to create a healthy environment to live in."

She unfolded the leather and looked at the symbols, "And the rest?"

"It is a formal request for me to come to adjudicate a dispute. However, it seems more likely they want me to come and make the decision rather than simply arbitrate between the two sides. It's easier that way. It's my fault if the decision is wrong and, either way, no one loses face. Unfortunately, it is a request I can't in good conscience refuse. You are safe here, and I am sure you will like Senden.

11

The Great Man Comes?

Lestze had set his internal clock and woke early. He was intending to wake up Yensen who had slept on the floor beside the fire in the family room and leave without fanfare, but Thsermi had beaten him to the draw. She was already bustling around the room preparing an early breakfast while, under her direction, one of her daughters was carefully wrapping and packing dried food into a woven bag.

"Good morning, Lestze," she winked. "I guessed you would want to be on your way early, so we are working on an early breakfast for you."

"Thank you, Thsermi, I'm grateful for your help," he said, accepting defeat gracefully.

He sat to the side of the room, seeing nothing else he could do to help and not wanting to be in the way. Shortly after, Yensen turned up with two of the other members of the extended family while Thsermi had called Atawhai. She was obviously assembling the family to see him off, though a number where missing.

It was an hour and a half later before Atawhai watched Lestze and Yensen walk into the forest, both carrying full packs. The sun had been up for a while, though it was difficult to tell between the dense fog and the forest gloom they faded into.

Atawhai turned back wistfully to close the door and sit by the fire. The others peeled off in different directions to attend to their allotted chores. Apart from helping prepare and set the table for lunch, she had nothing to do so was alone with her thoughts and mounting fears.

Late in the afternoon, she heard an echoing, rhythmic cry, faint from the distance it had travelled. Thsermi looked up from her preparations and said, "He will be at the jetty soon. Would you like to come with me to greet him?"

She was alarmed for a moment but answered "Yes" almost instantly. Better to go meet the threat than wait unknowing and helpless for it to fall on her head.

Thsermi nodded, dropped what she was doing and walked out the door without a backward glance. Atawhai was surprised and had to hurry to keep up. She asked, "Who called out?"

"Our youngest boy. He was given a job downriver a little so he could keep an eye out for the boat. He will walk upriver with it as they come to make sure they don't miss the jetty."

They followed the winding path around the river's edge to the jetty where the boy was already waiting. The boat was almost there and was surprisingly small, tiny more like, with only four men in it. The sail was furled, useless in the breezeless afternoon of the river valley. Atawhai saw all four men were working hard at the oars, making slow progress against the flow of the river. She let out the breath she hadn't realized she was holding and laughed out loud as some of the tension ebbed. Thsermi looked questioningly, but Atawhai made no comment. So much for the governor of these islands, the man of great power and self-importance she had been dreading. At first thought, she couldn't even say which of the four was Senden, but as the boat reached the jetty she could see one man was considerably older than the other three and knew he had to be Senden.

The boat hit the jetty lightly and one of the younger men at the front leapt on to it with a rope, which he tied as the other two held the jetty to keep the boat stable for Senden to step up. Senden walked briskly up the riverbank from the jetty and hugged Thsermi, greeting her by name. They spoke happily for a few moments before he stepped over to Atawhai, saying, "Hello Atawhai, I am Senden. I have come a long way to meet you." He took her hand to shake it, paused as he assessed her, then gave her a light hug with his other arm before Thsermi took his hand to lead him back towards the house.

Atawhai stood silently on the riverbank, watching the three men and the boy take the boat back downriver where they could beach it and drag it into the cover of the forest. Eventually, after they had gone, she spun on her heel to return to the house as the afternoon darkened towards evening.

12

The Trial Begins

Atawhai woke early the next morning and left her sleeping nook as soon as she was dressed. Senden was already up, talking to a man she had not seen before, while Thsermi was bustling with breakfast in the kitchen area. Thsermi interrupted the conversation to introduce Atawhai to him. Once his conversation with Senden resumed and Thsermi had co-opted Atawhai to help, she told Atawhai he was one of the leaders of a clan who were mining coal half a day's walk to the north-west.

The man was given an early breakfast before he left, but another two arrived soon after. The pattern continued all morning with people constantly dribbling in to pay their respects to Senden. Thsermi insisted on introducing Atawhai to everyone who came and kept a running commentary, in her broken English, on where they were from, what they were doing and why.

Sometime after midday the flow of visitors tailed off. By now, Atawhai was more angry than tired. This was supposed to be important. Senden's visit was supposed to be about her and he had ignored her completely. Here she was, ready to bring an end to all the misunderstandings and bloodshed and she had spent God knows how many hours serving food without a break.

"It's time to take a break," Thsermi informed Senden as their most recent visitor left. "If anyone else comes, they will just have to wait." He acquiesced with a smile and nod, got up, stretched and walked out the door.

By the time he returned, Thsermi and Atawhai had organized the next stage of the progressive meal for themselves. Once they began eating, there was chatter between Senden and Thsermi for a few moments before Senden turned to look directly at Atawhai and said in almost unaccented English, "Now Miss Atawhai, it is probably time I paid some attention to you. How do you feel about the present situation?" She knew instantly from the good humour with which he said it that he was aware of her inner tantrums and for a moment felt ashamed to speak, then decided to put on a good front.

"I want to help negotiate peace between our peoples — to find a way we can coexist or grow, maybe even help each other."

"Any decision like that is a long way in the future. Until we really know what is going on here, the council cannot make any decision on whether your people and ours can come to an accommodation or, as a longshot, work together, whether to ignore your beachhead on our world for the meantime or whether to drive your people off our world now."

"You couldn't do that." She was shocked at the simple confidence in his statement.

"Even with your advanced weapons we have enough people in the forest and the other settlements all over this island to overpower yours if I call them together. The slaughter would be horrible, but we would win."

She felt a sudden stab of despair. "Nothing I can do will make a difference, will it?"

"You are right, it won't. But who you are is making a difference. Your willingness to listen, to be open, to be even sitting here talking to me has impressed Lestze, and me as well. However, I have to get the truth, or as much of it as you know, to help in making that decision."

"Why don't you read my mind, isn't that what Lestze did?"

"I would prefer not to. It is an act of violence for a start. Equally, it is unlikely I would get the whole picture without your cooperation and a good deal of my effort would be wasted on your resistance."

"But you will take what you want anyway."

He sighed. "Eventually, I might, but I have not decided at this stage. I am responsible for the lives and well-being of my people. Enough have died already and I won't order hundreds more to die if I can avoid it. I am here to talk to you.

"I will make you a promise. If you will answer my questions as fully and as honestly as you can, I will answer any of yours to the best of my ability."

Atawhai only thought for a moment. "You will answer honestly any question I might ask?"

"Yes."

A longer pause this time. "Okay. I agree to your terms — you are a telepath, aren't you?"

"Yes."

"Are you as good a telepath as Lestze?" (Part of her mind noted that it was odd she asked about Lestze.)

"Far better, or stronger if you like. He is not a particularly good telepath by our standards." Senden thought quietly for a while. "He is really a very advanced empath, but that doesn't describe his role or position in our society properly either." He thought quietly for a little more. "Perhaps the best way to explain it would be to say he is a psychic systems engineer. Clans like the one he comes from have been developed over many generations to strengthen the trait."

"What — do you mean selective breeding?"

"Yes, that's a good way to explain it."

"You can't do that to people. Selective breeding is morally indefensible," she exploded with righteous indignation.

If Senden was surprised by her vehemence, he gave no sign. "Why would you see selective breeding for particular talents or character traits as unethical? Surely an intelligent society would pick and train its leaders very carefully. In your world, the only qualification people need to become world leaders is an abundance of ambition and greed. A large helping of megalomania is almost certainly a requirement as well. In general, in your society only the most socially and morally corrupt individuals have any hope of achieving political power. They then jealously guard that influence and power by endeavouring to ensure their children follow them in the political framework and tend to marry within their elite.

"By setting up a system that gives power to the most narcissistic, cruel and ambitious, over the generations, your civilization is conducting an interesting scientific experiment in selectively breeding its leaders for the utmost amorality. How is that working out for you?"

Try as she might, Atawhai was unable to feel any sarcasm behind his comments but still felt irked by his attitude. "What if I decided to ruin your precious breeding programme and convinced him to marry me. It wouldn't be too hard."

To her surprise, Senden laughed loudly and delightedly. "And how would you know it wouldn't be too hard? Forget that. How long did it take you to figure out Lestze meant you no harm?"

"You mean after I got over being knocked out and tied to a tree in the pitch dark in your black hole of a dismal jungle?"

"Pretty much," he agreed happily.

"Half a day, I would guess."

"Don't you think that's a little unusual? Would either of your two male friends from the tank have reacted the same way?"

"They were not my friends! . . . Sorry, that was a tender spot. They would still be doing their best to kill him, and the rest of you as well."

"True. It should be clear to you that you are unusually empathic. Many people are to some extent, but you trust your feelings and act on what you feel." He started laughing again. "You would make a fine wife for him — if you are looking forward to owning only what you stand up in, going wherever you are sent by the council, sometimes without warning and, to make it really great, dedicating your life to the well-being of our people. Feel free to think it over before accepting this fine offer.

"As an afterthought, if I was unhappy with the idea, I could always send Lestze on a mission to what you would call Australia or, better yet, Europe." He started chuckling again. "On that high note, let's take a break. We'll talk more later."

Later didn't happen. Another person had arrived to see Senden, and also some of the missing members of the family started turning up. Looking back, Atawhai realized family members had been disappearing soon after

Lestze had told the family when Senden would arrive. The length of time it was taking people to arrive was an indication of how far away they lived.

The return of some of Thsermi's girls meant Atawhai was not needed to help in the kitchen, and Senden was busy again. She spent the afternoon trying to amuse herself as best she could, but the dark clouds in her imagination multiplied.

13
Are Values Valuable?

Atawhai got up early two days later to find Senden had kindled the fire and was alone, sitting by it. She sat beside him and poured out what was on her mind. "You wouldn't really order an attack on the station, would you? The people there would show yours no mercy and you don't even have guns."

"At this stage, no. But what if we see the only possible choices are we destroy the station or everything we are will be lost and destroyed. We haven't had a war in many millennia. It would go against everything our government has stood for, so it is not an easy decision to make."

"Then why are you making weapons? You are training some of your people as soldiers too, aren't you? The surveyors said your culture was completely peaceful, not even major arguments between individuals. It seems to me you have abandoned your values."

"We have never been intending to go to war with you. We are developing more sophisticated weapons as fast as developments in our science will allow, but only here and in a couple of other places."

"What other places, and why?

"If I was to say near where Washington, Leningrad, Shanghai and a couple of other major cities located in your world, what would you guess?"

"That's where the jump stations are, but there's nothing connecting them to this world. Why would you bother?"

"We know you need an anchor point, a managing mechanism in any parallel universe to be able to safely transfer objects larger than microscopic. If the amounts of energy or matter swapped are not exact, the results can be catastrophic. Bearing that in mind, when hostilities break out between our worlds, we intend to have a strong enough force around the station to storm it and destroy it. That would finish any chance of interference for some time. However, your governments would be unlikely to attempt to rebuild here and would try again from one of the other stations. We need to be ready for that on our world anywhere there is a jump station in your timeline."

"If you see the station as such a threat, why haven't you destroyed it already? It would have been easy when there were only the caretakers here."

"It would have tipped our hand, warned your governments and given them time to come up with other ways to get around our intervention."

"You said earlier you haven't had war in many millennia. For such a stable society, how come you haven't improved your technology and standard of living?

Senden smiled, then started laughing. "You don't seem to be getting the hang of this. I'm supposed to be interrogating you, remember." His mood was infectious and in a trice Atawhai was laughing too. Senden sobered up first and added, "A dozen questions crop up for every answer I give you. I'm not in a rush, your people are not going anywhere but, still, time is important. I could do with an answer or two."

"Okay. I guess I owe you one."

"If I have to make do with only one then it has to be the crucial one. Why are your people here?"

"To escape a plague that has killed over fifteen per cent of our population."

"What's the point? If the plague has already killed that many people, surely, with your highly mobile society, everyone will have been exposed already.

"It's not that simple. When the plague hit, every pharmaceutical company on the planet worked day and night and someone eventually developed a vaccine for it. We thought that was the finish of it, but nine months later, close to a month ago, a new outbreak started in Europe and the vaccine is useless. Some very rich men hired a private security company and took over the jump station. They came here with their families and some hired guns, then shut down the station at this end so they can't be followed.

"So we needn't be concerned about an invasion by a well-equipped army in the near future."

"No. These people are renegades trying to save their own skin. They will be treated very harshly if they are caught."

"That explains why they brought the tank with them. They wouldn't have been expecting us to give any great resistance. They are terrified of reprisals from your world."

"Yes. When the first plague occurred, civil disorder on a massive scale broke out as the disease began appearing all over the world in a matter of weeks. I said fifteen per cent of the population died from the plague, but huge numbers also died from the rioting and chaos in the cities. Basically, martial law was declared over the entire planet and still exists. The different countries' armies were united, in some cases forcibly, under the United Nations. Since then people have really tried to work together to get the world back on its feet and, among other things, the vaccine was developed as a result of collaboration between companies and countries." People have actually worked for the common good, not for their own country or their own profit. Now people are working together to rebuild. Those here will be hated for breaching the worldwide trust and solidarity that have been growing for the first time in our history."

Atawhai fell silent and Senden waited patiently, sensing a change in her mood. Soon silent tears were running down her cheeks. "Thank you for being so open. We really needed to know what we are facing," he said soothingly.

Atawhai began struggling to hold back sobs but between them managed to get out: "My thoughts have been totally consumed with what is happening here. I had forgotten about home, my family. The world is probably falling part again with war and riots, and people, everyone I know, could be dying." She trailed off for a short time then said, "This is not a question; it's a request. Can you help my people, my world? Will you, if you can? I am begging you."

Senden sighed. "Give me some time. At least we know what we are dealing with now." He closed his eyes and relaxed into his chair. Atawhai fed some more logs into the fire and sat back to wait. Thsermi came out shortly after, saw the two sitting by the fire and nodded to Atawhai before getting into her morning chores without a word.

Senden was motionless for most of an hour before opening his eyes and sitting up abruptly. "We will help as we can. The council has agreed. As to whether we can help, the healers I contacted don't have enough to go on. Were you infected by the plague during its first round?"

"Yes. Most people were. It was a kind of influenza that has an unusually long incubation period and then takes a long time to kill."

"Good. The consensus is they want Lestze to have a good look through your body and see what changes or effects are still visible to him."

"He's been away for a while now. He told me when he left he wasn't expecting to be away for long. Why haven't we heard from him?"

Senden smiled broadly. "If I had to guess, I would say he is doing something he thinks I wouldn't approve of. If he doesn't contact me, I can hardly say no."

"Couldn't you contact him?"

"Yes, but it would ruin the fun. That young man continues to surprise me."

"Would he really help me? After what I have done here?"

"Of course he will. He couldn't hold a grudge if he tried. We will all do what we can. Nothing held back."

She started weeping again, as much in reaction to the unconditional kindness she felt flowing from Senden as to the cold despair she felt as she thought of her world.

Atawhai slunk back to her nook and refused to join the family as they assembled for breakfast. When lunchtime came and went and she refused to come out, one of Thsermi's daughters brought something for her to eat and waited for her, refusing to leave until she had finished. To prevent further intrusion on her solitude, she spent the afternoon walking along the riverbank and the forest margin, looking for the paths the natives here seemed to follow so easily.

She had composed herself and was ready to be with people again when she returned to the house as the sun went down. Thsermi stepped over to hug her as she walked in, saying, "We are really sorry for your people." The theme continued throughout the evening with everyone offering their condolences.

Sometime after the meal, when most of the family had left for their own huts, Senden waved Atawhai over to the empty space next to him by the embers of the fire. "Feeling better?" he asked as she sat down.

"Personally, yes. About the situation at home, no."

"I would expect no less." They sat quietly, staring at the fire together.

"I have been feeling guilty about so many things. I thought we have destroyed your culture, that you had become warlike, learnt violence from contact with ours. I have been feeling so sad, me helping destroy the villages, Lestze destroying the tank, me being taken prisoner and seeing the armoury; it felt like your values had been lost and we, me and my people, were responsible."

"I see. I understand now why you asked about this earlier. Do you still feel that way?"

"No. The people here have only been kind to me while you and Lestze have treated me with nothing but respect. Even the ones who captured me did their best to look after me. I feel you are still what you should be, but I am worried even so."

"Part of your problem is you assume culture and values mean the same thing. Culture, a collective system of behaviours, can be an expression of values, but it rarely is. All culture is artificial, simply ways of making sense of the world and, hopefully, keeping the members of that culture able to live together without exploiting each other excessively or butchering each other. As an artificial construct, culture has no intrinsic value unless it is a source of genuine values — safeguarding the well-being of the people, and that is everyone, not just those who share that particular belief or culture, and the world around them. Eventually, a mature culture must ensure that everyone on a planet can live relatively peacefully together while pursuing their individual goals.

"It can be very difficult to discern what are the real values behind cultural behaviours and concepts. If it is simply that you need to follow the behaviours of your forefathers, then your value system is doing things that way because dead people did.

"As a culture, we have chosen to value people, their well-being, not ways of doing things. The way people do things here is very different depending on where you are on the planet, but the way they treat each other is always the same. Cooperation and respect, genuine caring and concern is paramount. Those are our values, not acting the way we have for millennia. Ultimately, you must decide what you truly value as a civilization. If we think we need to take up weapons to protect us, we will. When we need to throw them away again, we will. We have done so before and will do so again."

"You keep implying your culture has survived for thousands of years; is that true?"

"Yes, many thousands."

"Then why aren't you more technologically advanced? You must have made discoveries that would make your lives better."

"By better you really mean easier and with more things. That is not better. Yes, we have made many discoveries and suppressed quite a few as well when we have seen clearly where they lead. Your people have expansive houses and cars that can take you huge distances whenever you want. You have enough weapons to destroy your planet many times over and you still don't feel safe. Just the opposite. You can fly all around the world and live lives of unbelievable luxury by our standards. Some of you are intensely smug with how many more trinkets you have than your less well-off neighbours, but are any of you genuinely happy?

"We have intentionally chosen social evolution over technological evolution. You have developed total control of the material resources and wealth of your planet, but your culture is still as violent as you were in the Stone Age."

"We are not violent, and we are developing socially too. Most of our people get along together very well. War between nations has almost vanished."

"You are still talking about external actions and behaviours that have nothing to do with the hidden attitudes and values behind your civilization. The intrinsic assumptions your culture is built on are violence regardless. As an example, violent and anti-social behaviour obviously includes hoarding possessions for status purposes or controlling resources such as housing to force others to pay for what they need. Where people have to spend their lives working to pay others for the right to the bare necessities to survive, it is slavery. The wealthy who control you have worked hard to paint a pretty face on this new form of slavery and called it debt among other things, but it is slavery nonetheless. The assumption that if you compete better than your fellow citizens and amass enough resources you can force others to pay for their use so that you don't have to work and contribute to your society is nothing but violence. Your economy is built around the belief that you have what you take, be it by war, economic power or even using guilt for past events to extort money. The permutations are endless, but it is still the same violence and is based on taking from another. The will to exploit another is violence that is only removed from killing as a matter of degree rather than in essence. A sane culture can only be created from the will to contribute and give rather than the desire to demand and take."

"Okay. I think I see what you mean, but it still doesn't explain why you have prevented technological developments that would only make your people wealthier and happier. Our machines, the technology, gives us much more time; it sets us free."

"Free to do what? What have you done with all that time? As far as I can see your lives are incredibly complex and all you get is confusion and dissatisfaction. You are still equating having things with happiness, which is ridiculous. It's really hiding insecurity, but that's not the point. We have been here long enough to see that economics is largely a biological science, not a mathematical one. You are a biologist. What happens when you get a large concentration of any particular biological resource?"

"Like what?"

"Members of an animal species congregating at a waterhole or for migration would be good examples for my purposes."

"The first thing it would do is attract large numbers of predators of one kind or another. If they stay together in one place for too long, it would usually cause a rapid spread of parasites and disease among the population too."

"Exactly. The same thing happens wherever you get large amounts of capital. Humans have the unhappy knack of developing their parasites and predators from within their own species. Your governments are largely parasitic organisms that have even developed the power to generate their own resources through taxation. Your predators, the rich and the large corporations, even individuals, control your governments and the laws they make to enable themselves to make more profit. Individuals dominated by the profit motive are predators to their fellows as they are always looking for commercial advantage. When any sufficiently large population becomes rich enough, the predators among them will always notice it is easier to exploit those around them than to work for a living themselves.

"Haven't you ever thought it strange that you have laws to control physically violent offenders or sexual predators but encourage financial predators who, in the long run, cause vastly more misery?

14
Underestimating Your Opponent?

During breakfast the next morning, while the family were politely grilling Atawhai about the disaster on her world, Senden said casually, "Lestze is more obviously thinking of us. I suspect he will be back here by evening."

Later, when Atawhai was alone with Senden, she commented, "Everybody here knew everything I said to you about the plague and wars back home. Isn't that sensitive or strategic information you and your government should be keeping under its hat?"

"The notion a government should keep information secret from its citizens is one of the cancers in your society. It means the government either considers its citizens are too stupid and untrustworthy to make sensible decisions if given all the facts or makes it clear the government and its individual members are behaving so dishonestly that they couldn't allow their citizens to know the truth. Generally, both statements are true.

"On the other hand, from our point of view, the fact that your governments need to be so devious about their intentions and actions makes it likely the individuals in your general population are not as insane as the overall behaviour of your countries would suggest.

"Unfortunately, our own secrecy has become a sore point and a matter of shame or embarrassment in some areas of our own government. Since the station was first built we didn't pay your people the simple courtesy that any one of our people would receive, that is to treat them as equals, to tell them the truth so they could make informed decisions. There has been ongoing disagreement between members of the council on this matter for the last forty years. We could justify it by saying we were overwhelmed by your total technological superiority with an equally complete lack of social integrity and maturity. Effectively, you are psychotic children with nuclear weapons, but we never gave you the chance to prove you were better and as a representative of our government, I apologize to you for that.

"Even so, nothing is going to be easy. For any collaboration to work, your people will have to be willing to let go of who they think they are *and* who they think we are. Our people will have to do the same."

Senden left the house to find Dginze, who had been the last of the family to return, and neither were seen for the rest of the day. Lestze turned up mid-afternoon and was obviously disappointed not to find Senden there. By default, he spent the rest of the day talking to Atawhai as she told him about Senden and what had been happening, including those of the visitors she could remember.

When she had told him everything she could remember, including the reason for the incursion and particularly that Senden had agreed to try to help her people, she asked, "So what have you been up to?"

"The people from the destroyed villages that are living in the forest are finding it very difficult without their homes and belongings. It is already cold and wet and will get worse as winter comes on. They were arguing about whether to stay out of sight or to go back and rebuild their homes since the tank is gone, or whether to move away. They don't want to leave as they know they are supposed to defend us against your people if necessary and won't abandon the responsibility. They wanted me to make the decision for them.

"It took a while to meet everyone I needed to talk to, but I decided that rebuilding the villages would be too much provocation. Your people would know very soon if we did. I suggested sending the more vulnerable, children and older people, to the settlements along the coasts. Some of those who stay will go to the last intact village, but most, and a few injured who can't travel far, will move to the armoury for temporary shelter and build more shelter in the forest around it. We will have to think about getting food to them if they have to stay there too long."

He fell silent, so after a while Atawhai felt the need to prod a little. "Okay, so that took a couple of days. You have been away most of a week now. What else have you been doing?" She was watching and caught the signs of discomfiture that flickered momentarily across his face so pushed her advantage. "Come on, you know I'll find out anyway, so you may as well save me the effort." She smiled as another bit of leverage occurred to her. "Besides Senden said our cultures need to be open and honest with each other now."

Lestze appeared to admit defeat gracefully. "I was just observing the jump station."

"Really? For three or four days. What did you learn?"

"Your people are very disturbed. More than I expected. Probably by the loss of the tank, but there seemed more. I could sense the emotions."

"And?"

"And what?"

"What were you really doing?"

"Well, your people have cut down a large area of forest all around the jump station. It's hard to get close."

"I notice you said 'hard', so not impossible. How did you manage?" There was that brooding silence again. "I'm waiting."

"We caught some of the large birds in the forest and sent them running towards the station. We know how close they can get before the alarms are triggered. Also, your people checked the alarms to see what was happening so the defences do not automatically open fire."

"You said 'we'. How many is we?"

He looked at his feet. "Maybe four or five."

"Keep going."

"By watching where people walked over a couple of days we figured out where you can move and at what times without setting off alarms. There are only some elementary motion sensors and heat detectors, but the coverage or range is nowhere near complete. We can get around them easily enough. They have put up a lot of buildings, mostly from rough-sawn wood, and have tents as well around the station. Once you get near them, there are no alarms."

"So you can get in and out of the camp without being noticed then?"

"Yes, but it's easiest at night."

Atawhai's head was spinning. She held up her hand to stop. "Let's go for a walk. Show me something interesting."

Lestze went to the door and looked out at the hills, and deciding it wasn't likely to rain before nightfall, he agreed.

He simply walked into the forest with no direction in mind and kept up a running commentary on how he was navigating and keeping his bearings in that dark world. It was impossible to walk in a straight line as they had to follow the contour of the land. Going downhill always ended in a swamp. Atawhai said little, leaving Lestze pretty much talking to himself. He was perfectly happy with the situation, assuming Atawhai would say what was eating away at her when she was ready but equally unconcerned if she did not.

Lestze turned when there was still plenty of daylight. "Okay," he said happily, "lead us back."

"You can't be serious."

"Of course I am. Get going before we run out of light."

Within five minutes she was lost and stopped. Knowing she was more able than this, he commented, "You really weren't paying attention, were you? Want to tell me what's on your mind?"

The afternoon shadows were lengthening, if they could be distinguished from the general gloom. "If you get us out of here, I might tell you."

"Fair enough," he said amiably, though he started to trace a different route back just to prove the point.

Within a couple of minutes of resuming walking, Atawhai said, "I know that once our people realized there was a significant culture on this world, there was a ban on giving you any knowledge beyond your current level of technology, with pretty severe punishments for breaking the laws. The UN at home banned any kind of development here apart from the station, as that had already been built. Your technology here is basically Stone Age. You have the ability to work most metals and could be at least advanced Bronze or Iron Age but don't seem to be bothered enough to make the effort.

"Damn it all, you were just talking about heat sensors and motion detectors. There is no way you should even have the concepts for such things, let alone be able to work your way around them. Who told you about all our technology? Senden has a very thorough idea of our financial system and history to some extent as well. Your people shouldn't know any of this."

"As to how we learnt it, from your books of course. Some of your linguists decided communication would work better if they taught us English as we generally learn languages far faster than you do. They let us have access to a dictionary for while too. If someone trains their memory properly, they can flick through twenty or thirty pages and remember them completely, at least long enough to get them written down. As we didn't know your writing either, at the beginning, all the exact shapes of the letters were copied from memory until our language skills were advanced enough to read them. Some of our people did some of the manual labour of building of the station and helped with the first surveys. They looked at every book they could. There have always been caretakers at the station for the last forty-odd years. They are rotated about every six months to two years depending on whether they want to study anything while they are here. New caretakers always bring their favourite lightweight books on their specialties with them, physics, chemistry, biology . . . There has always been an effort by the station's personnel to maintain good relations with the natives, so our people are coming and going all the time. We are pretty much up to date with your latest scientific findings.

"Also, some of our people know how to operate your computer systems and pull up any files they want. It is only the memorising and reproducing them that is the problem."

"It's not possible. They would have been caught."

"Of course they were seen. But people don't see what is really happening.

They only perceive what their own expectations and beliefs allow them to see. So long as the primitive only pauses flicking through pages to stare when there is a picture and knots his or her eyebrows in a confused manner, your people only laugh. The irony is that primitive in the loincloth could have had a far higher IQ than that of the ones laughing at him. For something really important, looking through the computer system, for instance, a telepath would sense where the caretakers were and would not get caught."

"So the people who were randomly roaming the forest that lent a hand with building and the ones who called in as they passed, even the locals who come regularly to trade food or help with cleaning were all handpicked."

"Mostly, although random travellers often call in just to see the station. It is still a marvel by any standard here."

15
A Death Wish

Senden and Lestze brought each other up to date during and after the evening meal. Senden at first disagreed with Lestze, sending the bulk of The People to the armoury, saying it was much more likely it would be discovered. He felt it would have been better for everyone to disperse. Lestze countered, saying he particularly wanted the trained soldiers nearby as they may need to intervene with the rebels at the station at any time. The armoury was not important if they had no people to use the weapons. He pointed out later to Senden (when Atawhai had gone to bed) that he had kept back the assault rifles from the tank and secretly having these gave them a tactical advantage.

Next morning, Senden asked Thsermi for privacy for Atawhai, and she quickly sent the family on outdoors tasks and left herself shortly after. Senden sat Lestze beside Atawhai and took a seat opposite. He told Atawhai Lestze would look through her body for signs of disease or disorder left by disease and she nodded in agreement. Lestze took her hand, not that it was really important, but if the mind believed contact would improve communication, then it, apparently, helped.

In about ten minutes Lestze spoke to the world in general. "I don't understand. The vaccine has definitely helped her body to develop sufficient immunity to the disease, but it doesn't feel like she is healed. It's like when I walk in a forest and I can feel whether it is healthy or not. My initial feeling was Atawhai's body is fine, healthy, and on the functional level it is, but the longer I sit with it the more wrong it feels. I don't know why."

They talked for a while, getting nowhere before Senden said, "You two take a break while I see if we can get some help," and disappeared into the recesses of his mind.

Without a word they walked out the door where the early morning sunshine had not yet burned off the mist. Atawhai shivered, as much from apprehension as the clammy fingers of fog stroking across her face and hands. In her own way she could sense distress radiating from Lestze. She took his hand again for reassurance as they walked away from the house. "Will Senden be able to help?"

"Yes. There is a vast reservoir of skill and knowledge in the council. Unfortunately, I am almost sure the problem now is whether we will be in time." He walked a few paces before continuing. "I have been thinking of what you told me about the new outbreak of pandemic on your world and what I was picking up from people's minds at the station, the sense of panic there, and what I felt in your body. I suspect there has been a disease outbreak at the station."

They walked to the river and sat in silence on a wet, fallen tree watching the river, or perhaps the hand of fate, in its inexorable onward flow.

Lestze started from his reverie. "Senden wants us back."

They returned to sit in front of Senden. Lestze passed on his insight, causing Senden to pause once more. In a minute or two, Senden announced, "We are putting a quarantine in place around these islands. It will take time for word to get around, but that has to be our first step. Now some council members are going to help Lestze look again."

As he sensed into Atawhai's body, Lestze felt the presence of Senden's mind in his thoughts and other minds connected to his. One commented, 'Yes, the body's systems are functioning effectively as you said, so we will need to look deeper.' It took time, but the disembodied voice helped Lestze sharpen his perspective down to an individual cell. The elder commented again, 'It only seems tiny and ineffectual because you are still thinking of it from the point of view and relative size of a body. In its own way it is just as complex an integrated whole as a forest or a body. You must approach it in the same way.' Lestze spread his senses through the cell, which seemed an odd exercise for something so small. Again, it seemed to be functioning well, but the sense of disharmony was stronger. He allowed the point of his consciousness to drift with the feeling until approaching a large barrier within the cell. 'Ahh, the nucleus, focus your senses within it,' the elder commanded.

Lestze experienced large coiled structures where he could not determine ends. 'Chromosomes,' the voice said. 'Tell me what you feel.'

Lestze continued letting his mind drift, finally coming to a particular strand. 'Parts of this one feel wrong. This bit shouldn't be here. It's alien.'

'Imagine that part as a being with a mind. How does it feel or what would it be thinking?'

Lestze struggled for some time, his awareness of himself becoming more tenuous or disintegrating as he tried to find common ground where there was none. Finally, a coherent feeling or purpose passed through his awareness. 'It wants to die,' he thought emotionlessly, and blacked out.

16
Trojan Horse

Atawhai was disturbed from her reverie by a slight change in the hand holding hers, from relaxed to limp. Not much, but she squeezed his hand and felt no response at all. She opened her eyes and turned to look at him. He had slumped against the table and had no muscle tone. His breathing was shallow. Alarmed now, she checked Senden. He seemed in better condition but couldn't be roused. She ran to the door and yelled for all she was worth.

Thsermi arrived first, brushing past Atawhai as she rushed into the room. She checked each man with the skin on the inside of her forearm. "Lestze is getting cold. Wrap him in blankets." As Atawhai brought the blankets from her room, Thsermi said, "We should lay him down." She folded one of the blankets and put in on the floor in front of the fire then the two of them struggled to shift his uncooperative body on to it. Atawhai put the other two blankets over him then got her pillow to put under his head.

"Sit with him and tell me if there is any change. I don't know what to do apart from keeping him warm. I have never seen this happen before." Atawhai nodded as Thsermi checked Senden again. "He seems fine." Atawhai nodded again.

Senden stirred several times before sitting up a short while later. He looked at the empty bench opposite then refocused on the supine form of Lestze on the floor with Atawhai sitting beside him. "How is he?"

Atawhai shifted him and felt no resistance. "Completely unconscious." She put her ear to his face. "His breathing is weak."

"The fact that he is breathing is reassuring under the circumstances." Senden shakily made his way to kneel beside Atawhai and gently put a hand on Lestze's forehead. He paused then sighed. "He appears to be where he should be."

"What happened?" Atawhai's voice was accusing.

"We pushed him much further than we should have. However, it looks like we will have an answer of sorts in due course."

"Not now?"

"Engli wants to discuss what she learnt with some of the other healers before she gives me her opinions. We were too busy getting Lestze back to worry about anything else."

He moved to slump back down at the table. When Thsermi rushed to help him, he shrugged her off ruefully. "I'm fine or I will be shortly — really." She settled for making him a hot drink and bringing some food.

When he had finished and felt better, he returned to sit by Atawhai who had refused to leave her vigil. He put his hand on Lestze's forehead again and closed his eyes.

"He has warmed up. His breathing is more regular and deeper too," Atawhai remarked later. Senden relaxed and took his hand away.

"What did you do?"

"I reminded him who he is."

"No, I meant to heal him."

"I did what I said. His mind needs healing, not his body. Actually, that is usually the case with almost every form of sickness. Help me up, will you?"

Atawhai jumped up in surprise to help him to his feet.

"Don't worry, I'm just tired." He gestured towards the door and she helped him walk out. As she walked with him to the forest edge, she wondered idly, 'Why have I never thought of him as old before?' This was answered by a small laugh, "Older than you think, but that is just a body after all."

Senden sat on a damp log; everything was damp at this time of year. It was getting on her nerves, as there was nowhere she could sit without getting wet, but she felt guilty at the thought of leaving him alone here. "I want to be alone," he commented helpfully. "It is much easier to remember who *I* am if there are less competing thoughts and images. I will come back when I'm ready."

Atawhai gratefully returned to the warmth of the house, passing on to Thsermi that Senden did not want to be disturbed. He came back as lunch was being put out. Lestze was conscious and propped up but unwilling to eat. Nobody was prepared to break the silence during the meal, which turned into an unusually sombre affair.

"Do you have any idea how the disease developed?" Senden asked Atawhai as he finished eating.

"It took time for the epidemiologists to trace its spread to a starting point, but they are ninety-nine per cent certain it originated from another timeline. I helped with some of the studies of that world recently. It is very primitive. There is no intelligent life there, mammals are rare and the dominant animals on land are large reptiles."

"Engli guessed as much. I will confirm her suspicions." He looked at Lestze. "Go to my bed and sleep for the rest of the day." It might have been considered an order if anyone had felt there was a choice between doing it or not. (Senden had been given Lestze's bed when he arrived. Lestze had slept on the floor by the fire since returning.) He walked out to the forest again.

Lestze had followed the directions and having set his internal clock slept soundly till near sundown. He woke and instantly went to look for Senden but was disappointed not to find him. Atawhai grabbed him, literally, and walked him off to a quiet spot to grill him.

"What happened to you?"

"I blacked out."

"It was worse than that. Senden was really worried. Tell me all that happened."

"Some of the council's healers were helping me look into your cells. We found something inside that took me by surprise. I guess, effectively, I lost the will to live."

"Why?"

"What I found felt inimical, opposed to the well-being of the cell. The healers asked me to try to sense its purpose or intention. Basically, I allowed my mind to join with or mirror its purpose as a way of learning what it was. It doesn't think, so it was my mind that interpreted its purpose as 'I want to die'. Unfortunately, if it's not looked at clearly and rejected, a rogue thought in the mind is far more infectious than any disease. For a moment 'I want to die' was the only purpose in my mind as well. The effect of that for me was inevitable."

"But you survived."

"Not on my own, I suspect. I was linked to other minds that held mine stable. Effectively, they said, 'You want to live' strongly enough to make it so.

Senden arrived soon after, radiating confidence. "We have an answer of sorts," he announced as everyone gathered around him. "The epidemic that Atawhai's people suffered was not the real problem, just a symptom. Engli says what Lestze found were fragments of DNA that have become parts of the chromosome material of Atawhai's cells. It is reproduced whenever a cell replicates and will probably be passed on to offspring. The interesting thing is she could tell that part of the DNA fragments was from humans, but part was definitely alien, at least not human. The flu virus was simply a vector that spread the alien DNA through the population. It was the Trojan Horse with the real malady hidden inside.

"This gets us to the real problem. That DNA is causing your immune system to malfunction. To use Lestze's analogy, it is a death wish. Dealing with any specific disease may be life-saving in the meantime but essentially meaningless if that death wish is not removed. Any virally spread disease that replicates itself within a cell will spread the DNA so every person who has been in contact with the original disease or infected by new variants is eventually going to die. The process will accelerate as new infections spread the DNA through the cells of the body too."

"But can you fix it?" Atawhai burst out when Senden paused to draw breath.

"Given time, yes. But not in time to save your people. Or most of those living on these islands probably. Lestze has already spread out a reasonable number of the population from here. It was the right decision at the time, but anyone who has been in contact with you or anyone from the station could be carrying the disease. We can't say at this stage."

"So there's no hope."

"Not necessarily. Engli said it's a masterpiece of genetic engineering. It is mixed with human RNA, so it crosses the barriers between the nucleus and rest of the cell. It couldn't possibly be natural."

"We have been on that world for many years. I was there for two. There is nothing intelligent there."

"You will have to rethink that. In fact, you will have to find that intelligence and make peace with it if you want to survive."

17
End of Eden

Senden waited till after dinner to give people a chance to assimilate the information before continuing. "We know time is of the essence Atawhai; we will need your input in deciding what to do next."

"You are sure your conclusions are accurate?"

"Given the evidence, Engli and the other members of the council she works with are convinced it is the only tenable explanation."

"What do you want me to do?"

"Get us through the station to your world. It is the only way we can get to your government and that other world."

"The leaders at the station won't help us," Atawhai replied. "They will be executed as soon as they open contact with home. They would rather risk possible death here than face certain death there. The new World Government is not that forgiving to renegades at the moment."

"Understood, but we have to try. Would you be willing to take some of us into the camp to negotiate a way to get us through the station? They can close it down again afterwards if they are that terrified. We would want you to come with us to help us in your world."

"If they close the station, how will you get back here?"

"That's unimportant at this stage. Your thoughts Lestze?"

"We could just as easily storm the camp and station now. It would be easier when they have no reason to expect us. Once they know we are here and organized they will be watching. Particularly once they know we need to go through the station, they hold all the cards."

Senden sighed. "Agreed, but the council is unwilling to open our side of this with an act of war."

"Hasn't the war already started?"

"One side attacking can hardly be considered war unless the other side agrees by their actions it is. We would like Atawhai to take us in as soon as we can — the day after tomorrow as it will take most of a day to get there."

"I would prefer just Atawhai and me. Maybe one or two of the elders from the villages. It doesn't make sense to risk you as well."

Dginze interrupted. "If I get some men together by morning, we could row you up the river and get you there in about five hours. Say tomorrow lunchtime if we start early enough."

Senden looked at Atawhai who nodded, then looked down at her feet. "Thank you Dginze. Organize it please." Dginze got up and walked out into the night.

"Good. We need to decide who is going with the two of you."

"I have my own thoughts on that," Atawhai responded. "I need to go back alone. Those at the station are not going to listen to any of you. For a start, I will have to say we drove the tank into the swamp and only I made it out. After that I was captured. If they think you destroyed it, you are very unlikely to get any cooperation. I am going to have to convince them you treated me well and are sympathetic to our plight. Then I am going to have to explain how you got your knowledge and what conclusions you have reached. They need to understand we have seriously underestimated your civilization here. If they can accept that, then we can all start discussing reopening the jump gate. It's going to take time. I want them to at least listen to the ideas before they decide to shoot you.

"This is the only way I will accept being part of this. They will not shoot me out of hand. There is a good chance they will shoot any one of you or just beat you and throw you out. There's not a lot to discuss or decide until we see how they receive what I have to say."

...

The family gathered with Senden on the riverbank to see Atawhai and Lestze off. There was a short wait while the boat was brought up from the creek and they each hugged Atawhai, wishing her well. Senden took Lestze aside and reminded him, apparently not for the first time recently, that as a representative he should not take action without discussing it with the council or consulting him.

The men were fresh, and the boat moved relatively quickly upriver. When they passed the large tributary, Lestze ordered them to stop at a small jetty hidden under the trees. He jumped off and ran into the forest after saying he would be away awhile. The other men made themselves as comfortable on the riverbank as they could and waited. It was more than an hour before Lestze returned and they were rowing upriver again.

"Making plans, were we?" Atawhai probed cheerfully.

"I prefer to think of it as allowing for contingencies," he countered, and refused to be drawn any further. Later he took a turn rowing and the other men rotated periodically so each had some respite.

"Keep an eye out on the east bank," Lestze called to the other men while they were still more than an hour away from their destination. "There should be scouts keeping an eye on where the enemy are. They will stop us if necessary."

"Did you arrange that at the armoury as we were coming here?" Atawhai asked.

"No, they couldn't have got here faster than us. I asked that scouts keep an eye on the station when I was here a few days ago. If anyone comes out our people retreat ahead of them into the forest. If your people have come anywhere near the river today, we should get a warning before running into them." He noted to himself he hadn't mentioned the armoury, so she had remembered where it was and guessed that was his reason for stopping.

They were lucky and Lestze was surprised to get to the pier on the river where the track led to the station without being stopped. Before he and Atawhai started up the path, he asked the men on the boat to get messages to the families at the coal mines and metal smelters to be ready to come and help as they may be called soon.

As they walked up the path from the river, Atawhai asked, "Shouldn't we be keeping out of sight as you are with me, at least keeping off the path?"

"I don't sense any of your people around," Lestze slowly shook his head. "Also, your people move in groups and they are noisy and clumsy. The birds notice them. There is always a change in the forest sounds, a sense of alarm that surrounds and precedes them. They are easy enough to avoid. Even so, the station was making its presence felt with a periodic ugly, discordant drone."

Less than fifteen minutes later, a man stepped on to the path in front of them, appearing from nowhere out of the gloom. He made a signal to Lestze then vanished back into the forest. Lestze turned to Atawhai, held a finger to his lips then disappeared silently into the forest after him. Atawhai struggled to keep up, acutely aware of the loud noise her boots were making as the litter of the forest floor cracked with every step, and she felt thoroughly embarrassed.

They walked at right angles to the path until they reached a gap in the forest and stared at devastation. The jump station building, halfway down a rounded hill, was over half a kilometre away. Between was a wasteland of tree stumps, huge trunks, trash from branches and the remains of fires, some still with wisps of smoke. An array of tents and rough-sawn shacks could be seen on the flatter ground above the station and running down the hill to the left of it. Close to the tents, a man was cutting up a fallen trunk with a chainsaw, the source of the noise Atawhai had heard earlier.

The two men greeted each other, after which the stranger said, "There are guards near where the path meets the forest at the moment. They pay more attention to it, as if the path is the only way to approach the station," and laughed, shaking his head.

Lestze introduced Jintze to Atawhai then said to her. "When we take you back to the path you can go on alone. Jintze or I will be waiting in the forest somewhere near the path during the day. If we don't hear from you within three days, I will come to get you."

"Please don't. You can't beat the mercenaries they hired to protect this place. I don't want you to get hurt."

"We'll see."

"Make it five days then."

"Maybe." He started walking back towards the path. Jintze waited for her to follow Lestze, then fell in behind.

When they reached the path, she hugged him forcefully then turned and strode off before he could see the tears welling up in her eyes.

18

Seeds of Revolution

Atawhai paused, then stepped confidently into no-man's-land and kept walking. After a few steps she spotted the two mercenaries, James and Chan, who were technically on patrol, sitting on a stump in a hollow, out of sight from the station, sharing a cigarette. Obviously, their stocks were running low. Something else they were going to have to learn to live without, she mused wryly.

She was halfway to their refuge when one sprang to his feet, fumbling for his assault rifle. It was at his shoulder and sighted as soon as he grabbed it. They were not expecting anyone to come in from the forest. He paused as he looked through the telescopic sight, then exclaimed, "Hey, it's Atawhai."

"Hi James. Nice to see you too. Can you take me to Mr Marsden? It's important."

Uncharacteristically, he hugged her. "We were sure you were dead. Where are Andrew and Zhao."

"Both dead, sorry. It's a long story. I'll tell you later." They paused silently for a moment.

"Okay," Chan commented, "let's go," and took the lead back to the station.

He asked several questions to which Atawhai just replied, "Later."

Marsden had set up office in one of the rooms of the station building and his family were using another. Mr Lin's family had taken over another two rooms and two other families had a room in the building. The station caretakers had been evicted from their rooms and were living in a tent in the area above the station.

Chan surprised Atawhai by walking into the room without knocking and said, "We have someone to see you." He then ushered Atawhai in without waiting for permission.

Marsden appeared not to notice the informality. "Thank you, Chan. You may go." Atawhai caught a glimmer of surprise on his face, though it did not show in his voice. "Tell me what happened."

"We ran into a swamp. I was driving. Zhao had the hatch up and was looking forward, telling me where to go. I just had to trust him as the visibility from inside the tank is very bad in the darkness under the canopy. He decided to go across some flat land as there were no real trees and it looked easy. He was wrong. Although there were plants growing on top it was pure swamp. The tank sunk in seconds. Zhao was out immediately and ran forward into the swamp. We knew we were being followed by the natives, so I guess he was afraid to try to go back. I got out next and saw him disappear into the muck. I doubt he got ten paces. I jumped off the back of the tank. I still got stuck in the shallower mud on the edge, so they caught me. Probably saved my life. Andrew didn't make it out."

"He was not a lot of use anyway. I sent him with you on the assumption he couldn't mess up anything out there." Atawhai was not surprised by the contempt he showed towards his son-in-law. It was typical of the man. "What happened then?"

"They took me to one of their homes. Most of those I met speak far better English than I had expected. They have a good working knowledge of our sciences."

"That's ridiculous," he interrupted. "They are not far removed from brutes — Neanderthals that evolution didn't have the sense to replace."

"It's not like that. They have a working planetary government. I met their representatives. They are willing to help us."

He laughed derisively. "How can they help us? Repair the water treatment plant? Give us petrol for our generators?"

"Not technological repairs. But they know other things. They told me what caused our epidemic and why it was so hard to cure. It hasn't been cured. Just put off for a while. We still have the sickness in our bodies."

He started suspiciously at that. "Have you been talking to the doctor?"

"No. I have been stuck in that jungle for over a week. How could I?"

He held up a hand. "I need to think." Then "I can't have you spreading lies and rumours at the moment." He walked to the door and yelled, "Get Chan."

Chan was there before Marsden got back to his seat. He had obviously waited, probably listening.

"I need you to put her under armed guard. She is spreading dangerous rumours. Do not let her speak to anyone."

"Where do I have a prison, or even a cell? She will be visible to people anywhere I put her outside. Some of them must have seen me bringing her here anyway."

"Get rid of her anyway you see fit. I shouldn't have to tell you how to do that. Put her in a tent in the forest with a guard if that makes you happy."

"I'll do that for the moment, but you had better be able to give me a good reason later," Chan grumbled. "I'll be down the river path where it meets the forest. Send me James and Henare and make sure anyone James has spoken to doesn't talk either."

He led Atawhai out and back down the path towards the forest so they did not have to pass the tent village above the station.

"How much of what you said to Marsden was true?"

"It was all true."

"So we all still carry the disease?"

"I'm sure."

"And you think the natives can help us?"

"Yes, they can. But they need time and we may not have much. They need to get through the gate to another world to do it though."

"I can't allow that. We need to see if you can come up with another solution."

"Marsden said something about the doctor. Can I talk to her?"

"I'll think about it."

"I will need her help if we are to do anything."

They sat and waited far enough in the forest to be invisible from prying eyes. Chan checked up the path periodically. When he saw his subordinates approaching he said blandly, "Marsden doesn't care if I shoot you. Neither do I if you make things difficult for me. Don't make any trouble."

When the men arrived, he gave Henare the watch, then asked James to go back to get a tent. "Sure, Chan," he replied sarcastically. "Whose am I going to take?"

Chan sighed. "Okay. I'll come back with you."

"Henare, don't talk to her. If she insists on talking to you, gag her."

James arrived back an hour before sundown with what was obviously a compromise, a tarpaulin and a hatchet, along with some rope and a sleeping bag. He walked out to the trash where the trees had been felled and cut a long straight branch. Walking back down the path to where Atawhai and Henare waited in the forest brought another problem. The trees in a mature forest are huge. He had to cast around for some time and was some distance from the path before he found two saplings that were close enough for his branch to reach between but still big enough to hold it up. He tied it at chest height.

James walked back to the others to retrieve his equipment but cut a large blaze on a tree on the side of the path the camp was on. He brought the other two back to his camp, throwing the tarpaulin over the branch. Henare sat quietly watching Atawhai with his rifle on his lap while James collected stones. He pulled out the sides of the tarpaulin and put the stones on the edges to make a shelter, then unceremoniously threw the sleeping bag inside. He took the backpack off and pulled out a set of handcuffs. Walking over to Atawhai, he clipped them around her ankles. His embarrassment got the better of him as she looked at him without protest.

"Sorry Atawhai, Chan insisted. He doesn't want you running back to the natives, and if I put them on your wrists, you can still run." He handed Atawhai a small amount of food from the backpack then took some to Henare. "I will be back to relieve you at twenty-two hundred."

"What about my sleeping bag?"

"If you want it down here getting wet, you are an idiot. Besides, if you go to sleep or lose her, Chan will skin you alive."

Atawhai lay awake in the bivouac for much of the night. She heard the rain start around ten and was glad she had some cover, although there was no ground sheet so her sleeping bag was damp where it touched the ground. She heard the change of guards at ten o'clock and made no sign of being aware. She heard a change again and looked at her watch. Four in the morning – six-hour shifts, a long time for sentry duty. A little after seven in the morning, Chan turned up to relieve her current jailer. Atawhai poked her head out to see what was happening. Both men were wearing wet weather gear, though the rain had stopped temporarily. The canopy kept dripping huge, heavy drops.

"I hope you brought me breakfast."

"Maybe. You will have to answer my questions to get it, though," Chan replied.

They talked for half an hour. Atawhai gave him the gist of what she had learned and how, filling in the gaps of what she had told him earlier, while emphasizing that the real problem was now within their own cells. They would all die from one disease or another if nothing was done, and she said repeatedly she needed to speak to the doctor. At eight, after half an hour's silence, a new jailer, Raj, turned up to relieve Chan, who gave him the same lecture about talking to Atawhai that Henare had received the night before. Atawhai retired to her boudoir.

James turned up as midday passed and, to Atawhai's surprise, with the doctor in tow.

"Hi James, Sylvia. Lovely day for a stroll," Atawhai took the initiative.

"You are to speak only when asked by me and you need to keep to medical matters," James countered tersely. He formally relieved Raj and watched him go, held up his finger to his lips, then trailed off after Raj, silently, into the bush.

Returning, he said, "I had to make sure he was gone. Didn't want him listening. I talked with Doctor Armstrong coming down here. I trust her. I'm on your side; you can say what you want."

"What do you mean 'on my side'?"

"Just talk to the doctor. She can explain it better than I can."

"Okay. Sylvia, why was Chan giving the orders? Is he in charge of the mercenaries now?"

"No, Brandon, Mr Marsden's head of security, is still in charge of the mercenaries while Chan as Lin's head is second in command, though they are pretty much equal. But the reality is they are working together on their own agenda."

"In what sense working together?"

"Well, the social fabric in the camp is really volatile right now. Most of the people, the young people and families, have had enough of building a brave new world and just want to go home. This forest is very inhospitable, it is hard to find food, so we are running low. The lot of them are spoiled brats anyway and are extremely unhappy living in damp tents without their usual opulence.

"Then there's the power structure problem. Back home Marsden and Lin and the others here like them are immensely powerful. They have huge amounts of money and influence. They can hire and fire thousands of people. An entire social system with police forces and armies and all the other support structures is built around maintaining their power and comfort.

"Here, the gold and diamonds they brought are worth nothing. Now they consume food and other resources but have no survival or other skills worth a damn and think they are above having to work manually to make shelter or grow food. They are actually a liability — weak men whose only authority was the power that a different society conferred on them.

Sylvia paused briefly, barely breaking stride in her explanation of the situation.

"Then there's the mercenaries. Any one of them with an automatic weapon now has more real power than all the rest combined. Why should they follow anybody else's orders? They have figured that out.

"The camp is divided into three blocs with inherently incompatible aims. By far the biggest group only want to go home. The news you brought could completely destabilize an already tense situation as it makes returning home vital in the long run. On the other hand, the mercenaries and those ruling are very keen to suppress your information, which puts you in a very dangerous position. While on the face of it Marsden and Lin are tacitly governing and making the decisions, the mercenaries are the ones really in control now."

"By mercenaries you mean Brandon and Chan. The rest of us don't have a look in," James butted in acerbically.

"Does that mean some of the mercenaries might help us get back through the gate?"

"No," James shook his head. "Most people enjoy having power over others, even if it is just the satisfaction of knowing you are right and the other person is wrong. Holding a gun when someone else doesn't is a lot more addictive than that. Also, although the families may be regarded as innocent victims back home, the men who engineered this will not. We mercenaries freely accepted their money to break the law forbidding the use of jump gates. We will be executed too if the gate is reopened."

"So you won't help us?"

"I will, but the others will fight you every way they can. Let's leave it at that."

19

By Negotiation?

Atawhai went on to recount her experiences and discoveries once again for Silvia so she understood what they were up against with the epidemic. "Why did Mr Marsden accuse me of talking to you when I told him?"

"I have a case of bronchitis up there that should be getting better. Treatment has slowed it from getting worse, but it looks to be heading for pneumonia. It's not the flu from the epidemic, but it looks like it is following the same pattern. I had spoken to Marsden about it a few days ago. We are having lots of colds crop up because of the cold, damp living conditions, but this feels different. You are just confirming something I had already guessed."

An uneasy silence ensued. James broke it brusquely. "All well and good. So what can we do about it?

"The Neanderthals have agreed to help us," Atawhai replied. "They believe if they can get to the world where the epidemic originated they should be able to stop it."

"Our people couldn't."

"They have skills we don't."

"You're sure?"

"They solved the epidemic riddle in less than a week."

"Okay, I'll follow your lead. Sylvia?"

"I will too. We have to do something quickly. Marsden sees the sick man as a threat and could exile or shoot him anytime. It won't make any difference as we have all been exposed, but it would certainly stir up those who want to go home."

"Speaking of time," James said, "now we are down one mercenary, there are only three of us to split guard duty for Atawhai as Brandon won't and Chan thinks it's beneath him. That means two shifts a day at four-hour shifts. It won't last more than a day, two at most, before they decide you are not worth the trouble. They will shoot you rather than let you join the natives."

"Okay," said Atawhai. "You are both convinced neither Marsden and Lin nor the mercenaries will help us get through the gate."

"Yes," Sylvia replied, while James said, "Absolutely certain. They will block any attempt. For the meantime anyway."

"So are we committing to taking control of the station by force?"

James laughed happily. "You are sitting there in the mud with handcuffs around your ankles and telling me you are about to storm the station, kill the mercenaries and force Marsden and Lin to cooperate. I love your optimism."

"No, I am asking, if I make the attempt, live or die, will you trust me enough to help me?"

"Yes," Sylvia answered without hesitation. "Everyone will die eventually, both here and at home, if we don't do something." James agreed.

"Good. Don't be too surprised." She let out a yell — "Lestze!"

He ambled up from the forest with a hunting bow over his shoulder as if this kind of thing happened every day. Ignoring James as he grabbed his rifle, Lestze walked up to her and reached down to help her to her feet. Lestze looked at her ankles and smiled. "I see the negotiations are going well," then hugged her happily.

"As well as we expected." She took some time to introduce him to the other two and help them get comfortable with the situation (James relaxed enough to aim the rifle down), then continued, "You were right about the problems at the station. The situation is very unstable. We need to do something as soon as we can."

"What and how soon?"

James interrupted, "There are too many variables to be sure, but it could all fall over anytime. One to two days maximum. We really need to defeat both the mercenaries and the ones in control at the station."

Lestze weighed up James and Sylvia for a few moments. "I am not sure of your motives, but I see you are sincere. I am going to call Jintze here." He whistled a few notes and Jintze appeared out of a patch of deep shade a surprisingly short distance from the group. Not only did he have a hunting bow like Lestze, he had a cocked crossbow in one hand.

James was appalled. "Has he been waiting there, that close, all along?"

"No, I moved here while you were watching Lestze's clumsy, noisy approach," Jintze answered for himself and grinned at Lestze. Trusting Lestze's judgement of the situation, he carefully uncocked the crossbow, commenting, "The trigger mechanism is still a bit unreliable and might go off unexpectedly," to no one in particular.

Silvia, Atawhai and James each gave the newcomers their assessment of the situation. James finished, noting, "There are not many mercenaries, but they are the crucial target. If we can't knock them out immediately, they are unassailable with their modern weapons. We would lose over time by attrition."

"No, the station has got to be the priority," Jintze stated firmly. "The only reason we are doing any of this is so we can get through the station to help Atawhai's world. If, while we defeat the mercenaries, someone damages the mechanisms for controlling the jump between worlds, it will be for nothing. We can't repair them. If we take casualties, even high numbers of deaths because of focusing on the station, we just have to accept it. We are assuming helping another world is worth it."

"There aren't enough of us to try for two objectives at once," countered James. "We could never hold off the mercenaries after we took the station."

"We have more than enough people to hold both."

"Where?"

"Spread out in the forest around the station. We realized you found the villages in the forest because concentrations of people show up on aerial heat sensors. We don't want to make the same mistake twice."

Atawhai glared at Lestze. "It seemed the logical thing to do," he commented diffidently. "I asked Apakta yesterday morning to get everyone who could fight up here as soon as possible. The fastest soldiers were arriving here late afternoon yesterday and the rest made it here bit by bit during the night. It could take a couple of hours to round them up though. I said I would come and get you. I just wanted to be sure I could."

"Your soldiers still can't beat assault rifles," James pointed out to Lestze.

"About that. We recovered the rifles that went down with the tank. Apakta has them with him. He has Atawhai's pistol too."

James shook his head ruefully. "You appear to be thinking of everything."

"I wasn't expecting to have to act this quickly and certainly wasn't anticipating having friends to help. What would you do, Jintze?"

"James' relief will be here in about two hours. We wait for him to come and James takes him prisoner before going back to the station. We won't have everyone ready by then, so I suggest we wait until the next change of the guard comes down four hours after that. It should be easy enough for us to disarm him as it will be dark then. We should attack after that."

Lestze turned to James and asked, "What do you think?"

"Sounds great. That would leave only Brandon and Chan in the command tent. I can handle them on my own. I suggest Sylvia should be in the station then, visiting Marsden or something. I will give her a pistol and she can lock herself in the section with the jump machinery. We time the attack for eight-fifteen. You can signal us before then if something goes wrong with catching Raj; wave a torch or something on the forest edge."

"No thanks for volunteering me James. I'm a doctor, not a soldier."

"Sorry Sylvia. There will only be you and me in the camp at that stage, and I will have my hands full."

"We should have people get there to help you within minutes," Jintze observed.

"Regardless, I have to get back to my clinic. I have been away too long as it is. You can come talk to me later, James."

Lestze sent Jintze to escort Sylvia back to the path to the station. When Jintze returned, Lestze asked him to send messengers to get the soldiers together for the attack. He disappeared into the forest for more than an hour, returning not long before the next change of guard. At a word from Lestze, the two of them melted into the forest.

Ten minutes later, Henare walked carefully into view carrying his rifle in the ready position. He spotted James sitting in the middle of the largest open space around the shelter to give himself the maximum all-round visibility. James raised his rifle as Henare approached until Henare identified himself. Henare muttered a few words and took a small packet of food to Atawhai before walking back to James complaining about pointlessly wasting time in the rain. James agreed wholeheartedly as he stood up, slung his rifle across his back and walked back and forth a little as if he had been sitting a long time. He nodded as he gave Henare the watch, but as James stepped past him, he pulled his knife from his sleeve, pivoting to bring it up to Henare's throat from behind him while pushing Henare's hips slightly forward with his left hand to unbalance him.

"Don't even twitch a muscle, Henare. Very slowly take your fingers away from the trigger . . ." By the time Atawhai reached them, Henare had dropped his rifle. She picked it up and James said, "Henare is about to kneel. If he makes any sudden movement, shoot. No hesitation."

Henare took the hint and made no move, while James tied his hands tightly behind him. As Lestze and Jintze walked into view from the forest, Henare spat, "So you are selling us out, James."

"No, I'm saving our lives, but I don't have time to explain or argue." James inspected him carefully, removing hidden weapons, and turned to the others. "I need to get back to the station or they are likely to come looking. I'm relying on you to support Sylvia and me."

"We will be there when the time comes," Lestze promised. James nodded and trotted through the forest back to the path.

20

The Peasant Army

 Atawhai could only hobble, so he slung her over his shoulder and strode off to rendezvous with Apakta, carrying Henare's rifle in one hand.

It was still light when they reached the assembling group. Apakta stepped over to greet Lestze warmly. Lestze said, "We need to get rid of the cuffs on Atawhai's ankles."

"We tried to come prepared," Apakta replied. "One or two of the men will be carrying a file." He walked into the group and spoke quietly, coming back with another man, not much more than a boy, who took off his pack and retrieved a blunt metal instrument from it.

"Are you sure that is going to work?" Atawhai wondered out loud.

"It doesn't look pretty as it is handmade, but we have learnt enough from you to know how to harden metal. It will work," Lestze insisted.

Atawhai sat over a log with a foot on either side to pull the chain tight while the young man filed notches in the links closest to the cuffs. Once that was done to the depth he wanted, he pulled out a small hammer and broke the links, supporting the ends between two bits of metal. While he worked, he got across to her in very broken English that his family ran one of the metal forges. Atawhai watched him carefully pick up the broken links and put them in his pack along with the rest of the chain, reminding her how precious metal was in this world.

The process had still taken more than ten minutes. She walked a short distance to find Lestze talking to Apakta who was dividing the arriving men into two groups, one to take on the command tent, the other to continue past it to the station. They were discussing coordinating the groups to reach their objectives at the same time.

"Feeling better I hope?" Lestze enquired of Atawhai. "Apakta has sent two men to keep an eye on Henare. Jintze should be back here any moment."

"You seem to defer to him a lot. Aren't you in charge?"

"Yes, I am. In charge means something different here. More like being responsible for achieving the optimal outcome for all concerned, but certainly not having things done my way. Jintze is a natural tactician, our best probably. He sees ways around things the rest of us miss, but if I was being uncharitable I could call him sneaky. I would be stupid not to respect his advice. Apakta has been responsible for training the young men how soldiers behave. He will be commanding them during the attack because that's what he is good at. Even so, he will listen to anything Jintze or I say, but the decisions are still up to him."

Jintze trotted up to the three of them ten minutes later. Lestze spoke first. "Apakta is going to take the group of men to attack the command tent. We think you should lead the group to take over the station and I will take some men to capture Raj when he comes to relieve Henare."

"I have been thinking about that. I would put Atawhai in charge of the group to occupy the station. There are a lot of her people there and they are far more likely to listen to her than to one of us. It will make it much less likely they will panic and do something unusually stupid. You should go with her as you speak their language well and you have the authority to deal with the rulers there. We don't. Also, she is the only one here that really knows how to use one of those assault rifles. She has to take one. Our theoretical knowledge of using them won't mean much when facing their professionals."

Lestze looked at Apakta, who raised his eyebrows with a smile then nodded. Lestze turned to Atawhai. "Okay with you?"

"I will if you insist. I'm not happy about the idea though."

"We are not happy with any of this, but we are doing the best we can regardless. I agree with Jintze. You are by far the best choice to lead that group. It just hadn't occurred to me. We will do it that way."

Jintze dropped the bundle he had been carrying on the ground between them. It was Henare's jacket wrapped around his helmet and all the equipment he had been carrying.

"The helmet has a torch that would be useful for Atawhai. There is a little hand-held torch there too, which Apakta should take. Anything not useful we can leave here to pick up later." Turning to Apakta, he continued, "I will deal with Raj. I will need all the ropes you have with you and three or four men good with bows in case what I have in mind does not work. I need to go now while there is still some daylight to work in and enough time to set up."

While Apakta and Lestze looked for the men detailed to carry lengths of rope, Jintze sidled across to speak to Atawhai. "I suggest you go and talk with the men you will be leading. They will follow your orders because Lestze and Apakta will tell them to, but I think it will be important they get to know you and trust you as a person. They will realize quite quickly if they can trust you and won't hesitate later when it's critical." After a moment's silence, he turned slightly to look straight at her and whispered, "Take care of Lestze. He is precious to us," and followed after Apakta.

Lestze returned shortly after, carrying a rifle and her pistol and handed them to her. He led her towards one of the groups of men. "Most of the men are here now. We will take our groups to the edge of the forest so the men can get a look at how the land lies and obstacles that can be used as cover before it is completely dark." He signalled with his hand and the men followed, spreading out through the forest enough to almost disappear in the gloom. All of them carried hunting bows, while some had crossbows too.

"Jintze said I should talk with the men in our group."

"Okay. We can do that later."

Atawhai's group moved further up the hill so they were in the forest on the right side of the station just above the command tent. Apakta's group would be slightly downhill from them. They would avoid the sensors that were mostly on the downhill side where the track led to the river. The men found different vantage points or took turns observing to minimize the risk of being seen. They moved back into the forest and, using candles to see, Lestze drew pictures in the dirt. Other men corrected bits from time to time while they discussed strategy. Lestze translated for Atawhai.

When they paused, Atawhai whispered to Lestze, "What am I supposed to say to them, something heroic?"

"What do you feel right now?" he replied conversationally.

"Afraid it will all go wrong, afraid for your people and mine and also very grateful you are willing to risk your lives to try to help us, my world."

"Then that's what you need to tell them."

Atawhai spoke for only a minute or two as Lestze translated, but when she finished the men silently nodded as some closer to her moved to squeeze her hand or pat her lightly on the back.

Lestze broke the spell by asking, "What is the time?"

She looked at her watch. "Seven-thirty."

"Good, half an hour before we need to move."

The candles had been extinguished apart from one in an enclosed container. Time seemed to stand still for Atawhai in the alien darkness. She inched back till she felt her arm touch Lestze, and whispered, "You will be amazed by our world. There is so much we can contribute to your people."

"Really? What specifically would you contribute?" he asked.

"We can give you machines to do your work for you, better ways of making houses that last longer, electricity to keep them warm, cars and planes that could take you anywhere on the planet, the list is endless."

"So, toys then?"

She was angry at hearing her largesse spurned. "No, not just toys. Knowledge. Hundreds of years of industrial and scientific development, maths and physics, philosophy too."

"Intellectual toys as well? Wonderful."

She was beside herself with frustration. "Damn your smug superiority. You are just the same as Senden!"

Lestze stopped short, startled by the level of anger she was radiating.

He sat immobile, thinking for long enough that Atawhai asked if he was okay, worried she had really upset him. In answer, he took the cover off the candle and held it up.

"Look at these men and tell me what they really need. They have a happy life with their families and friends. They are only here because they have been asked to help and trust those who have asked them. The fact that they are not full of illusions about themselves and the perceived nobleness of their motives means they see others very clearly too."

Atawhai's frustration had not abated, but she kept quiet as he went on.

"These people are content, they don't need anything more to be at peace with who they are, rather than defining themselves by what they have. They are whole. To contribute to that wholeness in a meaningful way, or even to understand it, you would need to be whole.

"People teach and contribute who they are. It is impossible for them not to. That is what your people would contribute too — the will to compete. Call it hard work to get ahead. Ahead of what other people have, of course. To be special, more important. To prove yourself superior simply because you have more in one way or another."

Lestze continued, despite a slight sigh from Atawhai.

"The first thing your people would teach here is 'there is not enough to go round,' and they would reinforce that by trying to grab resources for themselves alone. Ideas are far more infectious than any physical disease. Very soon there actually wouldn't be enough to go around as the rich hoard resources and deny the poor access to them. That is the first thing your people will contribute and what I am afraid of."

A small, birdlike noise came from a sentry watching the station. Atawhai and Lestze moved out to his position. "A man has moved from one of the tents to the command tent."

"That will be Raj," Atawhai noted. Sure enough, as he came out a few minutes later the light silhouetted a figure in full combat gear. Without a word, the rest of the men silently gathered behind them as they watched Raj walk down the path. She waited a few moments after he disappeared before turning and handing Lestze the pistol he had brought her earlier. She showed him how to unlock the safety, stating quietly but emphatically,

"You need to take this. Use it without hesitation; you have a duty to your people to survive. I can tell this venture won't succeed without you." To forestall argument, she continued, "It's time we got moving," and stepped out of the forest.

21

Night Terrors

Jintze had taken three men and was leading them through the forest at a run. They were headed back to the tree beside the forest path where the developing track to Atawhai's bivouac branched off. The mercenaries always turned off the path in the same spot, close to the trunk of the tree. It was the best place to set a snare. They had to tie a rope around a rock and throw it over a branch, then climb the rope just to get to the lowest branch. One of the men climbed up, taking more ropes with him, while the three on the ground gathered the heaviest broken pieces of fallen branches they could carry. When they had a bundle several times heavier than a man, they lashed it together and tied it to ropes lowered down. The men on the ground climbed up and Jintze had one of the ropes passed over a suitably smooth branch close to the trunk and passed down to him, lower on the trunk. He tied a loop in the end and, pulling the rope tight, he put a foot in the loop and acted as a counterweight, lowering the tree trunk as the others pulled on the other rope lifting the bundle. When he reached the ground, he called up and although he kept his weight on the rope by holding on to it, he took his foot out of the loop in case they made a mistake while tying the rope holding the bundle of branches to the tree trunk and dropped them.

As two of the men climbed down, he committed the sacrilege of cutting their last precious rope into a number of pieces and the three men on the ground made a number of nooses, each tied off to the loop at the end of the rope going up the tree. The nooses were spread along the track, concealed as well as the men could in the litter of the forest floor, and the trailing rope was pushed as close as possible to the trunk of the tree.

Jintze was not fool enough to think they could time things to guarantee to catch a walking man as he stepped through a single noose. As it was, they had done what they could using a candle to see by when the ubiquitous forest twilight turned black, and had been forced to retire into the forest with no time to spare — the man waiting in the tree had seen Raj's torchlight reflecting off the tops of the trees back towards the station.

■ ■ ■

The men followed Atawhai and Lestze out into the devastated land. She marvelled that a group of men were moving with her, but she couldn't keep track of them, even though she knew they were there. Only a few moved at a time, in and out of the shadows cast by the waxing moon, nearly halfway to full, but never repeating a pattern or assembling in a noticeable group. Every move a man made was influenced by an uncanny awareness of what the other men were doing, each one simply filling in the gaps. She stopped just before she reached the cleared area close to the south side of the station. The light at the front door facing the forest path to the west seemed absurdly bright after so many days without artificial lights. Lestze crawled into position beside her where they could communicate at a whisper if necessary but said nothing.

Atawhai swore as a single shot echoed from down in the forest. "That will stir them up. Should we attack now before they get organized?"

"No. It's still more than ten minutes before we agreed to attack. We should wait to see how this plays out."

A man hurried out of a small tent and into the command tent less than thirty metres downhill from them. It was clearly James. His voice carried in the still air as he entered: "That sounded like trouble. Should I go check on

Raj?" Two voices joined his in discussion.

"Brandon and Chan are both in there," Atawhai whispered.

"I'll get my gear," James spoke loudly.

There was some shuffling and the sound of a metal cabinet being unlocked followed by a short silence. "Down on the floor. Both of you!" An imperative command. "What the hell . . ." Brandon's outburst was cut short by a dull thud and grunt. "Face down, hands on the backs of your heads! Another short silence followed by "I'm done here. Get to Sylvia."

Atawhai jumped up and ran for the door to the station. Lestze ran with her and she could see some of her group keeping pace and fanning out beside them. She bolted through the unlocked door and turned to the right down the short corridor to the workshop and jump mechanism. The door was locked. She ran back out and set two men to stand just inside the corridor with arrows knocked to their bows. She noted two men had already positioned themselves, standing flat against the wall, one either side of the front door. As she detailed four men to check the large lounge room, used for entertaining visitors, and kitchens that lay ahead of the front door, Marsden stepped out of his office, the first room down the corridor to the left, with a pistol in his hand. His face twisted with surprise and anger as he saw the native men filling the foyer, but he swivelled slightly to aim the gun at Atawhai, both recognizing her and deciding the rifle she carried as the major threat in the same moment.

As he turned and Atawhai was turning to face him, an arrow hit him where his right arm joined his shoulder. Out of her left eye, Atawhai could see one of the men by the door fitting another arrow to his bow in a single smooth movement. The pistol fell from Marsden's hand as he lost balance and fell, as much from shock as the impact of the arrow. Atawhai jumped past him and ran to the middle of the corridor to where her voice was most likely to be heard in all the rooms. Wanting to prevent any further incidents, she yelled, "This is Atawhai. The station has been occupied by armed men. We don't want to hurt anybody. Stay in your rooms and don't open your doors. Do as you are asked, and no one will be hurt."

She ran back to the foyer as the four men she had sent to the kitchen returned with a group of nearly hysterical teenagers who had been hanging out in the reception room to get some space from their families. She repeated her message to them and finished, "These people are here to help us. Make sure your families understand that." It was not an easy message to get across with Marsden groaning on the floor in front of them.

As they were sent down the corridor, James burst through the door. He skidded to a halt. Nine arrows were aimed at him along with Atawhai's rifle. "Shit," he said, "this is not a good place to run into." Atawhai smiled and dropped her rifle aim so the others relaxed with their bows. "Apakta and a couple of his men have Brandon and Chan tied up and nailed down. He has sent some of the others to ground between here and the forest and some around the tents too. He has told them to shoot first if they don't recognize people with guns. We assume Jintze got Raj, but Apakta doesn't want to take chances."

"Why assume Jintze caught him?" Atawhai asked.

"Four men against him who are faster and more capable in the forest. Only one shot. What would you expect?" filled in Lestze. "I also suggest, in view of Apakta's order, that if you or James go walking in the dark again with your guns, you take one of us with you. It's hard for us to tell your people apart and most of the men haven't met you both either.

"Okay. That makes sense. Let's relieve Sylvia."

James walked with Atawhai down the corridor and knocked on the door. Atawhai called loudly, "It's James and me."

The door opened slowly and Sylvia peeked out. She was holding a gun and looked remarkably confident. "It went well?"

"Better than expected. No casualties on our side that we know of. However, Atawhai has a job for you." As they walked back to Marsden, Sylvia handed James the key to the jump room together with the gun.

"I told Marsden I needed some tools from the workshop in there to repair one of my machines. He gave me the key without a second thought." After checking him over, she said, "It doesn't seem too serious. He hasn't bled much and his breathing sounds fine. Send some men with me to get a stretcher and we'll get him back to my clinic."

As she was walking out the door with two men trailing behind, she stopped and took the arrow out of the hand of the sentry at the door.

Examining it, she pointed to Marsden and asked, "Is the head on that one the same shape?" On getting an affirmative reply from Lestze she handed it back, almost with a flourish, to the bemused man and commented, "At least I know now not to try to pull it out," as she walked out.

"She's enjoying the excitement," Atawhai whispered to Lestze.

"In a way," he replied. "She is feeling like she is fighting for something of value, the reason she wanted to be a doctor in the first place. She hasn't felt that way in a long time."

22

Break it to Them Gently

Atawhai and James went to each room in the station, calming the occupants where possible and promising to explain everything in the morning. James confiscated a couple of handguns, promising dire consequences to anyone hiding a weapon. There were no arguments. Word of Mr Marsden had been passed on. They then took a group of men as bodyguards to walk through the tent town and repeat the procedure.

Apakta and Jintze were waiting when they returned to the station. Jintze had left two of his men to take a very bruised and sore Raj deeper into the forest and was nonchalantly cradling Raj's rifle like he had owned it all his life. When Raj had stepped into the snare, Lukta hadn't cut the rope with the first stroke of his knife. Raj heard him move and swung his gun up to shoot. Lukta was clearly visible in his torch, but Lukta's second cut worked and Raj was jerked off his feet just as he pulled the trigger, so his shot missed. He hit the trunk of the tree hard and dropped his rifle, so the rest was easy.

Apakta had followed Jintze's example and detailed two men to take Brandon and Chan into the forest south of the station. "I'm making sure I keep the malcontents away from each other and hopefully where they won't find their way back to the station easily if they do escape."

"Why are you sending two men with each prisoner or group?" Atawhai asked. "It is very expensive on manpower."

"The prisoners can sleep any time they like," Apakta answered. "If there are two guards, they can take turns resting. Otherwise it would be a very long night for one man. Speaking of which, you and Lestze should take a break now. We will swap with you later." He called a couple of men and they helped him carry the desk and furniture out of Marsden's former office.

After the last night trying to sleep on the wet ground in the forest, the floor of the station was a luxury. Atawhai was asleep in minutes. She woke feeling disoriented and looked around uncomprehendingly for a few moments before remembering where she was. There was enough light coming through the glass panel in the door for her to see around her. Lestze was gone. Jintze was curled up in a corner and another man was lying asleep against the back wall. She walked quietly into the foyer. There were new men on the door and down the corridor to the jump room. She looked the other way. Three men were up the other corridor, one with a rifle. Apakta was taking no chances. All quiet, all under control.

For a moment she was afraid. Everything was wrapped up, there was nothing for her to do. She wasn't needed any more. She pulled herself together. Accept the moment. The fact that she had no control of how this was going to turn out. For her or all of them. She would do her best regardless, no guarantees and no obligations or expectations.

She was too keyed up to go back to sleep and the sentries at the door had no idea where Lestze was, so she decided to sit in the lounge to wait. Stumbling around in the dark out there was not likely to be a healthy choice. It was half an hour before Lestze arrived and, despite her intentions, she had dozed off, starting awake as the door opened. She jumped up and hugged him. "Where did you go? I was worried."

"I have been talking to Senden, or more particularly the council."

"Are they angry? Are you in trouble?"

"No. Senden was more open than usual, letting me see some of his deeper thoughts. He is pleased with how things are working out. He will be here sometime in the afternoon."

"Where is James?"

"In charge of security for the command tent and the weapons there. He will be around there somewhere."

"What do you want me to do?"

"Nothing. I'm going to get some more sleep. You should too."

- - -

Lestze waited till ten o'clock before getting the reluctant émigrés together to discuss their current situation. They were confined to quarters apart from emergencies. "There is no rush," he had commented in response to Atawhai's impatience. "It's a rare sunny morning. Give them time to get over their fears from last night. Let them see that we are in charge and nothing terrible is happening. It will make it easier when we do talk to them."

Jintze walked around the tents with a couple of guards ten minutes before to tell everyone to meet outside the front of the station. Atawhai walked down the corridor of offices hammering on the doors and telling the occupants to come to the meeting. James had been warned and was at the station early. Lin had refused to come out with his family or answer Atawhai's knock. James took two guards and when he got no answer, shouted, "I don't want to force my way into a room where I know there will be guns. If I don't get a reply, I will shoot the lock a few times, but if I am feeling really angry I can always throw a grenade through your window from outside." The door opened almost instantly. James thanked Lin politely but checked each person as they came out and took two pistols from the family.

There was a large crowd waiting expectantly when James had checked all the rooms were clear and walked out the front door of the station. Atawhai and Lestze were sitting on chairs facing them with an empty seat beside Atawhai. Jintze and another man were sitting on the ground beside them. James hesitated — he didn't need to be an empath to read the fear and resentment simmering in the crowd, waiting to explode. Rather than stand behind Atawhai, he walked to the side of the assembly and up the hill a little so he could look down and see the whole assembly, not just those in front. It looked like at least half of Apakta's men were in unobtrusive positions around the crowd, but behind them where they were effectively invisible. He knew that while his people were waiting impatiently for something to happen in front of them, they knew him and couldn't help but wonder what he was doing and would have an eye on him. He brought his rifle to his shoulder and scanned through the crowd, clearly able to see individual hairs on eyebrows with the magnification of his scope. The not-so-subtle hint was not wasted, and the restiveness of the crowd vanished. They started sitting down to wait.

Sylvia bustled around the corner of the station and hurried up to sit in the third chair. Atawhai said a couple of words to her then stood up, saying, "We have asked Doctor Armstrong to speak to you first as you know her and know she is trustworthy. It will help you understand why we have done what we have done."

Sylvia told them she had a patient in the infirmary with another disease that was showing all the symptoms of the plague that had ravaged their home world. It was happening here. They had all brought the seeds of it with them.

Atawhai stood next and told them about the original plague affecting their immune system and DNA so they could not fight off new diseases. They would all die over time without intervention. Their families back home would die too. Then the pivotal point, the World Government here had agreed to help them. They needed to open the jump gate and get to the world that was the source of the contagion to see if they could produce a cure quickly.

Some reacted ecstatically to the thought of the jump station being reopened and some with dread. Most didn't believe Lestze's people had anything to offer or could help. Atawhai made it clear that in social and mind sciences they were well ahead.

A belligerent older man who had challenged Atawhai several times stood up. "Prove it," he sneered. "You, smart boy," he pointed at Lestze who had taken no part so far, "tell me what I am thinking."

"I doubt you are accustomed to thinking much at all," Lestze commented innocently. A chuckle ran through the crowd. Atawhai scolded him.

"I was just telling you what I see," he tried to apologize. "Your mind is filled with resentment and jealousy towards your older brother. You have been blaming him for your plight here, even though he was only trying to save your life. You envy him his success when you have not been successful and blame him for your failures. Even here in a totally new environment, you are still envious and resentful and bitter. There has been no change. It is the same completely unconscious loop of past ideas and emotions that replay in every situation you find yourself and through which you filter every new experience. There is no actual thinking happening at all."

The crowd was silent, stunned, trying to integrate the incongruity of the sight of the barefoot, poorly dressed savage with the sophisticated thoughts they had heard. They were too embarrassed to ask another question. Eventually, a teenage girl put her hand up and, addressing Lestze politely, asked, "Do you speak for your people?"

"Yes, I do."

"What will happen to us?"

"That is up to you. You can go home to your own world when the time is right. You can stay here if you want, but you will have to learn to learn to live by our laws if you do."

She sighed. "I really want to go home. How soon can I?"

"I can't answer that just yet. It is a big decision that our government will have to make, but it will have to be very soon if we want to stop the new plague on your home world."

"Why are you trying to help us?"

"Because Atawhai asked us to, and because we should. It is the right thing to do."

23
Understanding Takes Effort

Senden arrived by boat early afternoon. A messenger came running from the jetty and Lestze ran off with Atawhai to meet him. Despite his age, Senden was almost halfway to the station when they met him, walking up the path on his own. He had told the men who brought him not to worry about him and to go on with their own duties.

It was a joyful meeting. He ruffled Lestze's hair and laughed. "You have managed to surprise the council again." They continued laughing as they ambled up the path, making small talk as Senden happily chided Lestze about not listening to his elders or doing as he is told. The mood vanished as they walked out into the open of the ruined forest. Senden stopped to take in what he saw for a minute before continuing to walk up the path, silently, though still looking from side to side.

When they came close to the station, he sent Lestze to continue with his responsibilities and asked Atawhai to escort him around the settlement, saying to her, "I want you to explain all this from your point of view. Take me to the people you think I should talk to as we go. The wise rather than the powerful. Let me see it all through your eyes."

Her first stop, the outlying tent furthest from the station, housed Neela and Andrew Robinson, biologist and physicist, the dispossessed caretakers of the station.

Later, as twilight stretched the shadows of the forest over the land, Senden called a strategy gathering with representatives from all the interested parties, which he insisted included Brandon along with Andrew and Neela.

Atawhai again opened the meeting, set in a rough circle in the lounge of the station. She spoke a little about her experiences after she was captured then introduced Senden as the primary representative on these islands for the ruling council that governed the planet. He started by reassuring them that while the council had its own objectives it would try to achieve the best outcome it could for the castaways here, and his purpose for the meeting was to listen to their opinions.

"You have attacked us, invaded our homes and taken control by force of arms. There is no way we can trust you to look after our best interests!" It was the bitter man from the morning, Mr Marsden's older brother, Samuel, Lestze now knew. He chose to reply.

"If you look honestly, you will see your society here has collapsed in only a few weeks to a despotism ruled by the mercenaries. You are running short of food already and are desperately under-prepared for the winter that is upon you. You have the first case of a new outbreak of plague and you have all been exposed. If we wanted to do you harm, we would have done nothing. The bulk of you will be dead in under a year in very unpleasant circumstances." Lestze waited to let the truth sink in.

"As for the council looking after your best interests, if you were given the fame and power you crave tomorrow and all the other things you lust after, you would still not be happy. You would feel smug and superior but would still feel small and empty inside. You have no idea what would make you genuinely happy so are completely unable to judge what is in your own best interests."

Lestze could feel Samuel's anger rising towards another outburst but continued anyway. "Don't be driven by the poison that has overtaken your thoughts and react from its anger. You are now in the position of speaking for your family and your people. Put them and their well-being first. Decide for them from the goodness of your heart."

The room went silent as everyone paused to see what would happen next. Samuel took a few deep breaths and looked around, noticing no one was going to speak and that they were politely waiting for him, even Brandon and Lin. The bravado drained away and he finally nodded his head, saying, "I understand. I will listen to what you have to say."

Senden continued, "Good. The council intends to send both Lestze and me through to your world as representatives from this world and of its planetary government. We will expect full ambassadorial status and will not enter into dialogue with your government with anything less."

"They are unlikely to accept that," Samuel stated.

"Agreed, under normal circumstances. However, we may hold the key to stopping the plagues. That changes everything. We will take Atawhai with us to act as go-between and interpreter in case we misunderstand some nuances of the language. We will insist our sovereignty be publicly acknowledged along with our right to govern our own affairs. As part of the negotiations we will endeavour to ensure there will be no reprisals against those of you who want to go home."

"If you are the leading representative for the planetary government of these islands, it is clear appearances have no meaning for you," cautioned Brandon. "Back home appearances, not substance, mean everything. If you want to be taken seriously, you will have to look like it. You will need a security chief for a start. I recommend you take James with you. Despite the current situation, I still believe he is trustworthy. I am beginning to understand his actions."

"I am planning on leaving him jointly in charge with Apakta and Jintze. They will need his help and experience in dealing with your people."

"In that case, I volunteer, but I think you would be better off with someone younger. I suggest Chan. He is professional and reliable."

"Is he one of your mercenaries?"

"Technically, though back home he is Mr Lin's head of security. The very best."

Senden turned to Lin. "How do you feel about this?"

"If he is willing, I support the suggestion too."

Senden looked over the heads of the attendees to a guard. "Get him for us, please."

"How soon do you want to do this?" Brandon asked.

"As soon as we can. Tomorrow morning, early. Time is simultaneous across the world lines. It will give us a full day on your world if the station is manned on that side and they respond immediately."

"It will be manned alright. They won't have let us go that easily and will be delighted at any chance to humiliate us," Samuel broke in. "You speak of bargaining with the World Government but have no idea what negotiation means on our world. There is no goodwill involved. I was never good at business; I don't have the ruthlessness. My brother Daniel is indisposed so the only person here with the skills you need is Wei-Shan Lin. I think you should appoint him as your chief negotiator."

Senden paused then said something regarding Samuel as an aside to Lestze. He replied in English, "Samuel is sincere in wanting to help."

Senden couldn't help but laugh. "This is not going as I had expected. Do you have an opinion on this Mr Lin?"

He laughed too. "Wei-Shan, please. I would be honoured, and I give my word I will support your cause faithfully. You are obviously surprised that we want to help. Even if Daniel and I are executed as the ringleaders, if our children are going to die from the plague anyway, they want to go home and face it together with the rest of our families and friends. If your people can find a cure for these plagues and maybe negotiate some sort of clemency for us, that is a godsend for us all. Why would we not support you?"

"I hope you have finished with adding members to our party. Are there any other questions or concerns then?"

Instead of interrupting, Samuel lifted a hand and waited for Senden to look at him and say yes.

"I have a question first then possibly a request. You are the representative for your government here. Where does he," pointing to Lestze, "fit into your governmental structure?"

"It is a little more complex than that. The leaders of any village or city represent the council too, and most are in regular contact with the council. Apakta and Jintze also represent the council in their areas of expertise. There are many people who can speak for the council.

"I am a member of the council. We make and maintain the laws, among other things, though many of us don't hold or no longer have administrative positions. Lestze and the few like him have a different role in our society. It is their duty to speak for what has no voice to speak for itself. In all our decisions, they speak for the rights of the fish in the sea or the forests and their creatures. Who can put the value on a clear mountain stream or the sigh of the wind through the trees? When they are gone, you cannot understand what you have lost because the part of your being they represent has already died in you too."

"I'm not sure I understand," Samuel furrowed his brow.

"No. You don't have the experience to."

"I suspect that brings me to my request, an idea your intentions bring up. You are right; I have been angry for a long time. I want to change that and don't want to go back home to being an also-ran in a race I will never win. If you are going set up diplomatic relationships with our world; you will probably need to appoint a permanent ambassador there. They will need to appoint one here too. I would like to be that ambassador, or on his staff if that is too difficult. If my family agrees too, of course."

Senden looked at Lestze, who pondered for a while. "It could work," he finally commented.

"Alright. I will do what I can. We can continue discussing the finer points of our mission, but if there are no objections I will send Andrew and Neela to make sure the jump equipment is ready for tomorrow." There were none.

24
No Small Step

Lestze watched Neela send the request to transfer a group of five people to the counterpart station with the total mass to be transferred. The almost instant reply stated it would take an hour to assemble the correct ballast mass to send back.

"That should take ten minutes if I was being generous. They are organizing a special welcome for you," she noted. Lestze could only shrug.

A five-minutes-to-transfer warning came through and the five of them assembled on the square, polished stainless-steel floor. He watched the seconds count down to zero on a monitor mounted outside the cubic volume that would be swapped between timelines. A body trying to occupy the same space as the equivalent volume of air in the other timeline would be lethal to say the least.

It was a disappointment at first, as there was no sensation of change. However, the much brighter lights in a much bigger room put things into a different perspective, as did a number of fully armed and armoured men, rifles pointing inwards, surrounding their square of floor. Chan, standing in front of Senden and Lestze, put his hands up instinctively. Lin and Atawhai followed suit.

"Get your hands up!" It was the sergeant in charge of the squad. Senden had made no move to raise his hands when Chan had, and Lestze was following his lead. He still stood calmly with his hands down. The sergeant shouted the order again, louder. Senden turned to look at him.

"These Neanderthals are the legally appointed representatives of their planetary government. They are here as ambassadors to our planet. You have no authority over them," Chan yelled back.

"If they don't put their hands up, I will fire."

"This is our planet's first official diplomatic exchange with another sentient species and you are going to shoot the ambassadors. I hope the station cameras are recording this historic moment. It will certainly make you famous."

Chan could see him reach a less drastic solution. The officer pointed to him. "You. Walk over here." Chan obeyed. As he reached the line a man beside the officer spun him around and pulled his arms down behind him to handcuff him. The pattern was repeated with Atawhai and Lin.

The captain moved close to Chan to keep the exchange low and unheard by the microphones. "What the fuck do I do with them?"

"You could try asking them, politely, to come with you."

He snorted derisively but walked closer to Senden to say, "Come with me." Senden didn't move. "Please."

"Certainly. Where are we going?" The man's initial shock at being spoken to in good English turned to confusion. The cells at the police station probably wasn't the right choice if these two genuinely were sent here by their people. "Wait a moment." He decided to shove the problem up the chain and called the station, speaking to the superintendent awkwardly.

"I have to take you to the police station. They can sort it out there." The three in handcuffs were led out to separate cars. Senden and Lestze were allowed to ride together in another. They were frog-marched into the station with no respect for dignity and taken to separate interrogation rooms. Both were interrogated for more than hour but refused to give any information, then they were allowed a break and given some food. A few hours later the Resident Coordinator for the recently formed New Zealand United Nations Country Team, Adrian Norris, arrived from Wellington to take control of the situation. He tried Senden first who refused to comment until his entourage was returned to him. Adrian returned over an hour later with a new issue.

"I've just heard the Neanderthal B station is refusing any further contact with our station. I'm sure the others have no idea why."

"Our people will not respond until I send a message with the correct words."

"So your people are in control there. We have no contact with your world."

"Not until I allow it."

"What do you want from us?"

"Nothing. We are only here to help you, and your people on our world."

"You don't want them punished for invading your world?"

"What would that achieve but more pain and misery?"

"Supposing I believe you?"

"Get my people together. We can go from there."

"They are criminals by our law and deserve everything they get."

"Then you will have to learn to let go some mistakes and forgive, just as we are doing."

"You really expect us to give in to your every demand?"

"As we have said, over and over, you need our help to stop the plagues killing your people, so yes, I do." Senden refused to say more. Adrian gave up and left a little later.

Time passed, another meal came. Adrian came back and escorted him to a conference room. Lestze was already there, flanked by two officers. "Your interviews have been examined by experts overseas. They say you are all telling the truth, or believe you are. We will be bringing the others shortly. Atawhai tells me your culture is much more advanced than we thought. You are able to communicate globally and were able to tell from examining her the cause of the plagues. She also says some of you are telepathic."

"Yes," Senden replied.

"Then you must have known Sergeant Waitere was prepared to shoot you if you didn't raise your hands."

"Of course."

"Are you crazy? What were you thinking?"

Senden turned a little towards Lestze, who was clearly uncomfortable. Lestze noticed the scrutiny and there was a pause as he tried to remember what had been said, what he should say. He answered the question.

"In that moment your culture, your race, was choosing its collective future, its fate. We were interested to see which you would choose."

"So if he had shot you, we could have doomed ourselves to oblivion and by not shooting you we made the choice to survive?"

"Exactly. For the moment anyway."

"That really is insane. How could you let the fate of billions of people rest on one man's decision, his state of mind?"

"That one man was simply a projection of your conscious and subconscious racial beliefs, hopes and fears as all the others are. You made him. You make them all what they are, the good, the bad and the indifferent. Besides, every nuclear arsenal you have built becomes a point where one man can determine whether your race lives or dies. You do it all the time. It is not always obvious. Why blame us if you keep doing it to yourselves?"

"But how could we have known that you were going to be there, that this event could be vital for our survival?"

"You chose the path that could have led to your destruction when as a race you chose how you would treat the rebels. Would any gesture from them be met with condemnation or compassion? The reception we received made it clear which choice you made. Whenever you choose condemnation you choose self-righteousness, fear, hatred, death. All that differs is the degree to which they show up consciously and visibly. Regardless of the choice your government had made, your officer did not choose self-righteousness and condemnation. For whatever reason, he chose to see a wider picture. Perhaps he is just a symbol of your race collectively choosing not to commit suicide. He made a good choice for you all."

25
Setting the Stage

Close to midnight, they were moved to the Ambassador Hotel tower block. Adrian had commandeered the top floor. The city was under curfew, so no one was walking the streets, but they still had a police escort and the Special Air Services had been called in by Adrian to provide security. In the car, Atawhai was trying to describe to Lestze the difference between the Armed Offenders Squad who had met them and the SAS who were now shadowing their every move. He was becoming increasingly restless and uneasy. When they reached their floor, she put him in a bedroom then took her concerns to Senden who was talking to Adrian in the conference room, while Chan and Lin looked on.

"Lestze is too agitated to sleep. He won't be much help tomorrow if we can't settle him down."

"He is reacting to the stress of too many undisciplined minds around him. He is going to have to learn quickly to protect himself."

"What are you talking about?" asked Adrian.

"He is a reasonable telepath by our standards, but people who are in his position are the best empaths on our planet. He feels emotions extremely acutely. If he walks into a forest, he can feel minor disturbances to the ecosystem many kilometres away. He found being around Atawhai on her own very distressing, as, like you all, her emotions are strong and chaotic. Now he is surrounded by thousands of you. The man guarding the lift has had an argument with his girlfriend. He is very angry with her and feels he is in the right but doesn't want to argue further and make matters worse. You started off being totally contemptuous and were sure we were fakes. Now you are terrified we may destabilize a very volatile political situation and plunge the planet back into war. You have no faith in your superiors to handle this situation honourably and not turn it into a political football. You are worried for your family. You are all screaming emotions at him and he doesn't know how to handle it."

"Yes to all that, but what do we do now?" Atawhai interrupted.

"At home, if he was feeling overwhelmed, he would go into the forest for a while. He can't do that here."

"I started university in this city. I know it well. The river is less than two minutes' walk from here. There's a path beside it with trees."

"Worth a try. Take him there."

"I can't allow that." Adrian was adamant.

"Am I officially the ambassador from our planet to yours?"

"That hasn't been decided yet."

"Then decide. Decide for yourself and your government. Now. If the answer is no, I am taking Lestze and going home. You will have to shoot me to stop me."

"I don't have the authority."

"As the United Nations Resident Coordinator for this country you have a great deal of authority. Your decision is binding and sets a precedent that your superiors will find very hard to publicly overturn," Lin corrected. Senden started walking to Lestze's room.

"All right." Senden turned back. "With whatever authority I possess as a representative of the United Nations, I ratify your status as the official ambassador from your planet to ours."

"That includes diplomatic immunity for me and my staff."

"It looks like I have no choice."

"State it," Lin commanded.

"All the responsibilities and privileges that would go along with your status are extended to your staff."

"By the laws of our people, Lestze has equal status to me and so has full ambassadorial status here."

"I don't know how that will work, but I grant that too."

"As an official delegation, are we under arrest?"

"That would be diplomatically unacceptable, I think."

"Then I am sending Atawhai to take Lestze to the river."

"You will need to contact the police so they don't get arrested," Lin added.

"It honestly isn't that safe at night. With the new outbreaks of the plague, quarantine barriers between continents and the threat of the collapse of our global economy there is a lot of social unrest."

"Then give Atawhai a gun," Senden insisted. "She is going anyway."

"Yes, I am," Atawhai piped up.

Adrian sighed resignation to the situation. "I will talk to the soldiers and get one for her." He led the way and the others followed. "You are pushing this to the limit. You have intended this all along, haven't you?"

"That's very perceptive. Of course, I have in one way or another. Once we are moved to your headquarters it could take days or weeks of negotiation to get to where we are now. All the strutting peacocks would have to display their authority and we would have to be careful not to ruffle their collective feathers. All the egos would have to be mollified. Your people are dying. They can't wait while we play political games." Senden smiled an impish smile. "As it stands, the only person everyone can be angry with is you. That can be easily kept under control. While we are on the subject of guns, my head of security had his gun taken from him at the station. He would like it back." Chan grinned behind them.

Adrian shook his head in disbelief but laughed too. "You just don't give up. You have already destroyed my career, while you have wheedled out every concession you wanted. This is no negotiation. I have been completely railroaded."

Senden smiled. "I'm happy we both see this the same way."

There was a short pause while Adrian argued with an SAS lieutenant, but soon after Atawhai scuttled off holding a pistol.

"I think we need to get this written up, signed and sent to Adrian's headquarters before his superiors fly in tomorrow," Lin advised. "We should have a copy ourselves too."

...

Atawhai was watching Lestze's reaction to the river. "What's wrong?" she asked quietly.

"It's just moving water. Its connection to life has been broken. It feels like a moving corpse. He walked over to a large tree and put his hand on its trunk. "It is alone. Its sense of self is not connected to anything, and it's so small it barely exists."

He didn't respond further so she took his hand, saying, "This isn't helping, is it?" He shook his head. "Let's go back to Senden." He trailed along after her without resistance.

Atawhai left him in his room and went to find Senden. He was sitting in a chair dozing in the conference room while Adrian was sitting at a table typing on his laptop with Lin breathing over his shoulder. It felt unkind, but she woke him.

"It didn't help. He's worse."

Senden paused, looking distant. "He will go into shock if we are not careful. This all happened so quickly I had no chance to prepare him. Can you think of a way we could get him to an undamaged forest? It would need to be someone you trust completely."

"Why can't I take him?"

"I'm not breaking up our group more than necessary and I need you here. He is actually less vulnerable than you as the authorities here don't know how to treat him. We know what they want to do with you."

"My brother Patu would help. I trust him with my life, but he lives in Rotorua and he has bad eyesight. His girlfriend, Juanita, would have to drive him."

"That's fine. We will get them here now."

Senden called Adrian over and told him what he wanted.

"They would be arrested being the only car on the road after curfew."

Senden looked at Atawhai, eyebrows raised. "A police escort?" she suggested.

"Do I have to?" Adrian asked. Senden nodded.

He pulled out his phone to organize it, then gave his phone to Atawhai to call Patu. He arrived an hour and a quarter later, Juanita in tow, wide-eyed and excited. He hugged Atawhai. "I can't believe you're back. I thought you were making this up, but the police car was at our flat five minutes after you called. We got to speed as fast as we wanted. It was cool."

Atawhai explained to them quickly why she was back, then Senden told them what he wanted him to do as Atawhai went to get Lestze.

Atawhai introduced Lestze to Patu and Juanita and as they walked to the lift told him Patu would take him somewhere away from people to reduce the emotional noise. Senden followed. As they waited at the doors, he said "Lestze" loudly. Lestze gave a lackadaisical reply. Senden stepped closer, looking Lestze in the eye for a few moments. Lestze was withdrawn, not really meeting his gaze.

Senden hit him close to his left shoulder. Hard. Lestze rocked back, his gaze meeting Senden's in shock.

"Good. I have your attention. You have the rest of tonight. Get over what you think you see and feel. They are just images. You are giving them all the meaning they have for you. I need you tomorrow. This world needs you much more. I can't do this without you. Understand?" Lestze met his eye and nodded.

Senden turned and walked away as the lift doors opened. Atawhai followed him, feeling shocked and angry for Lestze. "That was a bit harsh, wasn't it?"

"It was the most loving thing I could do under the circumstances."

"Give him a break. He was ready to die with you this morning to prove a point."

Senden laughed. "Dying is easy. Any fool can do it. In fact, we all do. The hard part is living every day with total honesty, kindness and self-respect, not giving in to anger or resentment or self-pity even if we have lost everything and the whole world has turned against us. That really is something."

"But he is suffering."

"No, he is caught up with the feelings of thousands of people thinking suffering, who believe they are suffering and he is believing it is real. Regardless, he will be himself tomorrow."

"How do you know?"

"Because he made the commitment. He has the courage and integrity to make it happen and will not accept anything less."

26

Politics 101

The autumn morning dawned clear and cold, a little too early for a frost but not far off. It was a welcome relief from the clammy fogs of the alternate world. Atawhai looked out the window of the room over the Waikato River. She was home and should have felt happier, but in some way it felt alien. It hadn't changed, but she had.

Breakfast was brought up to the conference room and they ate together. "What are we going to do this morning, Senden?" Atawhai asked.

"Nothing until we hear from Adrian. You may as well relax in the meantime." Relax-yeah right. Atawhai felt like the canary in the cage as the cat is pawing at the door.

Patu and Juanita arrived back with Lestze in time for lunch, all three looking tired but happy. Patu walked over and hugged Atawhai. "We took him up the Mangorewa track. He was happy once we got in the bush where the old trees are."

Atawhai looked at Lestze. He smiled back diffidently.

"So you are feeling better?"

He felt the concern behind her words. "Yes, much. I was a fool to let exterior appearances decide my state of mind. I do know better, so I'm sorry for upsetting you."

She stepped over to hug him. "You don't feel the pain any more?"

"No, it's still there, but it's like when you look straight at a bright light you are blinded and it's all you see. Fear, suffering, evil are all the same. Look away and you see there is still a world of goodness around you they are concealing. Sometimes I forget I can look away, see the world differently. Your family are decent people."

Lunch was delivered by two soldiers in combat uniform. While they were eating, Adrian walked in. He sat down opposite Senden at the table. "We have certainly stirred up a hornets' nest. After my rash declarations last night, I have just been informed by my superiors that I have so many pressing issues they need me to take care of I have been relieved of all responsibility for your situation. They will have the army fly you out on a military plane after dark this evening. Nothing public; they want this kept secret until they decide how they want it to be handled."

"Where does that leave you?" Lin asked.

"It has been tactfully suggested that there will be no consequences for my unilateral actions if I let the matter go and forget my rash jumping to conclusions."

"So they don't want Senden's world's help?"

"No. They would just send them back or lock them up if that was the case. The government will take any help it can get where the plagues are concerned, but in this case not publicly. The absolute ruling about no interference with any intelligent culture is to make sure no other world line ever gets the technology to compete with us, rather than to protect other cultures. Accepting Senden and Lestze as ambassadors and making their help public would make them our political equal and recognize the sovereignty of other worlds, which would affect current exploitation of them. It would also lead to ongoing contact with their world, making it very hard to stop information and innovation leaking back to their world."

"Where do you stand with this?"

"My hands are tied. I can do nothing to help you."

"I mean you personally. Will you do anything to stop me doing something that would contravene the silencing of these people?"

"No. Senden and Lestze were willing to give their lives on the off chance of helping this world. I will do anything personally I can to help; it would be dishonourable not to."

"Good. I suggest you have urgent business to attend to for ten minutes." Adrian nodded, and Lin waited for him to leave. "Patu, Juanita, do you have your phones with you?"

They chorused "Yes."

"Excellent. I want you to take some pictures of the people here and a couple of short videos." Lin organized Patu to record a brief statement from Senden while Juanita recorded one from Atawhai. He then recorded a slightly longer one himself with instructions for several people and gave Patu a number of email addresses and websites to send all the information to. "These addresses should be secret, but some will be watched even so and the files may be blocked before they get to the recipients, but I'm sure some will get through. Download the files on to memory sticks and send them from as many other devices as you can quickly. Not from your phones, which will be traced to you immediately if you use them. Then disappear for a few days. Get going." The last was spoken as a definite order.

They were back within seconds. "The guard won't let us down the lift."

Lin ran off to find Adrian, who came back with him. "He may let them leave with me if I insist it's my orders," and he walked with Patu and Juanita back to the soldier who chose not to question Adrian's right to take them with him.

Adrian returned ten minutes later when he was sure they were gone and spent the rest of the day with the group in the conference room, turning off his phone and shutting his laptop. Early in the evening, the lieutenant in charge of the SAS detachment came to see Adrian, saying he had orders Mr Norris must contact his head office immediately and he was required to make sure it happened. He waited as Adrian made the call.

After a tense few minutes of argument, the call ended. Atawhai was using the computer and projector in the conference room to show Senden and Lestze images from around the world. Adrian had given permission for her to use it so long as no one made contact with the outside world. He asked Atawhai to pull up a news channel. He commented, "Apparently I have committed treason against the World Government. The government of Taiwan has very publicly demanded access to the ambassadors from Neanderthal B as Taiwan has been denied representation by the UN. They therefore wish to talk with Senden and Lestze separately."

As he spoke, an image appeared on the screen of a news presenter who was animatedly asking whether this was a hoax, before Atawhai clicked on links taking them to the photos and videos Patu and Juanita had taken that had been released by the Taiwanese government.

Everyone turned to look at Lin, who smiled and shrugged his shoulders. "It seemed the only way to protect our friends. The World Government can hardly deny their existence now."

Several hours later, the lieutenant returned. "You won't be flown out tonight after all. We have been ordered to shift you to the SAS headquarters at Papakura. We will have vehicles here shortly."

"What does that mean?" Senden asked.

"It is a small army base in Auckland. About an hour's drive from here." Atawhai answered.

"So we will be shut away from your world still?"

"It is for your own protection," the lieutenant insisted.

"I don't think so. I am not willing to leave here."

"I will carry out my orders." Senden sat looking at him. Lestze moved to sit beside him.

"Is this another one of those moments?" Adrian asked Senden. He smiled with a nod.

Adrian sighed and addressed the soldier. "Lieutenant Shaw. As my superiors have refused to accept my assessment of this situation and are now giving you your orders through your military chain of command, you had better make sure your superiors are well aware of what they are ordering you to do. These people are here to help our world and for no other reason. They are here as ambassadors to our planet and when I represented the UN I legitimately accepted their status as ambassadors, including granting diplomatic immunity. To my knowledge, that ruling has not been rescinded and Senden will accept no other status. Get in touch with your local superiors before you set off a diplomatic firestorm. Get them here to decide for themselves if necessary." The lieutenant nodded and walked out.

Atawhai walked over to sit opposite Senden. "I thought the plan was to get to a jump station in the United States as soon as possible."

"Yes, I had thought that, but not at any cost. Our mission is really to help you heal your world. Maybe help you heal your world-view would be a better way of looking at it because your thoughts and actions spring from that. Just finding a cure for a disease will do little or nothing towards that goal. A government that will not trust the decisions of its representatives on the ground to do the right thing and that forces strict obedience to its central directives and power is already a tyranny despite seeming to be based on democratic or any other socialistic concepts. I notice that, so far, when your people are forced to really think for themselves and not simply follow orders, they usually choose for the good of their planet and their people, not their own political advantage. It is very encouraging, but I can see that will not happen as we get closer to the centres of power. I think we are better here out on the fringes while the wrangling happens."

Sure enough, when Lieutenant Shaw came back almost an hour later he said, "There appears to have been a problem at the motor pool. We are unable to get transportation for you at present but will reschedule it when the problem is sorted. Have a good night."

27

Trial by Media

Once the night curfew ended, the car park below the tower block began to fill with reporters and camera crews. A group of soldiers had been rapidly sent to close off the ground floor of the hotel when the first few arrived. Senden and Lestze looked down on the mounting chaos from the balcony with bewilderment.

"You say they are here to talk to us?" Lestze asked Atawhai again. He could not feel any genuine interest or concern for them from the throng.

"Not to talk to you; to interview you to get a story they can send to the company that employs them. I've explained that."

"So they ask us questions about things they don't really care about to get answers that they are not really interested in with the hope the stories and their fake excitement might cause other people to buy their papers or watch them on television."

"That about sums it up."

Lestze shook his head. "Do you have any idea how silly that is?"

Senden walked back to the conference room to Lin and Adrian who had stayed the night in the hotel with them. "Why don't we give them what they want? Go and talk to them. They could go away then."

Lin laughed. "I don't think it would happen like that."

Adrian was shaking his head. "And just when I thought you couldn't make it any worse for me. Can I talk you out of this?"

"I don't think so. It feels the right thing to do." He sent Chan to get Atawhai and Lestze. Then as a group they walked to the lift.

The soldier stood resolutely where the lift doors met and refused to step aside. Chan pushed the button to call the lift, so the soldier said, "I am ordered to stop anyone leaving, which I will do, up to and including lethal force, if you insist. Step back, let me call Lieutenant Shaw and you sort it out with him." Senden agreed.

When the lieutenant arrived, Senden met him with "I have decided to go to speak with the . . ." He looked questioningly at Atawhai. "Reporters," she filled in for him.

"There is no way I can allow you to do that."

"Well, I have been reviewing my options. Shouting at them from the rooftop seems a little undignified so I might have to try climbing down. That might look bad on . . . TV . . . particularly if I fall, so thought I would try this first."

"I will restrain you if I have to."

"In that case," he said, looking at the others, "any of you who are free are to run to the balcony or roof and shout that the ambassadors are being held against their will and physically restrained to prevent them helping the citizens of Earth." He started walking back towards the exit to the roof.

"Stop! Give me some time and I will see what I can organize."

"I am either going down in that metal box now or climbing down the wall. The choice is yours."

"The lift it is." He told the soldier to let them pass and follow them down. As they went down, Senden said to the lieutenant, "I have nothing but admiration for your dedication to duty and honour. Remember Lestze and I are also under orders from our planet's government and are perfectly willing to do whatever it takes to fulfil our mission."

"When we get to the foyer I am asking you to wait while I get my men assembled and briefed. I am not trying to stall you."

"If it makes you happy."

As the soldiers were rapidly assembled from other parts of the hotel,

Lieutenant Shaw told Senden, "I will send my men out first to make sure it is safe for you to leave."

"No. Hiding behind soldiers here does not seem right. It is not what we would do at home. Trust me, please. I am not reckless and do not take unnecessary risks."

Senden and Lestze took a few steps out the door with Atawhai between them while Chan, Adrian and Lin followed behind. There was a sudden silence as the school of piranhas noticed their prey then they started to surge forward, shouting questions. One of the two soldiers who were on duty outside the front doors fired a shot in the air as two of Lieutenant Shaw's soldiers flanked the group on each side. The lieutenant stepped around them. "These people," he gestured to the group, "have decided to speak to you and very much against my better judgement," he shouted. "I have agreed reluctantly, but if any of you make any more sudden moves I will put an end to this."

There was an embarrassed hiatus. Lieutenant Shaw looked from the camera crews filming back to his charges, standing somewhat forlornly in front of the doors. Might as well make them comfortable. "Give me a few minutes to get this organized," he yelled at the journalists, followed by "and you two get me five chairs out here now" to the soldiers still standing either side of the doors.

Chan moved beside the lieutenant and said quietly, "I would rather stand where I can see what's happening if that's okay with you. Get someone upstairs to look down on them." Lieutenant Shaw nodded, so Chan walked to the side where he had a reasonable view of both groups.

Once the four from Neanderthal B were seated, the lieutenant moved to one side and invited the crowd to move a little closer. There was a spare seat so Senden called to Adrian, who had stepped aside with the lieutenant, to sit with them. He shook his head, but Lieutenant Shaw politely nudged him back with a few whispered words. He sighed and gave in, walking back to sit down. This provoked a storm of questions and shouting as reporters competed to be heard. Senden did not move or reply.

Lin held up his hand for silence then stood up. "This will have to be organized too. We can only answer one question at a time. Put your hands up when you have a question. I will get to you if I can. I will ask the lieutenant," he turned and nodded to Lieutenant Shaw, "to remove anyone who calls out out of turn. This is Mr Adrian Norris, the UN Resident Coordinator, as most of you recognized. I will take questions for him first."

Lin needed to explain his own position as several reporters had recognized him as one of the leaders of the group of rebel fugitives before introducing Atawhai and getting her to tell a little of her story to provide background. He then introduced Senden and Lestze as joint ambassadors from the World Council of Neanderthal B.

When an hour was well passed and there was no respite from the reporters, in fact as most were on satellite link and were getting feedback from their studios, the interest was intensifying. The lieutenant stepped in front and called an end to the impromptu press conference. His men quickly escorted the group back into the hotel.

Back in the conference room, Adrian organized the hotel kitchens to send up breakfast while Atawhai put up some of the news reports from the internet through the projector.

"Well, it looks like we are the number-one story worldwide. That puts you in a very different bargaining position than you were in yesterday, Senden," Lin stated.

Senden only nodded, looking tired, while Lestze appeared to be in shock again. Atawhai sat by him and took his hand. "Remember to look for the good," she whispered.

He squeezed her hand and she could feel his spirit rally. He started laughing. "Thank you, teacher," he quipped.

"It's a difficult job but someone's got to do it." They sat quietly, feeling, if not happy, at least pleased circumstances seemed to be moving in the direction they hoped, to wait for breakfast.

Later, Chan chatted with Atawhai and Lestze while Adrian spent the morning talking with Senden and Lin. Adrian had commented, "If I leave the building, the chances are very low I will be allowed back in."

Atawhai kept an eye on the international news reports. A couple of hours later, a press release stated a group of UN officials led by Mr Adrian Norris, the New Zealand UN Resident Coordinator, were working with the ambassadors from Neanderthal B and developing a mutually beneficial collaboration. She called the others over and replayed the clip.

"That's good to know," Adrian remarked a little caustically.

"Why would they say that?" Lestze asked.

"Because the people of this world are afraid and desperate. The illusion of government and control is hanging by a thread and could easily break again. At the moment, public opinion is very highly in our favour and my superiors want to ride that wave and appear part of it. If events don't work out well, they can distance themselves from this later, and of course find a handy scapegoat."

"But it's not true. How can we work with people that don't mean a word they say?"

"I think the people mean well regardless," commented Senden.

"He's right," Adrian chipped in. "Individually people mean well. It's unfortunate that the collective intelligence of any large organization is usually inversely proportional to the number of people in it. The inertia of these organizations means they can't respond in a creative way in real time and tend to react out of reflex or instinct to preserve themselves. The individuals who are part of the organization become compelled to turn a blind eye or cross an unclear moral line more and more often to maintain their individual positions and power, their perceived security or safety, that depend on maintaining the power of the monolith. Individual morality or intelligence gradually becomes meaningless."

As lunch was delivered, Lieutenant Shaw came to see Adrian. "Mr Norris, among others, the prime minister and the New Zealand Chief of Defence Forces have asked to meet the Ambassadors. The UN Government has told them to contact you to schedule an appointment. I suggest you start paying attention to your phone and emails again, sir."

Adrian noticed the slight emphasis on 'sir' in a way suggesting respect rather than contempt (ah, the swings and roundabouts of political fortune) and thanked him, then commented, mostly to himself, "Après nous, le déluge." He paused for a moment, then asked the lieutenant to wait. "Senden, I take it you are not willing to be moved from here at this stage. This would be much easier if we moved you to Wellington, but Auckland would do as it has an international airport."

"I think it better we stay here on neutral ground and close to the jump station in the meantime."

"As you wish. In that case, Lieutenant Shaw, can you have the hotel remove the beds from one of the suites and have two office tables installed with phone and internet connections.

"Yes, sir." He turned to Senden, momentarily coming to attention: "Mr Ambassador," then walked out. Atawhai suspected there would be a grin on his face if only she could see it.

28

An Observation Perhaps?

Adrian moved his office manager, Graham, up from the Wellington office; he brought some of his team with him. He had commandeered a small Air New Zealand jet and was at work within a couple of hours. Not only was he here to organize a burgeoning social calendar but immediately felt affronted at the appearance of his charges. "You can't meet world leaders looking like that," dismay dripping from his tone. A few phone calls and despite the lateness in the day clothing retailers were soon knocking on the door or, rather, being repelled at a distance by soldiers with guns. This meant having to appraise the lieutenant of who to let in. Security had been more than doubled since the morning press conference with more SAS teams called in.

Lestze found the idea of having more clothes than he stood up in disturbing. He had been on the move for more than half his short life. "If I have to carry half the clothes they are giving me, I would die in a few days. I couldn't carry food or my hunting weapons," he said to Atawhai during a free moment, being too polite to argue with his hosts/benefactors. "It is immoral to take more than I need if others don't have what they need."

Atawhai just laughed. "Everything is seen differently here. It doesn't mean what you think it means. Let it go without trying to make sense of it because it probably doesn't make sense to any sane being anyway." It was good advice as shoe sellers and hairdressers followed in quick succession.

The next morning started early with a visit from the mayor of Hamilton who formally welcomed them to the city while the prime minister, arriving for a midday meeting, then joined them for lunch. Other dignitaries were fitted in between, but Graham soon learned to run his schedule past Lin who had looked at the list of people wanting to meet the ambassadors and insisted many of them would have to wait. Senden and Lestze needed some respite time to themselves between visitors. Lin had also bumped up the list a request from Waikato University for some of their staff to speak to Senden and Lestze, seeing this as equally or more important than forging political alliances. As a result, a group of professors arrived late in the afternoon along with the chancellor.

The conference room had been set up for them and a small group of reporters had been allowed to cover the event on condition anything released would be vetted first. It was the first concession to the media apart from official statements since the previous morning.

Lin took charge as master of ceremonies, fielding questions, while Senden and Lestze in particular had been warned to keep their answers as generic and short as possible.

It started with "Why do you speak English?"

"Every child on these islands learn it as their second language. It is used for science as well as it has so many words for concepts that had never occurred to us," Senden answered.

Then questions about how their government was organized as it had been a revelation they even had a government. The questions developed from there.

"So you use telepathy to coordinate and hold together your government?"

"Among other things. A stable government doesn't need the level of communication you have here where you stumble from crisis to crisis on a daily basis. Really important decisions may not arise in generations," Senden answered.

"Then why are you so primitive."

"Look at your treatment of your fellow human beings and decide who is primitive."

"Sorry, I was meaning technologically."

"Any society that values technological development over social and psychological or interpersonal development is doomed to destroy itself."

"If telepathy is real, why don't we experience it?"

"Your fear of the unknown keeps you locked in a tiny part of your mind."

The questioning continued with both Atawhai and Lestze answering questions sporadically too until a professor of physics asked, "We have found so few parallel worlds. A Neanderthal and an Australopithecine world. A Palaeozoic and a Mesozoic world. It was a huge surprise when our small facility at the university discovered your world, a second Neanderthal world. Do you have any thoughts on why two Neanderthal world-lines exist?"

"We are not a Neanderthal world. On our world an exceptionally cold period during an ice age forced the Neanderthals out of Eurasia and back into Africa. They recolonized Africa but integrated with rather than exterminated the developing *Homo sapiens*. We are a hybrid of the two species, but our world-line is a very low probability occurrence so would not be easy to find."

The physicist nodded his head. "Still, why so few world-lines? Every significant choice point should lead to world-lines splitting off or diverging and new world-lines appearing. There should be myriad worlds."

Senden shook his head and smiled. He was obviously feeling tired. "I will leave this to Lestze. He is much more interested in physics than me."

Lestze instantly perked up. "Well, quantum entanglement for a start."

The physicist laughed with surprise. "You know about that then? Explain please."

"Yes, we know. We have had forty years to look at your discoveries from our point of view. You know an entangled particle is influenced by a particle it is entangled with. Consider two parallel universes that have just diverged but still essentially exist together in the same place or meta-space at the same time. Every particle is mirrored by its twin particle throughout both universes except at the point where the divergence occurred. The entrainment and entanglement forces forcing them to converge again and collapse back into a single world-line are huge.

"Parallel universes are constantly diverging where one choice occurs in one and the opposite choice occurs in the other all the time, but quantum entanglement will generally force the two universes to collapse back into a single world-line in an instant with only one of the two possible choices having been made."

"Why not both?"

It is clear from the Schrödinger's Cat principle that after any choice point, when the observer looks the cat must be either alive or dead. It can't be both. The act of observation causes the space–time field to collapse into a single, definable, specific event. If every possible choice is allowed simultaneously, resulting in an infinite number of worlds, it is the same as there being no choice being made. Forcing a choice and excluding other possibilities produces the observable universe."

"But that makes it seem like the act of observation is itself the choice, that we choose what we want to see, maybe how we want to see it. Or something does anyway."

"That is the way it looks. The observer effect makes it clear that the act of observing changes the nature of what is observed. If that connection is unbreakable, then either the observed world creates the observer or the observer creates the world they observe by their own expectations.

"Then why are there still separate world-lines?"

"Each represents a way of perceiving the nature of the universe that is, apparently, significantly different. We experience them as separate and hard to cross between, but if the way we perceive the world affects the nature of the world we see, it is likely that completely changing our minds about the nature of reality may automatically cause us to experience or be in another world-line."

"An interesting way of looking at it, but is it true?"

"Can any attempt to discuss multi-dimensional, non-linear time based, abstract concepts in three-dimensional, specific terms be considered true?"

The professor laughed. "Okay, I can accept that. So on the very rare occasions two world-lines have successfully diverged they continue to develop in different directions."

"Not necessarily. They will eventually converge again."

"But what happens when the two world-lines collapse into one. The past from one or the other must be built upon for a coherent timeline to continue."

"It is only an assumption that there exists a concrete and objective past that leads through a single arrow of time into an as yet formless future that will be formed in due course by our choices. This seems highly unlikely to us. Almost certainly both the past and the future propagate in opposite directions from the present moment along the timeline. The past that you remember in the physical world only seems to exist because it logically leads to the present moment the observing consciousness experiences.

"If that moment is substantially changed by a collapse point between timelines, you will still experience, call it remember if you wish, a logical past history leading up to your present moment, even if events and people in that history didn't exist in either of the timelines that collapsed into the one you believe is 'real.'"

"Do you think there is a limit to the number of timelines?"

"We are not sure it is important. It looks like the universe began as a single timeline that has diverged into many as billions of years have passed, but convergence will ensure it ends as only a single timeline."

"Why?"

"When it becomes obvious to the observer that all temporal choices lead to the same end."

Lin called a break for refreshments at that stage, expecting the university staff to leave. Instead they unanimously requested to stay and Senden reluctantly acquiesced. After a break, as the hotel staff brought food and drinks for the incumbents and their guests, the careful organization degenerated into transient groupings constantly reforming around one or more of those from Neanderthal B until late in the night.

29
Metaphorically Speaking

Senden summoned the five to an early morning meeting, extending the invitation to Adrian and Lieutenant Shaw. "I think our position is secure enough for us to start the next stage of our mission. I am happy enough to continue to solidify our status here with Lin and Chan as advisors. The scientists are sure the plagues originated in the Palaeozoic World, so I want to send Lestze and Atawhai there as soon as possible. I don't want to be making hollow promises, so I need to know where we stand and if there is genuinely anything we can do."

Adrian frowned. "All traffic with other world-lines has been suspended since the pandemic outbreak. As the Palaeozoic World was where it came from, the chances of getting the UN to agree to sending people there is close to zero. The risk they might bring something else back would be politically unacceptable."

"If you could get on to it as soon as you can please. I think it would be easier to arrange if a representative from your world goes with them. I doubt Atawhai would count as that any more for many people here. Give some thought to that as well please."

There was nothing more to add so the meeting ended.

Later, Atawhai sought out Senden. "If what Lestze said is true, I could lose everything I am."

"It's not quite as dramatic as that. It seems that the longer timelines have been divergent the longer it would take for them to converge again. It may take lifetimes, then again maybe not."

"But I wouldn't be me any more."

"Define 'me'."

"I don't know — my body, my thoughts, my emotions, my attitudes, my experiences. All of it I guess."

"How about none of it?"

"But my thoughts are me. One of our greatest philosophers said, 'I think therefore I am.'"

Senden laughed. "Why would you identify yourself with your thoughts? Your normal thoughts are nothing more than artefacts, recycled memories and images you have made from your experiences and imagination or wishful thinking. Your people are particularly good at recycling your emotions, I notice. They play the 'I am sad, I am a victim' role really well. As your thoughts or emotions are your own constructs they cannot define what you are in any way, and you are completely responsible for what you are feeling or thinking. They are arbitrary and ephemeral. You have made up the thoughts. It is no more profound to say, 'I think therefore I am' than to say" — he looked at the almost empty plate in front of him — "'I make sandwiches therefore I am.' Would you therefore decide you are a sandwich and say this is me?" He started chortling again.

Her face fell. "I don't understand why you are laughing."

Senden was suddenly sober again. "I'm sorry, child. I didn't mean to hurt your feelings. I was not laughing at you. Just that absurd human hubris that believes it understands what it sees and makes such arrogant comments. I am as guilty of it as anyone else. The older I get the more I see that this persona, this role I play, doesn't know anything at all about what is real. It is part of what is made rather than the maker. When you say, 'my body' or 'my thoughts', the real question is, who is the 'me' that those things belong to, what is it that is making or rather observing and identifying with the thoughts?"

Later that morning, Adrian updated them. "I have passed Senden's request on and it was received more positively than I expected. Most of the major countries had stations on the Palaeozoic world-line. There is no sentient race there so there was no UN ban on exploiting its resources. However, it looks like the plague came through one of the US stations so using Washington Station makes sense. As a result of your antics yesterday, there are a couple of people coming from UN headquarters in New York and one from Geneva. If they are satisfied with your intentions and your credentials, whatever they are, we should get permission fairly quickly."

As there was time to kill, Atawhai got Senden's permission for Lestze to dodge the day's engagements and asked Adrian to get her a car. They were careful to avoid the paparazzi and she took Lestze to a west coast beach that was deserted at this time of year, then to Bridal Veil Falls and later walked a trail up Pirongia Mountain. It was late in the evening when they arrived back at the hotel.

The UN representatives from New York arrived early next morning, the Under-Secretary-General for Political Affairs and the recently created Special Envoy for Global Pandemics, Robert Baudelaire. After a breakfast in the hotel and a long briefing from Adrian, the three UN officials then met with Senden, Lestze and Atawhai. Mid-morning the Director-General of the World Health Organization arrived from Geneva and joined the meeting. After lunch, when the visitors were convinced that Senden and Lestze were worth taking seriously, Senden asked for Mr Lin to join them and negotiations began in earnest.

By the end of the day, they had agreement in principle for cooperative development between worlds with both worlds having equal standing but, most importantly, agreement to get Lestze and Atawhai to the Palaeozoic World. It had been decided that Robert would return to the US with them and act as chef de mission. Adrian's brevet conferring ambassadorial status to Senden and Lestze was formalized along with the extension of diplomatic immunity to their staff.

Atawhai and Lestze escaped to a balcony when no one was looking, closing the door behind them. They sat in silence, watching the colours change as the sun set, letting the tensions of the day drain away. Atawhai looked across at Lestze. "Are you happy?"

"Yes."

"I mean with how the day went. You have been given what you wanted, what Senden had hoped for."

"I thought Adrian had already agreed to all that. A simple yes or no would have worked. Why waste all day to agree to what we have already agreed to and then agree to eventually come to an agreement?"

"The UN representatives want an ironclad agreement from both parties, something set in stone that can't be backed out of easily."

"Why?"

"So we can set out a framework for how we can cooperate. What we each need or have to give so we get a mutually beneficial exchange. Think of it as a map of how we can proceed from here."

"We don't need anything from you."

"You keep saying that. We don't have to change your culture. Look at your people living in the forest, like that family we stayed with. Better axes and saws would make their lives so much easier. One person with a chainsaw could cut as much building timber in a day as a whole village could in a week."

"Chainsaw?"

"What we used to cut down the forest around the jump station."

He nodded. "I remember that. In a few days you destroyed a huge number of living things without any feeling or care, some that had lived more than a thousand years, trees old enough to have a sense of themselves, a voice of their own. Have you thought through the real consequences? People would find it easy to build houses far larger than they need. That would soon be expected and everyone would do it. What happens to our world when everyone cuts down many times what they do now? Look at what you have done to our forest and multiply that by half a billion. How would that be progress for us?"

He waited. Eventually, she replied, "It wouldn't be, would it?"

"No, but soon the forest would just be a source of wood to cut down. What we would really lose is knowing our relationship to the forest. It is our friend and our kin; we share life together, not independent lives. The forest provides what we need, and we return that gift by our care and consideration for it. Losing our connection with the life around us would destroy who we are."

They fell silent for a while. Atawhai knew Lestze was just making observations, there was no sense of blame or guilt in his comments. A little later he started snickering to himself.

"Okay, what is it this time?" she demanded.

"I was just going over what we have been talking about in my mind, trying to be sure I understood what you were meaning."

"And . . ." she insisted.

"I was just wondering how far I could walk carrying an ironclad agreement and a map set in stone," he offered innocently.

"They are only metaphors, you oaf," she retorted, exasperation evident in every word.

He laughed even more. "You know that describes your culture perfectly. You really believe the stories you tell, you are totally enslaved by your metaphors."

"What do you mean?"

"Well, for instance, what do you think the purpose of all these negotiations are?"

"To make sure we reach an agreement that is fair to both sides."

"That is the myth, the story you are all telling yourselves. I was watching the byplay of emotions all day. The real motivation of the negotiators, their ulterior motivation, is to make sure we don't get any advantage, get more than they do. They are more disturbed because they can't see what we want than if we were to openly trick them and gain some huge advantage from the agreement. At least that would be understandable from their world-view. Behind the veneer of common cause there is still the thought — how can we get access to what we want, their help, their resources, their world and give as little of what we really value as we can? They are caught up in the myth that the only possible interest is self-interest."

"How would you write an agreement then?"

"I would say let's have free and regular communication between our governments, nothing binding, then accept or ask for help as the need arises and is agreed to by both governments on a case-by-case basis. It is impossible to predict how contact between worlds will affect either of them. We will have to make the decisions as we go along."

"But we need to know how we can cooperate."

"You mean we need to think we can control in advance what will happen. It is all based on fear that we will be exploited or lose something. We are walking into an unknown forest towards a distant goal. Our map in stone that we have to carry says that we have to follow a straight path. What happens when there is a tree in the way? Do we cut it down so we can follow the agreed path? Do we fill in the ravines and flatten the waterfalls rather than walk around? The only binding part of any agreement should be enough goodwill from each side to do what is appropriate as each need arises."

"It's not possible to work together without deciding first how we can. Both of our peoples will have to be willing to compromise if we want to get along."

"We aren't here to compromise. Compromise assumes the only possible outcome is loss for both parties and the purpose of the agreement is to limit it. We are only interested in a win–win outcome, some way we can both benefit." He grinned. "We don't see how we can manage that where your people are concerned, but it must be possible somehow."

"Of course, but with your superior wisdom, maturity and insight showing the way, how could we possibly fail?"

He paused, unsure how to take the comment. Atawhai waited a moment then said matter-of-factly, "Do I need to add good looks to the list?"

He relaxed, realizing she was teasing him. "I'm sure it would help."

"Big-headedness should be the only quality on that list." She poked him in the ribs and he winced away. "Why are you really here, Lestze?"

"For friendship, of course. For us to share our happiness with you and you to share your happiness with us. What could be more important or valuable than that?"

30
Hypothetically Speaking, Actually

It wasn't long before Chan found them. "Senden wants you to hear what they are discussing. He wants Atawhai's opinion on how she wants it to go." She sighed as they stood up to follow Chan back to the conference room.

Adrian paused as they entered, then addressed Atawhai when they sat down. "We are checking flights. There are two reasonably straight flights to Washington tomorrow that still have seats. The first at two-ten p.m. has a four-and-a-half-hour stopover in Los Angeles, the later one at seven-thirty has a six-hour stopover in Houston. Are you both happy with the earlier flight?" Lestze shrugged, having no experience on which to make a decision, and Atawhai nodded. "Good. Robert will stay behind in Washington to hopefully manage the political implications of your visit, though we intend to have you through the gate before news gets out. At this stage, we haven't been able to decide who to send with you as a representative from our world. Do you have any preferences?"

"We need survival specialists. We don't know what we will find even if the automated jump mechanisms are still working," she replied without hesitation.

"Okay. We have already sent a request for an update on the Washington Palaeo Station's status. If it tests out safe, we will send technicians through to check it out and get it prepared for you."

"Do you have that kind of authority?"

"Together, the three representatives here do, but Robert will still run it by the Secretary-General when he gets back to the US for her approval. What sort of survival specialists do you have in mind?"

"People with big guns. The caretakers were withdrawn and there has been no contact with the Palaeozoic stations for over six months. The lizards, sorry — giant reptiles — will have almost certainly broken through the outer defence lines. There were lots of people working at Washington Station who would qualify when I was there."

"I doubt that would be the case now. People with those sorts of skills have mostly been spread out around the world on peacekeeping duties. I will look into it."

After dinner, Atawhai decided to show Lestze a movie and agonized over choosing one. She finally settled for *The Incredibles* as it seemed innocuous and was funny. Watching it emphasized for her how much background knowledge she took for granted, the cultural divide between them. Apart from getting across what animation was — no, it was not real, but then it was definitely a parody of real life for many people. Why would people keep working at jobs they didn't like then? Why do you have to drive every day to work? Why were people angry at them for being different? If the makers of the movie can see life here is stupid, why hasn't something been done about it? Many good questions without answers apart from "that's the way it is here". He was enthralled regardless.

The weather turned to heavy rain that continued through the next day. It matched the sombre mood of the group at breakfast, each with their individual concerns for what might happen next and the melancholy of parting. While understanding Atawhai's concern for their safety, Senden had later vetoed sending a squad of armed soldiers with them, telling Adrian, "We are going there to ask for help. Sending in a war party would only give the wrong message."

As a compromise, Adrian said to Atawhai in the morning, "The simplest thing for me is to send one of Lieutenant Shaw's soldiers with you. He can get whatever weapons he wants when you get to Washington."

Not long after, Adrian returned with the UN representatives to collect Lestze and Atawhai. Two cars had arrived to take them to Auckland Airport. As Lestze and Atawhai hastily said their goodbyes, Senden hugged Lestze and said, "Our people are proud of what you have done. Don't put yourself in unnecessary danger to try to fix things. However it works out is okay."

On the way out, they were introduced to Corporal Jeff Wilder, a nonchalant and friendly young man, waiting patiently in the foyer of the hotel as if this was just another day. Atawhai and Lestze were sent to the front car, while Jeff and Robert were sent to the second, both vehicles having an armed soldier in the front passenger seat.

They had been on the expressway for only a few minutes when Atawhai leaned forward to tap the driver on the shoulder. "Can we pull off at Taupiri for a few minutes?"

The driver said nothing but nodded towards the guard beside him who commented, "Sorry Miss, I have orders to get you straight to the airport."

"Are you in phone contact with the other car? Can I speak to Robert?"

"I will check for you." He spoke into his phone for a moment then handed it to Atawhai.

"Hello, Robert, Lestze wants to stop for a few minutes at Taupiri and we have plenty of time." Lestze glanced sideways at Atawhai with his eyebrows lifted. She held a finger to her lips then after a moment stated peremptorily, "Yes, it is important." Another pause, then "Yes I promise it will only be five minutes." She handed the phone back to its owner who listened for a few moments then told the driver to take the Taupiri exit when they reached it.

The driver followed Atawhai's direction through the hamlet to the old highway and turned left into a tiny park by the river. As they stopped she jumped out of the car, pulling Lestze out the door with her in her excitement as she was unwilling to let go his hand. She towed him around the park then pointed out the mountain, exclaiming, "You know where we are."

"Yes, I do but I'm wondering if you do."

This is where the house is, where the family I stayed with in your world lives. You know this place well."

He gently placed a finger to her lips to quiet her. He waited while he took several long, slow breaths. Taking his finger away, he asked, "Remember how it felt when you were at the house? Then look at all this again but without using your eyes or your preconceptions. Tell me what you actually feel in yourself as you look; don't tell me what you think should be here. What has changed?"

Atawhai was silent for a while. "It's too quiet."

"In what way?"

"The house was part of the forest. There was always noise from the birds and people coming and going, but underneath that it was still peaceful. It felt good and happy and somehow right being there. Here, now, it's not peaceful, it just feels like death. It is alienated from the essence of life and living; it's so sad. It's not the same place at all."

Tears were welling up in her eyes, but Lestze could see they were out of time. Robert and Jeff were standing together by the cars, not sure what weird ritual they were seeing enacted, but were about to intervene nonetheless. He gestured, pushing his hand towards them to tell them to stay back.

"What did you expect me to see here or rather what were you wanting to be here?"

"I don't know, I was just wanting you to see somewhere you know well."

"Not really. You were wanting to feel safe and cared for, the way you remembered it when you were in the other world. Unfortunately, what we see is what there is here and now. All there is. Neanderthal B is an alternate world. Effectively, it's a 'what if' scenario: what could be here at this point in space and time if different choices were made in the past? In that sense, like all the other timelines, it can only be hypothetical."

She digested this pensively. "But doesn't that mean this world has got to be hypothetical too?"

Lestze laughed. "Absolutely. But it is the only one that is real to us while we choose to experience it. We need to go." He put an arm around her and walked her back to their car.

Back on the expressway, they were passing through one of the rare patches of farmland left, as, in general, new housing developments had sprung up where the land flanking it offered the illusion of rural living, while the road still gave easy access to the cities in either direction. "Tell me what I am seeing," Lestze asked abruptly.

"It's dairy farming. Raising cows to produce milk. We can graze cows here all year round so the land is very productive. Some of the most productive in the world," she finished proudly.

"That doesn't make sense. All I can see is grass and cows. The grass couldn't stay fertile for long without other species providing inputs and I can't see anything that could recycle the wastes from that many cows. That should poison the environment over time. It can't be that productive if everything was taken into account. Even a desert would have a lot more diversity than this. It all looks very lush and green, but it is a desert nonetheless. From the point of view of the health of your planet, it can't be a lot better than all the houses being built on the land."

They continued to the airport in brooding silence.

31
Crossing the Rubicon

They were hurried into a private lounge to wait the two and a half hours before boarding. The guards from the cars waited with them, one sitting in a chair by the door, one outside in the corridor, and later they escorted them to the front of the plane after the other passengers had boarded.

Atawhai nudged a completely relaxed Lestze in the ribs as the plane taxied out on to the runway.

"Feeling nervous?"

"No, but I notice you are. Those people," he gestured back down the plane. "Cabin crew," she filled in automatically without even noticing. "They are not worried at all. Do you know something they don't?"

She sighed, "No. But aren't you at least excited?"

"To not find an event exciting is simply a decision you make that it is not important to you. All situations feel the same if you are in the habit of giving each one your full attention. I am very interested in what is happening." Atawhai sighed again and dropped the subject.

They touched down in Los Angeles in the early hours of the morning and were ushered off the plane. They were fast tracked through immigration only to be confined to another faceless lounge and put back on the plane a few hours later without having any real contact with anyone, including the Internal Affairs agents escorting them. They landed in Washington in the early evening. Again, they were taken to a small, empty transit lounge to wait, though this one had windows looking out to the runways. Robert surprised them when he eventually turned up. "I've decided to leave you here in Washington tonight. I am catching a flight up to New York so I can discuss our requirements with the secretary-general. We need her approval to take the next step and I think it would go down better face to face. I have an appointment with her first thing in the morning. You are being sent to Andrews Air Base. I will get other experts to meet you there, if I can on such short notice, but if not, Atawhai, you will have to brief Corporal Wilder on what he is to expect on Palaeo World. He will have to decide for himself what weaponry to take. The base can supply anything he could ask for. Your transport is waiting. I hope to be back tomorrow, lunchtime."

He walked to the door at the back of the room and opened it. After a brief conversation, four armed soldiers walked in. "This is your escort detail. They will take care of you from here on," Robert stated.

Two of the soldiers walked back out the door while the other two waited stoically for Lestze, Atawhai and Jeff to walk to the door then followed. They were ushered out to the front of the terminal where two L-ATVs were parked close to the door and quickly shut inside.

As they drove off in close formation, Atawhai leaned forward and asked the woman riding shotgun who hadn't lowered her gun. "This is a bit dramatic, isn't it?"

"No," she commented unemotionally. "We are getting sporadic outbreaks of civil disorder as people are getting more desperate or angry with the movement bans from new quarantine laws and the outrage with the introduction of food rationing in the US this week. Things are not looking good for the World Government."

"Civil disorder?" Lestze asked quietly.

"Rioting and looting, I suspect. We didn't see any signs of that in the news bulletins we were watching back at the Ambassador Hotel. Censorship of the media must have been tightened while I was away," Atawhai whispered.

It was a sombre drive through Washington to the base. Atawhai tried to explain the nature of an airbase as a place where soldiers and pilots kept aircraft for fighting in the air and attacking ground targets. While understanding the concepts, Lestze had no experience to be able to grasp the scale of warfare on this planet.

After a careful check of the vehicles by sentries on duty at the entrance, they were taken to the Presidential Inn, an on-base, military-only hotel. As they went up several floors and followed along the corridors to their rooms, the place was buzzing with activity. Atawhai asked the woman who had spoken to her earlier why the hotel was so busy.

"The national guard and military reservists have been mobilized locally, while regular forces are acting more internationally. The airbase is one of several staging posts for flying peacekeepers to assist local security forces anywhere in the western hemisphere as incidents occur. There are similar operations being mounted by other armies in Europe, Asia and Africa."

When they reached their rooms, she continued, "Our orders are to consider your safety the highest-level priority. We can't let you leave your rooms at this time, so food will be brought to you. Have a good evening." Atawhai had a quick look in her room then stepped back into the corridor to see if she could walk around the hotel. Unsurprisingly, there was already a guard just past Lestze's door. Back the other way, the corridor ended immediately past Jeff's room.

Atawhai knocked politely on Lestze's door and waited a moment. She didn't get a reply so, after waiting for a couple of breaths, tried the door. It was unlocked and she went in.

Lestze was standing at the window with a blank stare, gazing out into nothing. He started slightly when she spoke his name. "I can't feel the land at all. Back where you came from the land had been devastated, but it still remembered what it once was, what it should be. There's nothing here."

Atawhai shuddered. "You aren't going to give up on me, lose the plot again, are you?"

He shook his head, smiled. "No more so than usual. I'm over the shock of it now." He turned away from the window to face her. "It looks like you are incarcerated again. This is getting to be a habit. It must be some subconscious wish-fulfilment thing."

"What? You mean, like, bondage?"

"I'm not sure what that means in this . . ."

He broke off, not sure how to finish, then flushed with embarrassment. "Oh. No, that would never have occurred to me."

Atawhai laughed. "You're blushing. You should know better than to read a girl's mind."

"But I wasn't. You are always shouting thoughts and feelings at me. Everyone here does, and it doesn't seem to have occurred to any of you to be quiet and simply listen. The concept is probably too scary. You have no idea how the way you think about your world affects the world or those you are thinking about. I just forgot to mentally put my fingers in my ears when you came in." He looked away. "I didn't mean to intrude, and I was only joking earlier."

"So was I dummy. Stop taking everything so seriously. Let's see if Jeff wants to talk. I would like to know him better if I'm trusting him with my life."

Jeff turned out to be a natural entertainer and they got on like a house on fire. Dinner was delivered not long after, so they ate together but retired to their rooms as soon as they had finished to recover from the long trip.

They were roused next morning as breakfast was brought to their rooms. Atawhai brought hers to eat with Lestze, after which they went back together to Jeff's room to wait. Nothing happened. For Atawhai the anticlimax was as nerve-wracking in its own way as almost anything in the last few weeks. She was getting jumpy as the day slipped into afternoon. Jeff, in the opposite corner, was at his phlegmatic best. "Relax," he advised. "Any day I'm not being attacked by protesters because I'm enforcing martial law somewhere, or maybe being eaten by prehistoric lizards, has got to be a good day. You have to make the most of your downtime — however it turns up. Besides, these rooms are nicer than my house and, also unlike home, there's room service if you bother to pick up the phone." He laughed at that thought.

Robert phoned them mid-afternoon. The gist was Jeff would be taken to get whatever weapons he wanted and while there was nothing more for them to do today they should be ready to leave with a moment's notice.

"Can we come with you to look at the weapons, Jeff?" Atawhai asked.

"I don't think they would be happy about the three of us wandering around the base. Robert must have given some sharp orders about our safety when he sent us here."

"He said I should advise you if he hadn't sent anyone else and I don't see anyone else, do you?"

"Okay. At least we can argue the point when they get here."

There was much less arguing than expected when an armed soldier arrived for Jeff. Robert's orders as a UN Special Envoy carried a great deal of authority in the new world order and Jeff insisted these were Robert's orders. After a brief call by the soldier to his superiors, an extra car and a couple more escorts were detailed to take them as a group.

After a quick look at a bewildering array of weapons and an even larger inventory including bombs big enough to do a lot of damage to a small city, Jeff turned to Atawhai and said sarcastically, "Okay, Madam Advisor, how many bombs should I take?"

She shook her head angrily. "This is ridiculous."

"How so?"

"There are packs of small carnivores that will quite happily take on a human being, but in summer there are reptiles there big enough to turn over a truck, and they have. One person can't be equipped to deal with it all. We really need a full combat team."

"That really makes it easy. Thanks so much."

Jeff mused discontentedly for a while then turned to Lestze. "Nobody tells me anything. I'm guessing you will be in command when we are on Palaeo?"

Lestze raised his eyebrows and looked at Atawhai. "Search me," she commented dryly.

"Sounds like an offer you shouldn't refuse," Jeff wisely counselled Lestze, who only looked confused. Jeff rolled his eyes in exasperation then sighed. "Someone must have some idea of who is planning to do what when we get there or what the hell's the point of all this trouble the UN is going to."

"I need to find a self-sentient species there somewhere," Lestze piped up helpfully.

"Self-sentient?" Atawhai asked.

"Most species are far more intelligent than your people seem to realize, but they don't experience themselves as separate from their environment or see themselves as not responsible for the consequences of their thoughts and actions. They don't think primarily about themselves."

"He really is a ray of sunshine," Jeff said to Atawhai, cutting off the discussion, then turned to Lestze. "So how do you intend to accomplish this impressive feat?"

"I am hoping they will find me. If not, we will have to go looking."

"Where and how?"

Lestze thought for a moment. "I don't know. I think we need help from our advisor to answer that."

"Don't you start," Atawhai replied. "We didn't see any sign of what you are looking for and we've looked at the whole planet by plane and satellite."

"How did you get around?" Jeff continued.

"On roads near the station, otherwise by light aircraft."

"Why?"

"You can't use vehicles easily in the forest and it's not that safe to walk."

"What do you think, Lestze?"

"Where did the roads come from?" Lestze asked Atawhai.

"We made them."

"In that case, they are no use for our purpose. It looks like going walking in the forest is our only option."

"Unfortunately, I agree," Jeff added. "That means all I can take is light weaponry. An assault rifle with grenade launcher, ammunition and a few grenades. I could take missiles for the launcher instead."

"The missiles are better, though you need a clean shot. Grenades often just make the bigger ones really angry," Atawhai commented.

"Thanks. That helps."

Atawhai decided to leave Jeff in the hands of the quartermaster to choose the best options now he had some idea what his role would be. She walked over to their guards, who had stood respectfully away while they talked. "Can you take Lestze and me quickly out to the runways while Jeff is busy?"

The corporal in charge just said, "Yes, ma'am," seeing no point in provoking possible disagreement.

She ran back to Jeff, saying, "Stay here till we get back," then trotted off with Lestze to join their escort.

They were taken between one of the vast hangars to the apron of the airfield. As they watched, a turboprop plane landed then a jet took off shortly after. As the jet left the ground, the corporal said, "That's a Globemaster. It's a really old plane, but they can land on unpaved runways so we are needing to use a few of them at the moment." Lestze only nodded, awed both by the vast resources and creativity expended here and equally that, ultimately, its purpose was killing other people.

They collected Jeff and were taken back to the hotel. As they were being escorted to their rooms, Jeff commented airily to no one in particular, "I have to say how pleased I am to be included in such an impeccably planned mission. I can't think of a single thing that could possibly go wrong."

"I can think of quite a few if you need the help," Lestze riposted happily.

'Excellent,' Atawhai thought. 'He's getting the hang of sarcasm after all. Who says there's nothing of value we can teach them.'

Atawhai asked Jeff to stay and talk with them in Lestze's room. She told him what had happened to her on Neanderthal B as she felt it was only fair he should know the background to what was going on. Dinner was brought to them a little after he went to his room. An hour later a messenger called to tell them to be ready to leave in an hour.

When the time came they were collected and taken with their bags to the front of one of the large hangars where a large helicopter waited. "Any idea why we are being shifted at this time of night?" Atawhai asked Jeff quietly.

"It's after curfew is the reason, but it's not for our benefit so your guess is as good as mine."

They were put on the helicopter and it took off immediately. "We are flying north, possibly north-west, if that means anything," Jeff noted.

"They must be taking us to the jump station," Atawhai replied. "It's built where Green Belt Park used to be."

"That doesn't mean anything to me."

They quickly reached a large, multiply fenced and guarded complex of buildings. The pilot searched for a moment, then landed at a lighted area beside the largest building. They were taken to a large, plush lounge and told to wait for Mr Baudelaire. A guard waited with them. An hour and a half later, Robert walked in with a coterie of assistants, guards and — most importantly — a tall, older woman he introduced without any fanfare as Leotie Berrymann, the UN Secretary-General.

"We have just arrived from New York. I have briefed Leotie as best I can, given the sketchy nature of your plans. She is coming with you to Palaeo and might accompany you on your mission. This is the only way she would give permission for you to go."

She smiled at him. "Thanks, Robert. I know you think this is a bad idea. It is, but I still have to go. It is the right thing for me to do. We do it now, without hesitation or regret."

Robert signalled the guard who led them down several corridors and into a large room with people at consoles behind windows. The machines reminded Lestze of the ones that first brought him here. As they were guided to the centre of the room, he said, "It's smaller than I expected."

"It's one of two mostly used for shifting personnel and smaller equipment. There's a big one that shifts the trucks and transports," Atawhai answered.

Leotie made a small gesture to Robert, who had stayed in the room outside the transport volume. "Hold the fort while I'm gone, Robert. Take care of all my people."

He nodded, turned to wave to one of the men at the consoles, then turned back to an empty room.

32
Last Hope Party?

A young woman in US military uniform was waiting in the jump room when they arrived.
"Welcome to Palaeo, ladies and gentlemen. I am Brenda and if you would like to follow me, I can take you to the rooms that have been prepared for you. Alternatively, there is a briefing room available if you need to talk first." She spoke as if this was just another normal day for her."

There was a surprised pause as no one was sure who was in charge and should be answering. Collecting her wits first, Leotie stepped into the breach. I was not expecting a welcoming committee. How many people are here?"

"About twenty ongoing and the jump technicians at the moment. When the initial scouts found the building was still secure, Mr Baudelaire ordered a security team in to clean up and restock the living quarters. We have needed to get the backup generators going for electricity for water pumps, and air-conditioning. The solar power units should be working again soon, so specialists are coming and going as required. Someone checked the vehicles yesterday too, so you will have transport if you want it."

"I see. It has been a long day for me and I would like to go to my room now. If it is okay with the rest of you, we can get to know each other tomorrow." There were no objections, so Brenda took them to their rooms.

Brenda called them early in the morning as Leotie had requested and left them at the kitchen where they made their own breakfasts before sitting down in the briefing room next door. They each introduced themselves, apart from Atawhai introducing Lestze who was obviously distracted.

"Any questions or thoughts before we discuss plans?" Leotie took the lead again.

"You are the secretary-general, the leader of our entire race, and things are looking desperate. What are you doing here?" Atawhai asked bluntly.

"Robert said the same thing. I am needed in New York as a figurehead to hold the whole thing together. The truth is if what you are doing doesn't work we can't hold the World Government together no matter what we do.

"It is human nature. When disaster happens, we look for something outside our own individual behaviour to blame. It can't be our fault. True in a way as it is never an individual's personal behaviour that causes the environmental or social disasters but our collective behaviours and beliefs.

"When the plague first hit with the wars and unrest that ensued, everybody blamed the national governments and rightly so. The World Government was formed as a reaction to that. It has been working out well, but now we have another outbreak and this time it is the UN having to enforce unpalatable laws to slow the spread of infection and prevent civil disorder. The people are blaming us, so our time is short. It would be kinder to hand power back to territorial governments early in a controlled manner than to wait till anarchy takes power away from us all.

"Your undertaking seems a long shot, but if you succeed I want to be part of this as head of the UN in what might be seen as a crucial part of the saving of humanity. It will reinforce the value of a world government again and I want that to survive as it has already wiped out international wars and can do so much more. If you fail, where I am will make no difference in the long run.

"All that said, mostly I am here to meet you. My parents brought me up to value living things or life as a whole. What Robert told me about Senden and Lestze piqued my curiosity. I think a collaboration between our worlds could offer a great deal."

Lestze finally spoke up. "I can get a sense of the land around here, but it seems as hurt or grieving as the land back at your home."

"Don't worry about it," Atawhai soothed. "You'll understand when you see outside."

"Okay." Lestze brought his attention back to those around him, letting the matter drop.

There was a pause before Jeff filled the gap, "I don't see any point in discussion or planning at this stage. We have no idea what we are planning for till we see the territory. I want to have a careful look around outside at the local conditions, then we can come back and discuss options."

The others quickly agreed so he continued, "I have my combat uniform and kit with me and I assume my weapons have been delivered. I need to get them. Lestze and Atawhai, you will need to get appropriate gear for whatever the environment out there is."

"What about me?" Leotie asked.

Jeff frowned. "Ma'am, I'd rather not take the risk of taking you out with us straight up."

"Call me Leotie, please." She looked at the other two.

Atawhai shrugged. "It used to be safe around the station. Now, I would assume it isn't, but it's not my call." She waited for Lestze to comment.

"Safe or not is irrelevant. We have to do this anyway and if Leotie wants to be part of this, it needs to be right from the start. If she only comes when it's convenient, there is no integrity to her being here. It makes it a sham. She comes with us."

"Okay. You're the boss. In that case, we will have to get her fitted out with an army uniform too."

"Why an army uniform?" Atawhai asked.

"Brenda is a veteran, not a wet nurse. It's easy for me to see that from the way she handles herself. I'll bet the twenty people sent here to clean up are two tactical squads with two spare, and probably one's an officer."

"I would assume the other one would be a civilian advisor. The whole operation here was run by corporations, contractors. The security team would need someone familiar with the place to show them the ropes," Atawhai added.

Lestze was frowning. "Senden made it clear he did not want our mission to be another military incursion of this world."

"Understood, but Robert would not want to be sending civilians into a dangerous situation and he probably wants you to have backup available if you need it. Hopefully, no harm done yet," Leotie calmed.

"Let's go sort this out," Atawhai suggested pragmatically. She led them through the maze of corridors to the administration section, passing two soldiers attending to different duties on the way. As predicted, she found Brenda in a spacious office where she acted as aide and go-between for Captain Jervois who was coordinating the operation.

After Leonie introduced herself and made it clear that any request from the mission personnel countermanded any other orders he might receive, Lestze asked that no one was to go outside the station without his permission while Atawhai asked for the magnetic pass cards for opening and closing the exterior doors. Brenda then took their sizes and left to get the kit sent through from the other world.

The wait was not more than an hour and a half. Atawhai asked Leonie if the captain had known she was here. "Not officially, but I'm sure Brenda recognized me and would have told him who I was," she replied. "Robert brought me here after curfew and has not sent any electronic messages about my movements. There will be public outrage and fear if they learn we have opened the station to the world where the plague came from, my being here too could multiply that."

They quickly returned to their rooms to change when Brenda delivered their gear. Atawhai suggested they go out on foot first to have a look around the building, taking them to a small human-sized door with the code A4 stencilled on it near the transport bay. She pushed the intercom button beside the card reader, saying, "Last Hope Party exiting door Alpha 4," then shrugged her shoulders, adding, "Probably no one there to hear, but it's the protocol." She put her card to the reader then stepped out into a glorious spring morning while the door was still opening. Once the rest had joined her, she touched the card to the external reader and the door swung shut again.

33
Prophet Motives

She laughed happily. Now they were on Palaeo and she had something to do, all the anxiety was draining away. "It just seemed appropriate. If you come up with something better, we can go with it."

The south side of the building was warm in the sun. A multilane road led from huge doors close to them, concrete where it ran to the large processing facilities on the high ground to either side of the jump station but turning to gravel and mud as it wandered a short distance to the south, or split east or west around the station. They looked south through the wire mesh fence that surrounded the complex over what had been a swathe of green, even in the middle of Washington City, and saw devastation, almost as far as the eye could see. Most of the large trees had been cut and the trash left lying where it fell. The scars of bare ground were still evident in many places, even though the general regrowth suggested this area had been milled some years ago.

There was nothing threatening so Atawhai walked towards the gate where the road passed through the perimeter fence. Her key card opened it and she chose to follow the west road that shortly crossed a small valley, then turned south and continued down the valley towards what could be considered a tributary of the Anacostia River. They followed the road for about half a kilometre, then took a side road that again led west. Lestze noticed the smell first, and when they crossed over the crest of the ridge, they looked down on what had once been a small, deep valley but now was a wide mound of garbage. It had been covered with a thin layer of dirt, but this had been washed off the higher parts by the winter rain.

Atawhai broke the stunned silence. "This is the oldest dump. They are filling basins further west as the closest ones are filled. It's because the jump needs to send equivalent masses in both directions. Rather than needing to pay for mass to send back here, this way Washington City is paying the corporation to get rid of its unrecyclable garbage. The corporation is making a killing in both directions and there are no environmental laws here."

Leotie was shocked. "The UN inspectors would never have accepted this."

"It's only a side road. There might be a broken-down truck just past the turn-off when the inspectors come to check, or they might be taken in one of the other directions. They would never know. Besides, the UN gave licences to governments to use the jump technology and it was mostly up to the governments themselves to control how it was used."

Leotie sighed. "It's clear we are not going to see anything of value around the station. I suggest we go back, have something to eat then take a ride out for the afternoon." They turned and started the walk back.

"If this is the Palaeozoic World, how come I was seeing birds down there around the garbage heap?" Jeff asked a few steps later. "They didn't evolve till much later, sometime when there were dinosaurs, I thought."

"Just because the Permian extinction didn't happen in this timeline doesn't mean evolution stopped. The reptile line that produced dinosaurs and eventually birds continued developing, but not everything that flies here is a bird either. Ice ages, constant climate change and continental drift forced lots of extinctions and speciation. The evolution in plant types forced changes in animal types too. Generally, the species here today are not those alive during the late Palaeozoic but developments from them. There are considerably more species here, but their ranges tend to be much smaller, isolated to continents or geologic regions, Permian-style fauna in some areas, dinosaurs or something else in others. Mammals did still evolve here eventually, but they are an also-ran rather than the dominant vertebrates. The giant reptiles still dominate in warmer climates." Atawhai was in her biologist element.

"So why haven't we seen any dinosaurs or anything?"

"The big ones learned pretty quickly to stay away from the station and there's not much left for food or cover for smaller ones anywhere around here."

Their direction walking back gave a good northward view along the west side of the perimeter fence, which appeared to have a gap part-way along. Atawhai didn't remember it looking like that so they left the road to walk north along the fence. It wasn't difficult as the ground had been bulldozed before the fence was put up.

Atawhai was shocked to see a short section of the fence had been squashed flat. Two of the heavy steel poles holding the wire netting had been bent over to the ground with the poles on either side partly bent over too. "The electric shock to the outriggers would have stopped when the power supply failed. Nothing has damaged the fences for years."

Lestze was looking at the trampled mess of the ground rather than the fence. "This was done recently; the tracks are still obvious. At least three very large animals — more than one species by the looks of it."

"The big ones learned pretty quickly to stay away from the station," Jeff parroted. Atawhai only glared.

They soberly followed the tracks towards the factory on the west side of the station. Atawhai was looking at the footprints carefully now as they were not as scuffed. "See this huge squarish footprint with five toes. It looks like a pareiasaur descendant. It's a herbivore, but these smaller ones are probably from gorgonopsids — they are carnivores and there are more than one. I wouldn't expect to see them together."

The tracks circled the blank walls of the factory, mud showing in places on the concrete apron, then continued to the station building. The footprint pattern became random when it passed the first window. "They stopped to look in the window," Lestze observed. The tracks circled around the station and back towards the flattened fence.

After a short break and some food, Atawhai took them to the transport bay and chose a compact electric four-by-four utility. She drove with Jeff riding shotgun. At the door, Jeff pushed the intercom button and announced, "Captain Oates exiting door T1. I may be some time," before opening it.

As Atawhai drove out the gate and around the fence to the north of the station, Jeff asked, "Why not have a door on the north side?"

"The vehicle doors are on the south here at Washington Paleo Station. When the trucks come in they are jumped to Washington Earth Station where the doors are on the north side, so they drive straight through on to Greenbelt Road and on to the Beltway. No confusion for the trucks coming back either.

"This track goes up past a lake. The area around it hasn't been cut and there hasn't been as much deforestation yet to the north."

No one spoke as they rattled down the coarse gravel road, passing regular tracks where logs had been hauled out. While the forest had not been clear-cut, all the forest giants had been felled; the damage done when they fell and the logs extracted left very little intact.

Lestze felt only grief as they passed the huge stumps. "You said there was less damage to the north, but the ecosystem here has been completely destroyed even so. It would take centuries to repair itself. Each time you degrade the environment, the life-giving capacity of the land is always less. You have already destroyed most of your own planet. You don't need to be prescient to predict the future of this planet. You already know exactly what it will be if you treat it in the same way. Why do you keep doing this?"

Beside him, Leotie sighed. "Because no one person is responsible. This place is run by a corporation. Its only purpose is to make a profit for those who invest in it."

"You need to see that you are part of the ecosystem, and its health is your health. Whatever you do to it, you do to yourself," said Lestze.

"We have known that for millennia, but to individuals it seems so abstract. Nothing changes. It's like the forces driving present human behaviour are not intelligent."

"That's true. There's a part of your subconscious that believes it is a victim and wants to play that role. It wants to see itself as special — tiny, alone and separate in a vast universe that is hostile to it. It is quite happy to exploit and destroy everything it sees to try to amass enough things to feel secure and prove its point of view. That part is insane."

"There doesn't seem to be anything we can do about it," Leonie replied. "Lots of people have tried. When I was young and running free on the prairies, I thought I was going to grow up and change the world. I tried and I was wrong."

"You keep trying to change your behaviour and that of others without changing what drives the behaviour. You need to change your self-concept and beliefs, how you define yourself in relationship to the world. Because you build your self-concept by making comparisons of the ephemeral, it will always be unstable and needs be maintained by constant effort against the fear of the world around you. It is a tragedy of insecurity that needs to feel special to try to gloss over its knowledge of its own transience."

Atawhai rounded a corner and they rocked forward as she jumped on the brakes. There was a huge quadruped walking along the road towards them. It stopped, swivelling its long neck to look directly at them. "What is it?" Leonie whispered.

"It's a titanosaur, a real dinosaur," Atawhai answered. "If we don't move or alarm it, it should leave us alone. It will most likely be a younger male moving north early with the warmth of spring, ahead of the herd to avoid the bigger adult males in the run-up to breeding season."

"Wouldn't a titanosaur be bigger and why migrate with the seasons, aren't they warm-blooded?"

"Too much competition and regular changes in climate reduce the advantages of size. Titanosaur is the closest description we can give, but the group evolved under different conditions here and are radically different in many respects to the ones from Earth. Bigger brains, for instance. The biggest of the species we see here are still less than half the size they reached on prehistoric Earth. I doubt there were bigger species of them here in the past. They move south for winter as they need less food if they stay warm."

Lestze got out of the car and took a few steps, stopping suddenly as the animal lifted its head, swinging it side to side, and rumbled a warning. "It was very surprised to see us at first but not hostile, but it recognizes the uniform as meaning dangerous," Lestze commented. "It is trying to decide what to do." He waited till the head stopped swinging then took another couple of cautious steps. Feeling the animal's alarm levels rise again as he did so, he sat cross-legged in the middle of the road. "Atawhai, back the car up to the corner, but keep it where he can see it," he called back to her.

She reluctantly did as he asked. The dinosaur waited to see what they would do next, but when nothing happened it slowly walked up, eventually getting close enough to sniff his outstretched hand before withdrawing a few of its large paces where it waited nervously. Lestze called to the others, "Come join me. Slowly."

When, after a few moments' nervous hesitation, Atawhai moved to get out of the car, Jeff put a hand on her arm. "Are you crazy?"

She turned to him and smiled, saying gently, "I've learned to trust him, Jeff," then stepped out.

Leotie opened the back door as Atawhai walked towards Lestze. "Come on, Jeff. You can't let an old lady show you up." He stepped out, wisely choosing to leave the gun behind. She took his hand cheerily, "Look on the bright side. This might even be fun."

They sat either side of Lestze and Atawhai. "What are we doing here?" Leotie asked quietly.

"Nothing in particular. It's a gesture of trust. We are putting ourselves entirely in their hands." Lestze looked pointedly at the huge reptile that even at a distance towered over them. "And thank you for joining me. It is equally a test of courage and integrity." The titanosaur was visibly starting to tremble. "As much for him as for us. Think kind thoughts towards him. I will make sure he feels it in some way."

"Like 'we mean you no harm'?" asked Jeff.

"No. Something simpler and more positive. The only word or concept that he notices or understands from your sentence could be 'harm', which wouldn't help at all. I can't know. Maybe 'you are safe' would be a better way to put it, but you can't conceptualize it. If being safe to you means being surrounded by your friends and he gets the feeling of being surrounded by humans, that would probably be the worst thing he could possibly imagine right now. The start of true communication between species and sometimes individuals is recognising that the thoughts, associations or physical conditions you consider necessary to evoke certain states of mind may be meaningless or anathema to them. Just look at him and feel happiness or kindness or admiration."

They sat there for some time, feeling awkward, not knowing if they were achieving anything or what to expect. The dinosaur slowly relaxed and its head drooped a little, then suddenly it spun around and bolted away from them. "That thing can really move," Jeff exclaimed in astonishment as he leapt to his feet. "What happened?"

"It responded to its instinct to run from danger is the short answer. The real question is why didn't it do that when it first saw us?" Lestze replied, obviously puzzled.

"What do you mean by that?" Atawhai asked.

"Give me some time to make sense of what I experienced please." He stood up and together they walked back to the car.

Atawhai continued to drive north away from the station, ignoring a turn-off to the lake to continue up a ridge from which they could look down to see the blue water of the lake through the trees to their right. She stopped at a clearing near the top where the road turned down the west side of the ridge to follow the river leaving the lake. "We may as well sit somewhere with a nice view while we talk," she said, looking over the lake and the pocket of forest that surrounded it, an oasis in the midst of desert.

"Okay," Lestze replied. They moved to sit by the edge of the road on some logs roughly carved by chainsaws as seats. "I could see two distinct lines of thought going through the dinosaur's mind. It came to the lake yesterday, taking a short cut through the cut-over area as it was sure there weren't any humans here any more. It was only going to stay a day or two before continuing north, but got a strong urge a short time ago it should come and look at the station, which it had carefully avoided up to now. That's why we met it on the road.

"When it saw us, its instinct was to flee, but that was almost immediately overlaid by a sense of curiosity and confidence. It was simultaneously wanting to run away while feeling the urge to walk towards me to see what I would do when I sat down. I helped it feel your goodwill, which it understood, and it relaxed to some extent. When the part of its thoughts that was holding it here noticed the calming effect without understanding its cause it seemed to withdraw in surprise or more likely shock. Left to its own devices, the dinosaur took the chance to run as it had wanted to all along."

34

Dances with Dinosaurs

The sun was close to the western horizon as they drove back to the station. Lestze was increasingly confident as the evening drew out. "I don't know what we encountered there but it definitely recognized us as human and was somewhat surprised by that. It wasn't automatically hostile to us, which really is a good sign," he commented to the others as they discussed the day's events after dinner.

"So what do we do next?" Leotie asked.

"I don't know. They need to make contact."

"How?"

He laughed. "We will know when they contact us."

Next morning there was still no clear direction so Lestze suggested they go back to the lake and see if they could find the titanosaur. They took a road that branched north-east off the north road they had taken the day before and drove down into the lake basin, stopping where the road ended within sight of the water.

"Do we go look for him?" Jeff asked.

"He is here somewhere, and he knows we are here. We should wait a while to see what he wants to do."

It took a while and he was moving cautiously through the forest, but they could easily hear his big feet and heavy body snapping twigs and branches well before they saw him. He stopped when he saw them standing near the car. Lestze guided them slowly away from the car as he said it was disturbing the dinosaur. They were angling in the general direction of the dinosaur when Lestze had an inspiration. "Let's walk down to the water."

They individually wound their way through the undergrowth beneath the trees and found comfortable places to sit down a short distance from the water. The reflections of the morning sun shining down the length of the lake gave a surreal glittering aura on the underside of the canopy trees. After watching them for a while and deciding they weren't doing anything threatening, the dinosaur started following them.

"We can't keep calling him it. We need to give him a name," Leotie stated.

"I think we should call him Dino," Atawhai was emphatic. Jeff laughed and Leotie smiled and shrugged.

"Okay, Dino it is," Lestze agreed. "Any reason why?"

"I will just have to show you sometime."

Dino lumbered to a stop a few metres away watching them carefully, his head slowly nodding up and down a little. Atawhai pointed out the movement. "We think that means he's happy or at least not feeling threatened." When nothing happened, he started grazing on the underbrush around him while still keeping a wary eye out.

Lestze was silent while as the others chatted quietly for some time then spoke. "Dino is feeling happy at the moment. He has done what the unusual promptings have asked him to do and there is a good feeling that comes with that. He also remembers the happy feelings from yesterday so is enjoying having us near. He is feeling lonely; he misses his herd." He got up. "Let's walk along the shore."

They walked for more than an hour, Dino following them at a discreet distance. When they turned back, Dino disappeared into the forest and circled around behind them. Lestze stopped when they were near the car and sat down again. It was back to the status quo. Dino wandering around eating while keeping a nervous eye on them while they watched him.

Eventually, Jeff took the bull by the horns. "Is this getting us anywhere?"

Lestze sighed. "Yes and no. I can sense his mind easily enough. I can sense there is something else watching us through his eyes at times but can't make sense of it and it can't make sense of us. There is no common ground for communication. We could waste weeks this way. If we want to break the deadlock, I think it might help if I could touch Dino. Better contact with his mind could give me better access to what is in contact with him."

"Can you ask him?" said Atawhai.

"I've been trying. He's too skittish — the idea makes him want to run away. He's only this close to us because he's being told to stay with us." They sat silently for a while.

"What if we all tried focusing on a message? They noticed us yesterday," Leonie asked.

"Worth a try but forget about words. Concentrate on an image of me touching Dino and everyone feeling happy. I will pass it on to Dino."

They got comfortable and each in their own way contributed a feeling of goodwill to Lestze's effort. After a few minutes, Dino paused his slow movement, nodding his head up and down nonchalantly then went happily back to grazing. Probably ten long minutes later, he abruptly stopped moving and lifted his head up to look directly down at them.

"We've been noticed. Keep doing what you are doing," Lestze encouraged. After a few minutes they all felt a surge of contentment. "And that was their reply."

"What was?" Leotie protested. "I was just remembering my father teaching me to ride my horse."

"Interesting, isn't it? If you identify with emotions or thoughts that appear in your mind, you will seamlessly call up supporting memories, emotions and preconceptions that justify and personalize the alien thoughts."

"But they were my memories."

"The memories may have been but the feeling that triggered them definitely wasn't. We live in a sea of contagious thoughts, opinions and emotions. It takes vigilance to know which are truly yours.

"It was very strong or focused. What you felt was the spillover from me experiencing what Dino felt. I'm going to him now while he is still feeling blissful. Don't move or alarm him."

Lestze stood up and smoothly walked through the forest towards Dino. He slowed as he got close, but Dino surprised him by lowering his head almost to the ground. Lestze took the last few steps and gently reached out to touch the giant snout. Rather than actively looking, he relaxed and allowed Dino's sense of being or consciousness to wash over him, enjoying its simplicity and lack of deception. He noticed the connection to the observer in Dino's mind and saw its awareness of him. Following the thread, he felt curiosity, a question. Less 'what are you' than 'help me understand'.

Instead of trying to explain, he recalled his earliest memories, his mother and father, his friends and the happiness of his small village. Then, while still a child, the start of his training with the village elder when she noticed his empathic gift developing. Lestze started one memory at a time, being careful to emphasize what he felt along with the memory, but individual memories gradually became a trickle then a torrent. His life was playing out in full detail by the time a member of the planetary council first visited his village to see him. He was not yet ten years old. He collapsed, not from strain but he had run out of resources to both control his body and process memories. After a few visits from the councillor, his family moved with him to a small city where several councillors mentored him. There were many roles he could have taken for his adult life, but he had been born into a small forest village and in a forest he felt at home. He chose to become a guardian of the planet's ecology, to devote his life to maintaining the balance and well-being of all life and living systems of his planet. At the end of his training his first independent responsibility was custodian of the islands where the invaders had built the jump station. He was given this task partly because he was young and could easily handle the rigours of the cold damp climate along with the untempered, wild environment and partly because, like many young people, he had been brought up with a good command of English.

Atawhai had watched him fall and jumped up with a cry. She ran towards him, but Dino was disturbed too. He nudged Lestze's inert body gently with his snout but took a step forward as Atawhai approached, his long neck over Lestze while his head blocked Atawhai's path. He let out a warning rumble and she stopped within metres of him, and spread her empty hands imploringly. She slowly took the last few steps and put her hands on his armoured skin, surprised that it felt smooth and faintly warm in the cool morning air. With all her will she asked, "Please!"

He waited then slowly stepped back. Atawhai darted under Dino's head and knelt by Lestze, checking him out.

His breathing and pulse were fine, though his eyes were half open and his muscle tone low. She sat and cradled his head on her lap and looked up. Dino had swung his head several metres away but was watching them absorbedly. He probably has trouble seeing things that are too close she thought, then slowly nodded her head up and down. He understood and lumbered around to squat with his enormous underbelly sitting on the ground beside them and wrapping his flexible tail and neck around to encircle them, his head on the ground.

Lestze felt the mental presence leave him with a sense of acknowledgment and thanks. He was aware of his body again and was surprised to be lying down and more surprised to find Atawhai cradling his head. He smiled and she jumped, feeling awkward.

"I'm sorry. I didn't mean to be impolite."

He reached up to touch her hand. "Don't worry, I understand. Thank you for caring."

"Are you okay?"

"I'm fine, I think. Effectively, I just forgot to stand up."

"Good. Jeff and Leonie will be beside themselves with worry. We had better go."

She shifted his head and stood up, steadying him when he stood up too. Dino lifted his head, having noticed them move out of one eye, and brought it close. Lestze walked to touch his nose again and reassure him. He stood up carefully then dashed around the nearby trees, leaving a wake of torn-up undergrowth behind him. You could have called it gambolling if he was fifteen tons lighter. They were both laughing at the incongruity of the sight as Jeff and Leonie reached them.

Lestze kept to himself as they drove back. Dino followed for a short distance but turned back as they left the forest fragment around the lake. As they sat back in the briefing room eating a late lunch, Leotie spoke what was on all their minds. "Okay Lestze, did you contact them? Tell us what you learnt."

"I am sure there is no 'them'. It seemed to be a single mind but abstract, not particularly associated with a body."

"What does that mean?"

"It seemed to be aware of the entire planet in a similar way that we are aware of our body."

"What is it? Where is it from?" Jeff asked.

"At a guess, I think it is the result of the collective thought of every living thing this planet produced or the thought that produced this planet. I can't tell which or if there is a meaningful difference."

"But is it willing to help us and why is it trying to kill us all?"

"Jeff, have you noticed these last two days what we have done to the environment around here?" Atawhai interrupted.

"Sure, but it seems a bit like overkill wiping us all out."

"It doesn't think like we do. In a way it sees species in much the same way we think of individuals. Not that it was communicating with me; it wasn't. It was absorbing or reading as many of my memories, my life as it could in that short time. I generally didn't notice emotions, but when it experienced my viewpoint of a forest as immense and essentially immortal, lasting thousands or millions of years, she found it funny. From her viewpoint forests come and go in the blink of a relative eye as climates and species change."

"You said 'she'," Leotie interrupted.

"Sorry, I was just remembering how the mind felt when it was amused. Saying 'she' feels right."

"No, don't apologize, it does sound right. But that means she needs a name and I'm hoping it is my turn to suggest one."

Lestze looked at the others and they nodded. "Go ahead."

"I would like to call her Tayanita. It's kind of a veiled reference to one of our creation myths."

"Sounds good, but finishing off, she was definitely surprised by the concept of your species coming from another world, then astonished that I came from a world other than yours. She hasn't got to understanding that we had been enemies, fighting each other, but now I am helping you, let alone things like timeline or parallel universe theory. I hope communication will be clearer next time we meet because we will have some common concepts to work with. We may even be able to talk about helping your people."

35
Into the Wild

After their discussion, Leotie went to Captain Jervois to send a coded message to Robert letting him know they were making progress. The surprising news she brought back from Robert was that the shock appearance of the party from Neanderthal B and ongoing publicity had captured the world's imagination and unrest had greatly decreased. Senden had just given a short press conference stressing the need for global unity while appealing for time for a solution to the crisis to be found. People were already wondering why Lestze and Atawhai were missing, but there had been no information leak so far.

Next morning, Lestze put off trying to contact Tayanita, saying it didn't feel like she was ready and said they may as well just wait. Despite Atawhai's impatience, he wasn't going to be budged. "Can you talk to her directly now or will we still need to get you to Dino?"

"It would be much easier if I was in contact with Dino's mind."

"But why? If her mind envelops this planet, surely you can contact her anywhere. Why not right here?"

He sighed, looking for words to explain. "Mind is a single continuum that infuses the universe. It seems to exist individually as discrete forms in discrete locations but ultimately this is only an appearance. This suggests

I should be able to experience any mind anywhere, but the reality is very different, partly because I experience myself as a discrete form. As an analogy, on your planet you had a bewildering number of broadcasts from satellites and those television channels I watched you flicking between and I have no idea what else. If you had no equipment, how would you find any particular one or know it was there? Every living thing here is attuned to Tayanita as she is attuned to them; it goes both ways. Even so, I would never have noticed her when communicating with Dino if she hadn't been consciously connected to him, watching through his eyes at the time. We were lucky, I could have lived here a lifetime and not noticed her, and it would never have occurred to her to try to communicate with an alien individual, assuming she ever noticed me. Her mind is of a different order to ours. She only noticed your species due to the extraordinary amount of damage you do in such a short time. That took her how long?"

"I don't know, but we found this planet a long time before we found Neanderthal B."

"Exactly." Atawhai decided to give up on the matter.

Lestze was still diffident the following morning, but later in the day he suddenly perked up. "I think she wants to talk to us. Can we go find Dino?"

"How do you know?" Atawhai asked. "Did you get a message?"

"No, nothing conscious, but on a deeper level everyone has intuition. It is really mind communicating in a non-conceptual, non-linear way."

Lestze suggested they walk to the lake to look for Dino as they could do with the exercise. He was nowhere to be seen when they arrived over half an hour later, but Lestze was sure he was on his way. "Dino knows we are here," he commented succinctly.

The titanosaur loped up to them ten minutes later as they waited by the water. Dino slowed to amble happily up to Lestze, then lowered his head and Lestze reached to touch his nose. He immediately could feel Dino's simple happiness at knowing they were friends, then felt another friendly presence. He reached with his mind to touch it, include it. There was a sense of welcome, then a question, effectively "What do you want?"

He was surprised at how easy it was to understand. An image came of him living his life, but his body flickered with images of trees, animals, the land and their connection. He indicated understanding.

He imagined people sick and dying, being given something to drink and becoming well.

Images of a tree dying, infested by caterpillars, parasites, the caterpillars being eaten by birds and the tree sprouting vibrantly. Then a world turning from blue and green to black. A very clear thought: "What is the difference?"

He thought of the people with him, the ones from Earth that he knew, Atawhai, Jeff and Leotie. He showed their essential goodness of heart and their willingness to help. Then the forest around his home village, how much he loved it. And the strange forest where he lived now, his care for it, even the smallest of the plants and animals and his joy in their shared life. He held out his hands to heal the blackened world image she had shown before. "I would do this if I could."

He felt her agreement, her happiness with the possibility of redemption for Atawhai's people, then a distinct instruction. There was a feeling of farewell for now before a clear, "We are not so different, you and I."

Lestze stepped back from Dino and turned to the others. "Tayanita has agreed to help. I'll tell you as we walk back." They started for the road. "She has been reliving the memories she has of my life, as if she was me. She has a better understanding of our perspective now so we could talk easily enough. She has asked that we go south, but not straight to the river."

"How far?" Jeff asked.

"No idea. She was a bit vague about that."

"Fair enough." There was a pause while they kept walking. "Is that it then?"

"Afraid so."

"Are we going this afternoon?" Leotie asked when they got back to base.

"I don't see why not," Lestze replied.

"I do," stated Jeff. "By the time we get stores and equipment together there won't be a lot of daylight left. It's spring and still cold so we will need time to set up a proper camp wherever we get to. We won't get much further overall than if we start from here early tomorrow and we will get a good night's sleep along with not having to carry extra food for tonight and breakfast tomorrow."

"I agree with Jeff," Atawhai stated. "We don't just need survival gear; some good maps and compasses for each of us in case we get separated would be good. RTs as well. You seem to have an unerring sense of direction in a forest, but the rest of us don't."

"You two are right, of course," Lestze agreed. "I would never have bothered for myself."

They started out as the sun was rising. Atawhai insisted they take a car down the well-maintained gravel road to the Anacostia River close to where it met the Potomac. A dock had been built at the confluence to give water access for boats and barges to the forests on the edges of Chesapeake Bay without the cost of building roads and bridges.

From the dock on the river they followed a logging track east for a couple of kilometres and left the car where it ended. With no particular place to get to, they decided to follow a south-easterly direction up and along the ridgeline to avoid dropping into the gullies carved out by streams. The maps were already proving useful.

The dimness of the forest enveloped them within a few steps. Lestze felt the sense of unviolated life wash through him like a cool drink on a hot summer's day. In contrast he easily noticed the others' increasing anxiety — the wary watchfulness he felt from the hidden denizens of the forest was not the same at all. It was a joy to feel the ancientness of the forest and know his senses were coming alive again.

A few minutes later, long enough uphill to stop the others talking, they surprised a large hairy animal, about the size of a pig. It ran off with a grating cry, stopping them with surprise too. "What was that?" Leotie gasped, alarmed.

"Don't worry, it's a herbivore," Atawhai replied. "Something descended from the dicynodonts, a warm-blooded not quite reptile or mammal. The forest species tend to be small as most of the food production is high up in the canopy. They go out to the forest edges where we cut down the trees to graze at night."

"So they are nocturnal then?" Jeff asked.

"No, at least not this species. The workers at the processing plants here think they are good to eat and there is a de facto trade in exotic animal meat back to Earth as well. They are safest at night. On the bright side, the hunting has taught the predators to keep well away from the forest edges."

With that cheering thought they resumed walking. The progress seemed agonisingly slow as there was no path and the undergrowth was dense enough in some places to make it easier to backtrack and go round. Lestze was happy regardless. Some of the tree species were recognizable, but many were subtly different to anything he had seen. He commented on this to Atawhai.

"There is virtually no biological difference between your planet and mine, but this one diverged so long ago it is different in most respects. In places the topography and continental shapes are different too," she added.

Leotie was finding it hard going so Lestze and Jeff shared out the heavier items in her pack between them. She was very apologetic, but Atawhai waved away her guilt. "You have done more than we hoped, and we are honoured to have you with us," she countered.

They stopped not long after for an early lunch. Jeff suddenly registered that the irregular, quiet background sounds of unseen animals moving was now constant and getting louder. He was up with his rifle held ready in an instant, circling to get the exact direction of the threat.

"It's all right," Lestze calmed him from where he was sitting, "I'm sure it's only Dino. He's been trying to find us." He stood up and let out a drawn-out yell. The sound of movement paused for a moment, then continued.

"You could have warned me."

"Sorry. I could feel he was looking for us but couldn't say where he was until we just heard him."

They sat and waited for him to arrive. Lestze called out again as they heard him get closer. Dino rumbled a greeting when he saw them, then slowed down to walk carefully up to Lestze and give him a slight nudge. Dino was so happy to see them he swung his head around to check on each of the others, sniffing Jeff closely despite the fact he was holding his rifle.

"Tayanita has encouraged him to come and find us. She sent him in this direction after we left yesterday," Lestze commented.

"Did she ask him to or did she convince him subconsciously we are his surrogate herd?" Atawhai asked.

"A little of both. He has definitely imprinted on us, but as an individual he is still happy to be with us. He finds us interesting."

They got up and started walking again. Dino circled randomly through the forest around them but kept pace. After a while he wandered up to Jeff, who was leading at the time, and suggested by moving towards him they turn a little towards the south. They continued with occasional short stops until mid-afternoon.

Lestze stopped them suddenly. "There is something following us, intently. It feels like a hunter. Any idea what it could be Atawhai?"

"No. I am surprised that something is tracking us this close to station, but there are several possibilities, a number of them deadly."

They had been walking across a large area of flat land that the ridges had led up to and were beginning to work their way down into a stream valley that cut across their path. Lestze saw Dino was looking intently back the way they had come from and decided to act. He and Jeff both were both carrying a hank of rope. Lestze grabbed them both while looking forlornly at the old conifer trees where they had stopped, arrow straight with their first branches well out of reach of their short ropes. He spotted an ancient, broadly spreading deciduous tree on a hillock ahead of them and ran for it. Jeff automatically took Tail-End-Charlie position, walking behind the others while constantly looking back with his rifle ready.

Reaching the tree, Lestze looked at the huge low branches that curved down towards the ground before continuing to arc up to the light further from the tree's trunk and threw a rope over one of the higher ones. Holding both ends of the rope, he quickly worked his way up to stand on the first branch, then tied both ropes to the branch above. The others were waiting below by this time and Dino was walking towards them.

Lestze threw the ends of the ropes down, asking Atawhai to tie one around Leotie tightly enough not to slip up her torso. Then as she started to climb up the other rope, he was able to help pull her up and ensure she wouldn't fall.

While this was happening, a pack of six hairy animals that looked like a cross between a bear and a wolf had stopped at the crest of the hill as they caught sight of their prey. Atawhai looked at them. "Dire wolves. I hadn't expected that."

As Jeff drew a bead on the lead animal, Dino started walking slowly and deliberately towards them. Atawhai put a hand on Jeff's shoulder and said, "Wait a moment."

The wolves were not interested in attacking Dino and could see easier prey behind him. The alpha animal skirted widely around him, and the others trotted after him. Dino angled towards their line, turning his body while swinging his head back. As the pack passed beside him, he suddenly swung his head at them while stretching out his neck, his huge head smashing one of the middle animals high into the air. He followed the scattering animals, hitting another wolf a glancing backswing blow as it fled. It yelped as it was thrown through the air but found its feet after somersaulting when it hit the ground and raced after its brethren. The battle was over in seconds.

Atawhai looked up at Lestze as he helped a shaky Leotie to sit on a branch and waited for him to look down. When he did, she commented, "I like what you did there. It was very helpful."

"It was nothing really, I think it only looks good in comparison to your contribution to the affair," he replied equally deadpan. They both laughed.

As Lestze was helping Leotie down, Jeff said, "They didn't look much like wolves to me, Atawhai."

"The workers here call them that because they evolved from the same family wolves did. It's easier than coming up with new names."

They continued down into the valley and slowly worked up the other side from the stream. When they reached flatter high ground, Lestze called a halt. "It's getting late. I think we should stop for the day."

"Leotie breathed an audible sigh of relief. "Thank you, Lestze. I have spent too many years in an office to be ready for this."

Jeff chose a flat area with good visibility and minimal undergrowth so nothing could sneak up on them and they set up two tents and collected firewood. Lestze went back to see if there were fish in the stream while Jeff set snares on tracks he could see in the leaf litter. Atawhai, Jeff and Lestze rotated two-hour watches during the night while Dino could be heard and sometimes seen as he came and went, playi

ng 'watch dinosaur' during the night.

36
Time for Morning

In the darkness before dawn, Atawhai was on watch as Lestze left his tent.

"I'm just going for a walk. I'll see you after sunrise," he said as he walked past, not waiting for her to disagree.

The sun was well up when he returned. The fire had been stoked to heat water while Jeff and Atawhai worked on breakfast. Atawhai looked over her shoulder as Lestze walked up to them.

"Where did you go?"

"I wanted to feel the sunrise in the forest. I haven't for a long time."

"Why not from here?"

He shrugged. "It's different."

It was obvious he was not going to say more. "Please explain," Leotie pressed. "I want to understand what you see and experience."

Lestze thought for a moment. "Everything you see has something to offer you. But what you see and the value you give it is determined by how you value yourself and how you believe others value you. You have to give love to what you see if you expect love to be given to you. Only by being loving are you able to recognize love. Your state of mind determines what you are able to see.

"The trees reach out to the rising sun, bringing them new life each morning with such delight. The forest rejoices with them and the birds return the joy they feel in song. The great trees greet the first autumn rains after summer drought like the return of a lover. They have such gratitude to be alive. It is not the way humans feel emotions, but it is love and gratitude nonetheless. There is no resentment or deceit.

"The people of our planet live in and are supported by the gratitude of all life. They add to it their own happiness and appreciation and it is reflected to them again from the life around them. On your planet you believe happiness, love, is limited. It can only be found through a certain person or having the right possessions or security of one kind or another. In your need to possess what you see as the source of happiness for yourselves and prevent others from taking it from you, you inevitably destroy the conditions for love's presence and become more competitive, malicious and controlling as the last drops of love disappear. Your planet is a cry of pain. It is no wonder you are all deaf and numb. You couldn't stand to live there if you could really feel what you have done."

"That's all very well," Jeff commented. "But how do I know? I can't feel what you feel or see what you see. It's been said nature is red in tooth and claw, it's all about killing to survive in the end, isn't it?"

"That's a very human perspective. Normal living things aren't obsessed with dying."

"What do you mean?"

"Well, your people have no experience of the unity of life so in general the only life they understand or value is their own. Other lives are only valued by what they contribute to you."

"But doesn't everything fear death."

"Not the way you do. From the old trees all I sense is what I can only call wisdom, even though it has none of the complicated words or concepts of what you call wisdom, and a great reverence for life. Your people, on the other hand, only see how much money they can make by cutting the trees down and selling the wood. By your attitude and your actions, death is your chosen companion every moment.

"To put death in a different perspective, on average how long do your people live?

Jeff shrugged. "No idea."

"About eighty-five years in Japan down to about fifty years in Chad with a world average of about seventy-four years," Leotie chipped in helpfully. Jeff turned to look at her. "Well, I am head of the UN. I don't want to look an idiot for not knowing my own statistics," she offered in explanation.

"So how many days is that?" Lestze asked Jeff.

"Somewhere between twenty and thirty thousand is the best I can do without working it through," Jeff replied after a few moments.

"Good enough. So how many days do you die?"

"Only one for most people, though it's pretty drawn out for some."

"Agreed, but it is an interesting ratio, isn't it? Do you think most other living things spend their lifetime being too afraid to live because they are afraid to die?"

"I see that, but death is so final. You are dead forever."

Lestze laughed. "That is just another primitive cultural assumption based on your current world-view. It is part of what prevents you from being able to see what I see."

They ate quickly and packed up their equipment, dousing the fire with water. Dino appeared not long before they started hiking and waited impatiently. When Atawhai led off, Dino guided her in the direction he wanted then walked off into the forest ahead of them.

"He wants to make sure we don't run into any surprises ahead of us," Lestze said.

They followed Dino's tracks south for a relatively short time before they curved towards the south-east again. Dino checked their progress several times as they roughly followed this direction till after midday. Dino was waiting for them where he wanted them to turn south again. He strode off as soon as he saw them make the turn, but Lestze called him back, getting him to understand they needed to rest and eat.

"He is being directed," Lestze pointed out. "He is very focused so we must be close."

Unfortunately, 'close' turned out to mean hiking for most of the afternoon. Dino had later led them along a ridge between two streams, into the valley to cross the bigger stream they joined, then across the higher land to the south. He stopped where the higher land began falling towards a swampy valley bottom, waited a while after the humans caught up, then randomly walked off to graze on the undergrowth, all thought of leading forgotten.

"I guess this is it," Lestze said eventually. "We may as well set up camp."

This happened faster as they were familiar with assembling their equipment.

When they finished and were killing time, Leotie finally asked the question that was on each of their minds. "Are you sure this is where Tayanita wants us to be?"

"It feels that way. There doesn't seem to be any push to move. That's the best I can say."

"So why here?"

"I have no idea. As there's plenty of daylight, let's look around for a while."

They walked the area around the camp, back along the high lands and down to the swamp until the daylight was fading, without noticing anything significant.

As they were sitting by the fire eating, Atawhai asked Lestze, "Any the wiser?"

"Nothing specific. As a biologist, did you notice anything about the forest in this area?"

"At a guess, the trees here are older than average."

"Yes, and there is a larger mix of species than I have seen growing together anywhere else. I think it is significant. We will just have to wait to see why."

37

Invisible Allies

They talked late but didn't set a watch for the evening. Dino had not come back and Lestze was certain Tayanita would divert anything that might threaten them. He slept late, falling into the deep sense of connection that surrounded him and woke up knowing what they had to do. Lestze collected the others without waiting to eat, saying he needed to do this while the dream images were still fresh and clear. He led them downhill to a huge tree, easily recognizing it from the image in his dream, branches still bare but the buds beginning to swell. Walking around it till he saw the exact position he had seen in his dream, he started carefully scraping away the fallen leaves, then the soil itself.

Exposing a small nexus of tiny white threads, he asked Atawhai to come close. "Tayanita wants several drops of your blood on those filaments."

She pricked a finger with the point of a knife and squeezed out a few drops as the others watched.

"What is it?" Jeff asked.

"Mycorrhizal fungi. They live off the tree roots," Atawhai answered.

Lestze had placed a wet leaf over the blood and refilled the hole before covering it with leaves again. "I can't let the filaments dry out," he explained.

He repeated the process for Jeff and Leotie around the same tree before crossing to a neighbouring conifer and doing it all again.

As Lestze searched further downhill, Jeff asked, "Why are we doing this?"

"The fungi are chemical wizards," Atawhai answered. "Maybe with the right guidance they can work with DNA."

"Not just that," Lestze added. "They are the forest's communication system, running between the plants underground. Usually there are many species running from any one tree to the others. A healthy forest is a network of connections that dwarfs the complexity of the human brain by comparison. But getting back to your question, Tayanita is trying to get this done quickly as we are running out of time. Different groups of organisms will be working on different parts of the puzzle at the same time."

After they repeated the process at the third tree, Lestze added some of his blood to the ground before they returned to the campsite to prepare breakfast.

"Do you think Tayanita can cure us?" Atawhai asked Lestze as they worked.

"Not in the short term. It took her a long time by our standards to develop the initial virus. She can't undo it quickly. I am not sure I understood, but I think she wants to make markers that will make it easier for your damaged immune systems to identify and stop present diseases infecting you."

"Oh. Antibodies. She wants to make some kind of vaccine. We managed that for the first outbreak, but it takes too long."

"I guess that's it."

As they were eating, Leotie asked, "Why did she want your blood as well?"

"I have no idea."

"Are you sure you can trust her?" Jeff asked.

Lestze couldn't help but laugh. "That thought is so typical of your people. Firstly, what choice do we have? Secondly, in revealing herself she has already put herself at risk. Your people are quite capable of poisoning this entire planet out of spite or their fear of the unknown, and she knows that. What you should really be asking is, why has she chosen to trust you?"

"What do we do now?" Leotie asked as they cleaned up.

"Waiting is all we can do."

"Yes, but how long?"

He sensed the apprehension rising in her that people feel when circumstances are uncertain and can't be organized, planned and controlled.

"You want me to ask Tayanita?"

"Yes, please."

Lestze could feel her relief. He disappeared into the forest and was gone for over two hours.

"That took a while. Didn't get lost, did you?" Atawhai laughed.

"Only in translation. We were discussing quantum physics."

Leotie laughed. "You're not serious, are you?"

"Very. It got complicated. Tayanita wanted to know about parallel universes. I got across to her that after learning some of the discoveries of your physicists, philosopher members on the council decided a universe has all the hallmarks of any other virtual particle, so it doesn't matter if there appears to be one or many."

"A what?" Leotie interrupted.

"Transient, ephemeral particles that appear and disappear randomly that physicists find when they make a vacuum." Atawhai answered. "Lestze, are you saying a universe is no different?"

"Yes. The term virtual particle is simply a metaphor for the disturbance or fluctuation in the quantum field as other particles interact but is not there before or after the interaction. It has no objective reality. A universe could be the same."

"That can't be right. Our universe has existed for billions of years, not appearing and disappearing in an instant without changing objective reality in any way."

He smiled. "That's the point, isn't it? What you are experiencing is from a viewpoint inside the universe. Time and space are artefacts, products of the universe itself. They are determined by the way we observe the universe rather than being an intrinsic quality of reality. They have no objective reality outside the universe. To assume you could tell the difference between a universe and a virtual particle from inside one is ridiculous.

"Anyway, after I mentioned the council, Tayanita examined my memories of interactions with the council very carefully and decided the council has developed into a mind like hers. Independent of the individuals that contribute to its existence at any particular time. She wants full members of the council to come here to see if she can communicate directly with the council mind. She would also like to talk to some of your physicists with our help. She thinks the need to conserve mass and energy when jumping between worlds is essentially a limitation of your method. There should be much easier ways to cross between worlds."

Atawhai sighed. "To get to the point of all this. Did you think to ask how long Tayanita needed?"

Lestze had the grace to look sheepish. "Sorry. Three or four days probably. Maybe five. It is difficult for her to put a time on it."

"Why?"

"She wills something to happen, like you decide to stand up. You don't consciously control every muscle. She has a lot of what she needs already but needs to see how your bodies are reacting to the epidemics and work on the specific diseases affecting you now."

"That's a long time. Do we go back to the station to wait? It would be more comfortable."

"I'm happy here. It's easy to talk to Tayanita. What about you?" he asked Jeff and Leotie.

Jeff mused, "It's two days' tramping to get back and it's already late to start today, which could be hard on some of us too. So that's two days down anyway. Then I guess somebody would have to come back here?"

Lestze shrugged. "I don't know."

"Assuming that someone needs to come back here, I think we are better off waiting here." Leotie agreed with him.

They hung around the camp in the meantime. Dino came back later in the morning with mud drying down his legs, belly and tail. "Looks like he's been in the swamp eating. I guess he didn't get much to eat while he was looking for us and guiding us here," Atawhai commented. He looked them over, deciding they were okay, and walked off a short distance to rest.

After lunch, Lestze wanted to explore so the others decided to go with him. As Jeff slung his rifle over his shoulder (it was never far from him),

Lestze said, "We won't need it around here."

"I know, but it's my training. I don't want to compromise the discipline."

Lestze shoved his shoulder. "I understand. I respect that."

As they wandered back to camp, the sky was becoming progressively more overcast and the afternoon warmth was cooling rapidly. "We'd better hurry with dinner," Jeff suggested. They did, but heavy raindrops were already falling by the time they washed up. These were followed by lightning and a thunderstorm as the evening progressed. The rain continued moderately next morning so Jeff advised they stay in their tents as much as possible. There was no point getting wet and cold.

Lestze took this as a chance to be on his own and left to walk in the forest as soon as he could, taking a supply of dried food with him. On a whim, he walked towards the coast, noticing an almost imperceptible change from the peacefulness of their glade after a couple of kilometres. He stopped and walked back and forward a few times and realized he was feeling the edge of the bubble of Tayanita's conscious intention.

Lestze continued slowly away from the camp with no aim in mind, content to embrace whatever came his way. He greeted the giant old trees as he passed, waiting to hear their acknowledgments while enjoying the joy and hope of the early spring flowers and revelling in their beauty. He sensed a pit of still hibernating snakes and walked around it without fear, watched the birds flying in the treetops or sometimes scratching in the litter on the ground and listened to the music they made as they called to one another. He took the time to hide and remain immobile long enough to see some small, shy mammals scurry around the forest floor and realized he could sense their distant relatives living in the treetops.

Later he passed into a large clearing, the result of a flash fire from a lightning strike decades ago, where grazing had prevented trees from re-establishing themselves. The annual seedlings and small shrubs were feeling the rush of spring. It was almost a shock. The feel of life here seemed suddenly so frenetic by comparison. Not serene and ageless like the great trees but vibrant and wild, the eagerness of compressing a lifetime into a season.

He went to cross a deep stream but as he felt the water flow over his feet he experienced the life of countless small beings, fish, insects and plants for whom the flow of water was an ever present if unseen force that shaped and was their world. After a time standing motionless in the moving water, he sensed the stream had a life of its own, a sense of presence and continuity through both distance and time, as much as any other living organism, a pulse measured in seasons rather than seconds.

The coldness of his feet pierced his consciousness, forcing him to move. Without a deliberate decision he turned and started making his way back to the campsite. He could feel an ethereal connection to Tayanita in every life he touched, but as the concepts and barriers in his mind faded further he felt her presence in the living soil, then in the rocks stretching beyond awareness beneath his feet.

As he neared their enclave and moved into Tayanita's conscious presence, he greeted her with no sense of effort. He felt her react with wonder. "You have changed so much in a day. More than I have in aeons."

He laughed. "As I said yesterday, the passage of time isn't fixed, just a matter of perception." He understood the concepts and ideas flowing from her mind in a way he hadn't the day before, experiencing them more the way she did instead of trying to analyse them and force them to fit into the narrow box of his own point of view and was able to respond in kind.

The rain had turned to showers during the day, which was turning into a cold, overcast evening. As Lestze walked up to the tents, Jeff was outside, reconstituting some dried meals in boiling water over two tiny camping stoves — trying to light a fire would be a waste of time with everything in the forest soaking wet.

Jeff looked up. "Leotie and Atawhai are out stretching their legs. Where have you been all day?"

It was not meant as a rebuke but Lestze suddenly felt defensive, the need to justify himself, as if he had failed in his responsibility. His mind closed around him, and he was suddenly experiencing a personal life again, as if from inside a body.

"Just walking through the forest," he answered through a hint of loss.

The next day dawned clear and cold. They spent the day talking or walking, sometimes together, sometimes alone, as Lestze was able to show them the boundary to Tayanita's protection. He spoke with Tayanita several times during the day, finding it easier each time. To his surprise, after the sun had set she contacted him.

"Tayanita will have what we need tomorrow," he passed on to the others.

They dealt with the morning chores quickly with a strong feeling of expectancy.

"Do we pack up the tents and get our packs ready too?" Jeff asked.

Lestze checked. "Yes, I see what Tayanita has in mind. She is waiting for the air to warm a little."

"Why?"

"You'll see." Lestze was not just being mysterious but felt it would be better to wait and experience it.

After everything was packed, they moved to a patch of sunlight under the trees, moving again as the sun rose and the shadows shifted.

"Roll up your sleeves," Lestze suddenly commanded. "They are here, the mosquitoes. Don't squash them."

It couldn't be called a swarm, just a few paltry mosquitoes landing on each of their arms and quickly starting to feed.

"Well, this is a wee bit of a let-down when it comes to saving the world," Jeff commented sagely as he watched the process.

Atawhai laughed. "They have been forced out of hibernation early, specifically to save your arse. Show some gratitude."

"I am. My unusual restraint is my gratitude."

A couple of mosquitoes landed on Lestze's arm too. He heard Tayanita say, "Your healers will know what to do with this."

38
Coming Home

As they picked up their packs, Lestze felt Tayanita's focus disappear and knew they were on their own. Well, not exactly on their own as Dino joined their march fifteen minutes later. He mostly roamed ahead of them, changing directions when he noticed they had changed theirs. There was the sound of some sort of scuffle in the forest ahead of them on the second day, but they did not see what Dino had driven off.

The return trek was much easier. They knew where they were going, their bodies had adjusted and their packs were lighter. They reached their car early afternoon of the second day. They stowed their packs and Lestze led them back into the forest. He silently called Dino who walked carefully up to their group and gently sniffed each one of them. Lestze put his hands on Dino's nose and gave him their thanks for his help and protection. He tried to help Dino understand they were leaving and that he should find his herd.

As they walked back to the car, Lestze reached out to Tayanita, asking her to help Dino find his way, and heard her answer "Yes."

He stopped and thanked her, showing the gratitude he and the others felt for her help. He was suddenly surrounded by her presence, by her care and love for all that lives and felt her appreciation of their group for coming to help. "Remember when you stand for your people you now stand for me. In whatever is to come you speak as my representative. Farewell." She gave him her blessing in a way only a telepath could understand.

Tears ran down his cheeks as he started walking again. The others politely did not notice.

Atawhai had the bit between her teeth and drove back along the gravel road at breakneck speed. "I think we have enough time to be comfortable as we go back," Leotie yelled from the backseat over the noise of the bumping and rattling. Atawhai apologized and slowed down.

Lestze looked sideways at her and noticed she was feeling uncertainty, grief or fear that they had finished their mission and she no longer had a place or role. He placed a hand on her shoulder and leaned over to say quietly, "We are together in this, you and I."

They reached the station and while Leotie went immediately to contact Robert the others relaxed with hot showers and clean clothes. "We will jump to Washington Earth Station in two and a half hours. Robert will be there by then," she stated peremptorily on returning, then stalked off to the showers herself.

Four hours later, they were back at the Presidential Inn, but in a suite this time, waiting for a late meal to be sent up. Leotie and Robert had chosen to stay in nearby suites. Later, as they were finishing their meals Leotie joined them, accompanied by two uniformed medical personnel.

"These people are from the Walter Reed Army Institute of Research. I have asked them to test blood samples from us."

She rolled up her sleeve as she walked to the table and sat in a chair beside it. The man deftly put a pressure cuff over her arm while his female companion was selecting a needle, tube holder and naming evacuated tubes from a sterile case she had placed on the desk. She quickly filled two tubes, pulled out the needle and applied a pressure swab. Jeff was on his feet and took her place as she stood up, Atawhai following in quick succession.

Lestze stood immediately to follow Atawhai as her second tube was filling. Leotie made a surreptitious hand gesture in his direction to stop him. When Atawhai stood up and the others' attention was back on Leotie, she took a step towards him and said formally, "Mr Ambassador, no one here or on this planet has authority over you. Would you consent to giving us a blood sample please?"

He sighed inwardly, understanding she was teaching him the role he would need to fulfil and graciously gave his consent before giving his blood sample.

Leotie was back early next morning to update them. "Those researchers and their team worked through the night to analyse our samples. The good news is they found reasonably high levels of antibodies effective against the current epidemic. There are other antibodies they don't recognize there too. The other news is medical technicians are on their way to get a pint of blood from each of us. The more they have the faster they can get something ready for public release.

"I have also just authorized an initial press release about our visit. I am sorry, Lestze, but I had to wait until I received the call from Walter Reed to confirm we had actually achieved something. Despite what Robert said about everything being under control, we are still balanced on a knife edge. The fact that we have reopened Washington Palaeo Station has leaked, though it is not common knowledge yet. Giving false hope would have destroyed any vestige of control we have.

"Lastly, I am sending you back to New Zealand. Senden has turned down all suggestions of coming to New York. He says, with the communications we have, an embassy can be anywhere we want, and he has no interest in attending diplomatic parties. I will be coming with you as I think it important I meet him. A plane is being prepared. I thought it polite I tell you in person." She turned and left as hurriedly as she had arrived.

Two hours later, as Atawhai, Jeff and Lestze were being escorted through the empty and guarded foyer of the hotel, Atawhai watched the words 'Breaking News — Neanderthal B Ambassador and Secretary General lead diplomatic mission to Palaeo World' repeating across an electronic billboard.

Leotie, along with a group of UN personnel, met them at the plane. Apart from crew and two attendants, they were the only people on the mid-sized jet. Even including an extra refuelling stop in the Pacific due to the jet's shorter range, the flight was quick and efficient. They set down in Auckland earlier in the morning local time than they had left.

After a short flight to Tauranga, a convoy of cars took them to a conference centre in the Kaimai Range where Senden had been moved as a refuge from the mental noise of the city. He had been advised of their arrival and was sitting on the porch waiting when they drove up. He had known Lestze was back well before they told him anyway.

They spent some time over introductions while the conference centre staff rushed to organize an unexpected breakfast for them all. Nobody had thought to warn them.

As the group were finishing eating, Leotie called for silence then asked that they move to the conference room to discuss their next moves.

"Not yet," Senden said calmly but with a dignity and authority that is unchallengeable. "I need to speak to Lestze first to know where we stand."

Leotie sighed. "I can give you an hour."

Senden nodded, stood up and turned towards the door. Lestze, who was sitting a few seats away, stood dutifully but looked around uncertainly and saw Atawhai sitting in a corner with Jeff. He walked over and took her hand, without words, lifting her to her feet and leading her with him to follow Senden, who had turned to watch the process without comment or sign.

Senden led them away from the building complex down a small path into the surrounding forest. They came to a small lookout clearing with a large seat where he sat in the middle and gestured to Lestze and Atawhai to sit either side of him.

"I don't need to be here," Atawhai demurred, feeling embarrassed.

"On the contrary, my dear," Senden answered. "You had the strength of character and wisdom to see us truly, regardless of your preconceptions and the terrible situation you were caught in. You are the only true ambassador for your people our world has seen. Without your greatness of heart none of this (he gestured towards the complex) would have happened. Besides, Lestze was not a full member of the council before, but I can see he has made that step on his own while you were away. He has the right to make his own decisions. I am not in a position to tell him you shouldn't be here. Tell us what happened, Lestze."

"I was totally alive for the first time. Completely me. It was like coming home."

"And what did it teach you?"

"Life is continuous. It may appear as bodies or even other forms, but life produces them. Bodies don't constitute life."

"Why do you think you saw this?"

"I had no expectations, nothing I thought I was required to do and no need to defend an artificial image of what I am."

"As good an explanation as any but don't regret the loss of that knowing. It will come again."

Senden questioned Lestze about what had happened on Palaeo. Lestze answered verbally and showed his relevant memories at the same time. First, the devastation around the station then their growing realization that the planet had itself developed a consciousness that they named Tayanita through the unlikely intervention of a dinosaur.

Lestze cut off the narrative. "You didn't tell me the council has an independent mind," he stated accusingly.

"No. You had all the training we could give, but we wanted you to be able to relate to Atawhai's people in a normal way for them. You could call the council a species mind. We have a planetary mind too; they work together. It gets complicated to explain. We will go into it when we have time"

Lestze jumped forward in time, showing the essence of all of Tayanita's communications following her agreement to help them. At the end, he passed over her farewell with a small mention, feeling it was personal.

Intuitively, Senden stopped him, asking if he could see what happened in more detail. Lestze showed him the memories. Senden started laughing. "So she has chosen you as her representative. Chosen ambassador for two worlds now." He reached up and ruffled Lestze's hair. "And you didn't think this was important? From the worry I was feeling from Leotie, I think this is a lot more important than you realize. Atawhai, can you get Leotie here as quickly as you can?"

Atawhai dashed off to the complex to find her as they kept talking. She was back surprisingly quickly with an out-of-breath Leotie.

"Lestze was too shy to mention Tayanita has appointed him as her spokesperson, essentially her ambassador," Senden said to her as she trotted up. "He didn't think it was important enough to mention to me either." He shook his head then laughed again.

"Really? What did she say?"

Lestze repeated Tayanita's parting words for Leotie.

"That's not all," Senden added. "In his own words, she gave him her blessing. I am able to see what he means and can only take it to mean she has given him complete authority to act for her."

Leotie let out a deep breath. "Yes, this does change everything."

"I know time is short, but will you take the time to explain why this is so important?" Senden asked.

"Yes. We have been a world government for less than a year. It wasn't governments who made that decision. It was the mega-wealthy powerbrokers who make or break governments who saw it as the only way to maintain enough stability during the original crisis to allow them to keep hold of their wealth and lifestyle. They forced their puppet politicians to hand over their governments' authority to the UN to manage a global response to unrest and civil disorder. The UN has never had plans to take over as a world government, so the structure of the former national governments was simply assimilated holus-bolus as the local administrations for the world government. We had no choice.

"Those administrations have many spies and informers within the UN. While loyal people like Robert and many of the under-secretaries see the figures for incidents of rioting and unrest that we deal with they don't see all that I do. There are many people who are loyal to the ideal of a fair and free world government, if not to the haphazard attempts we have managed so far. I have my own organization and network of spies now. I know that the local governments and the people who pull their strings have been waiting on the sidelines for the right time to withdraw. They see huge opportunities for profit in carving out new trade empires as they re-establish and rebuild their world order. It will look like unilateral withdrawals from the World Government in the future, but it is all being orchestrated now.

"As a separate issue, we are still being resisted by those who remember globalization as a free pass for multinationals to pillage Third World countries and don't see how we can be any different.

"I came here to see if the agreement between Neanderthal B and Earth could be shaped in a way that ratifies the UN as the only governmental entity your world will interact with or trade through. Anything you could suggest that could give us some leverage. It did not occur to me that it could be an agreement between three worlds.

"At this stage I would like to have an agreement between the three world governments that on our part includes concessions to remove many of the powers of territorial governments and guarantees the continuance of world government here along with guaranteeing your planets' autonomy, for your safety, within two days. I would like to have it signed and ratified by the chief executives and other representatives of the territorial governments before the serum is released."

"I couldn't in good conscience withhold treatment from sick people if we have it available, or be associated with that," Lestze stated firmly.

"Understood, but they don't have to know that. That is why I want the agreement signed by each world's representatives within a day or two. However, the current epidemic is killing large numbers of people as we speak so I will have UN personnel dispensing the serum as soon as it is available. I will make is absolutely clear to the population it is only because of the UN and the goodwill of other worlds and we will need their continuing help. There are other ways I can continue to put pressure on local governments if they haven't agreed by then."

"Tayanita was thinking about this more than I was obviously. We talked about this planet obviously. At one stage she said any species insane enough to consciously destroy the system that it lives in would almost certainly have a pathological fear of death. She said she could think of ways she could extend people's lifespan if we brought them to Palaeo. I realize now she was thinking of ways we could influence your people's attitude by contact with Palaeo. We need to think more about that too."

"Tayanita called us insane?" Atawhai interrupted.

Lestze laughed. "Another time she said your behaviour was so obviously insane it never occurred to her you might be intelligent. If your species returns to its former attitude and behaviour, we can't stop it destroying itself and, now, probably other worlds along with it."

Senden nodded. "We can implement changes to your social and administrative structures, but real change cannot be forced from the top down. We would replace the current hidden tyranny where your true rulers are invisible with a very visible and obvious despotism. The concentration of power in a true world government would be ridiculously easy to subvert. If those with power are not able to bend your integrity, there are numerous ways they could replace you with one of their own quislings. Your loyal supporters would be replaced over time and the lot of your population would soon be worse than it is now. The unseen rulers would continue as before.

"The only thing that will bring real change is if your people choose to rise up and free themselves from enslavement. Of their minds rather than their bodies. They must choose individually and collectively to commit only to thoughts and actions that are beneficial to all those around them. They would have to willingly surrender self-interest and fear. Do you honestly think you can lead them to do that?"

Leotie hung her head. "You are suggesting I try for a far bigger and harder goal than even taking control of the world's governments."

"Yes."

"It is the only way that will work?"

"In the long run."

She looked away for a while, plumbing the depths of her spirit, then suddenly looked up, squared her shoulders and looked Senden in the eye. "I swear by all I and my people hold sacred I will follow this path you suggest, by example and expectation, to whatever end it brings me."

"We give our word to walk that path with you."

A little later the whisper of the wind blended with the melody of Atawhai's happy laughter. "And *you* were calling *me* insane? Let's go do this."